COURTS & CURSES

A COURT OF BROKEN DREAMS & CURSES

COURTS & CURSES BOOK ONE

MICHELLE HELEN FRITZ

A Court of Broken Dreams and Curses: Courts & Curses by Michelle Helen Fritz

Cover Design: Wanderlust Ink & Tomb L.L.C.

Interior Art: Samaiya Art

Developmental & Line Editing: Paranormal Depths Editing

Proofreading: Brittany Smith & Cathey Nelson

Published by Clear Spring Books LLC of Clear Spring, MD

DEDICATION

For my daughters. May you always remember the beauty of dreaming and to make your wishes upon the stars. You are beautiful and kind and have everlasting value. Find the place where you belong and shine brightly, my darlings.

P.S. This is my love letter to you. Whenever you miss me, pick this up and let me tell you a story.

CONTENTS

PROLOGUE

THE CURSE

Once upon a time in the Faerie Court of Spring, lived a spoiled and selfish prince who never had a kind word or thought for another. His mother doted upon him excessively and his father granted his every wish and whim. Wanting for nothing, he took every kindness for granted. He grew to be a cruel young man whom no one could please, and because of that, his kingdom suffered for his selfish ways.

The prince was blessed with blond curls and large expressive mossy green eyes. The tips of his ears were perfectly pointed. He had a tail with a fluffy tuft of white hair upon its end that he liked to glamour away. Wearing a constant sneer, all who addressed him cowered in fear. Being vain about his appearance, he spent an unfaely amount of time grooming himself.

In his sixteenth year, during the Faecrenzial Spring Equinox celebrations, a haggard, cobalt-capped crone addressed him in a wavering voice and asked for a favor. Sneering at the old woman, he told her that he didn't grant favors to peasants. She replied that she was a citizen of his Court and that he existed to serve her.

So incensed was the prince, that he called forth his best hunting hounds to tear her to pieces. The smoky ebony beasts were terrifying with their hunched backs, razor-sharp teeth which dripped green venom, and black hollowed-out pits where eyes should be, but never formed.

As the ghastly beasts descended upon her, gossamer wings, that shimmered in different hues of blue, sprouted from her dark-robed back, and her hood fell backwards to reveal sea-colored hair that flowed out around her. Throwing out her hands, glowing purple flames poured forth from her palms and she cast them upon the growling creatures. The hounds instantly burned to ash, but their haunting shrill screams remained for a few moments and lingered in the oppressive air. The transformed woman, who was beautiful to behold, locked gazes with the stunned prince.

"You and yours shall be punished for all time, for I sought one tiny favor and you scoffed and sneered at me. You could have gained wisdom as well as great power, but instead, you chose to shame and destroy. You aren't worthy of Spring and you certainly are not worthy to be the keeper of new life. I curse you to live forever in your castle. I also curse your Court to never be able to leave this kingdom. Every living creature within your domain shall never feel the joy or happiness that true love can bring. Any who ventures into these lands may suffer this fate alongside you. But, because I choose to be merciful, I shall grant you a way to earn your redemption. Learn to show compassion and care for your fellow creatures and, one day, you'll meet your one true love who shall possess the power to save you. You must get her to fall in love with you and break this spell with true love's kiss. But beware, you'll never feel contentment or love again for anything or anyone, so you won't be able to return her affections. You must reach past your limitations and show her true kindness and devotion. Only then will she fall in love with you." And with that, she threw open her glorious shimmering wings and sprang into the fluffy pink clouds that hung in the purple sky, never to be seen within the Spring Court again.

The prince sank to his knees as if the weight of boulders suddenly crashed onto his shoulders and were forcing him to bow down. He wanted to cry, to weep, to shout, but he couldn't do any of those things for he was now an empty vessel. Ripping the golden crown from atop his head, he threw it into the bubbling fountain behind him.

The Faerie Prince had not yet realized what his actions had cost his kingdom. He didn't see his castle behind him transform into a dark, twisted thing as it rose up from the ground to tower above the lands. Nor did he witness the transformation of the fountain and the obsidian crown laying within its depths.

Gargoyles descended from the pink clouds, rooting themselves along the twisted turrets. Their watchful gaze taking in every detail.

All the Faerie Prince could concentrate on was the vast emptiness that both overwhelmed and consumed him.

1

ONCE UPON A TIME

Briella hummed a melody of long forgotten words as she dusted the porcelain figurines with an old, tattered rag. The cloth had been torn from one of her dresses that had seen better days. The dress wasn't doing her much good since it had been so long since she needed to look like a daughter of the house of Dubois. Even when it was new it was far from fashionable, having been created from a serviceable material that would be long lasting and durable. So, Briella tore her dress to pieces that morning and went about her chores. Her list was never-ending. Her days and nights were growing longer the deeper the household fell into disrepair.

Sighing heavily before the cherry curio cabinet, Briella looked down upon the porcelain maiden cuddling the tiny sheep. This had been her Mama's favorite treasure. It was so small that it fit within Briella's petite, calloused palm. She smiled wistfully at the porcelain piece and carefully dusted its crevices and curves. The remembrance of her mother, who loved picking up her collection and telling her stories about each piece, pricked her heart.

Mama's stories were about adventures to far-off places where pixies danced upon the water, and fae princes fell in love with human ladies. There were even tales of wolves in sheep's clothing and villains with wily ways. There were kings and queens, peasants and nobility. The piece that she now held in her hand was a shepherdess who loved to guard her sheep from all the evils lurking within the meadow.

Briella ruefully smiled, wishing that fairytales were real and that there were princes who rescued fair maidens. She wished that happily-ever-afters truly existed. She wouldn't mind doing the rescuing if it meant that there was even a chance that true love was out there awaiting her discovery. But this was real life and 'happily-ever-afters' didn't prevail. There was no prince waiting for her. She wanted to hold onto such beautiful dreams, but as she grew older her mother's stories lost more of their shine. With each passing day, Briella forgot Mama's voice a little more. Magic was just a beautiful dream and curses were just ill luck. Villains always triumphed. *But how I wish it was not so.*

Briella missed her mother dreadfully. It had been so many winters ago that she had been snatched away from this cruel and unfeeling world. Mama had fallen ill after a visit to the village, where she handed out baskets of food to the villagers. They hadn't realized how terrible, nor how debilitating, the sickness would be. It didn't care if it claimed the young or the old within its despicable clutches. The fever was the worst of all its symptoms. It made its victims hallucinate, and the fever dreams, from which they could not be woken made them wail and gnash their teeth. It was horrifying to behold and especially so for such an innocent young girl.

Briella's thoughts swiftly returned her to that tragic

evening when all of her hopes and dreams turned to ashes as the light faded from her mother's eyes. *Briella had hesitantly crept into her mother's bedchamber on silent tiptoes. When her gaze caught sight of Mama, who was murmuring and thrashing upon the bed, she looked to Mama's lady's maid, Sarah.*

"There is nothing we can do for her except to pray, my little blossom," cooed Sarah softly with tears rimming her luminous eyes.

Briella swallowed back her emotions. She could not let sadness overwhelm her, or grieve a life that was not yet gone. There would be time for that later; to succumb to all of her feelings, but for now, she had to be the strong one. Looking on forlornly, Briella reached out to lay the tips of her fingers against Mama's forehead but quickly drew them back again as she winced. It felt as if her tiny fingers were being burned to a crisp. She didn't want to leave, couldn't bear the thought of leaving Mama's side, but watching the life ebb from her mother's frail, thinning frame was not an easy undertaking for a girl so young. Straightening her shoulders, Briella picked up the cloth that rested beside the bowl of cool water and dipped the cloth in. As she wrung it out over the bowl, she replayed within her mind how Mama had tended to her in times of sickness. I shall tend to Mama during these last moments even if it serves to further break my heart. I'm strong enough to do this, I'm strong enough to rise above my fear. Gently she bathed Mama's face and neck as she hummed their favorite melody. With loving care Briella tended to her mother as Sarah sat by her side. Even when the sight of her mother's distress and the writhing of her body threatened to cloud Briella's resolve, she continued to patiently offer what comfort she could. Mama had taken her last struggling breath long before the endless hours of night greeted the dawn. And only then, the never-ending flood of tears drenched Briella as her heart poured all of its fright and woe from her small trembling body.

Bowing her head, Briella took a deep cleansing breath. No wistful thoughts or bittersweet memories would linger within her mind or heart, taking up any more of her day. She had shed enough tears and buried enough of her broken dreams. It did her no good to dwell upon the past.

She couldn't count the numerous disappointments or unfair treatments heaped upon her by those who should have sheltered her from the cruelty that life created. She only really had herself to rely upon. Straightening her posture, Briella realized that she'd better stop daydreaming and finish another item on her endless to-do list. There would be other moments to feel grief and to mourn all that she'd lost and all that would never be. *I must put these saddening thoughts far from my mind.*

Briella placed the shepherdess onto the glass shelf and softly closed the wooden door. She turned around and gazed at the room, making sure that the throw pillows and seating were all in their appropriate places. The large bay window with its many carved rosettes didn't have a spot upon it and all of the hanging oil portraits were free of dust. True, the furnishings were all old and shabby. Some should have been retired long ago, but there simply weren't funds to be found to replenish such mundane things. If there were rips in the seating or tears in the drapery, it was up to Briella to mend. If she lacked the knowledge to accomplish the task, then she simply learned by trial and error. She loved her home, and every time she discovered another piece of it falling apart her heart broke a little bit more.

Of course, it didn't help that her stepfather, Alerion, had insisted upon perfection and nothing less would be deemed acceptable to him. He was a strict man with her, and he never failed to remind her of his *kindness* in not turning her out after her mother had passed. He inherited the chateau and the vast fortune that her father had brought with him upon marrying her mother. He had squandered the money away to cover his debts. Alerion had led an extravagant lifestyle and came into the marriage with a dark cloud of debt shrouding him. Briella had never learned whether he had gotten into so much debt because he had a penchant for gambling, or because misfortune had landed upon his doorstep, but she suspected it had happened because he liked the finer things and borrowed too much. *How my beloved chateau has suffered for it…*

Alerion also brought to the marriage two sons that were just as vile and spoiled as himself. Mama had not known what his true character was as he could be quite charming when the situation called for it. *He had fooled us all.*

Now the male trio sneered at Briella and never gave her a kind word. Her whole world had changed with her mother's passing and things only became bleaker and more sorrowful as the days went by and the house of Dubois continued to fall further into disrepair.

Briella walked to the cream-colored marble fireplace and reached for the dark wooden box that held the matches to light the logs within the large grate. Her stepfamily would take their after-dinner port here and they would expect the room to be toasty. Briella struck the match and watched the glowing orange flame for a moment. *I am the match and everything else is the fire waiting to consume me. How I feel the ever-hot embers that threaten my being.*

The kindling lit right away once Briella tossed the match into the fire as she sat back upon her heels. She looked up at the smiling faces of the pale cherubs which were looking down upon her from their molded places along the marble mantle. She had always thought that they looked so cheerful but also had a fair bit of mischievousness hidden behind those perfectly shaped eyes. She wistfully smiled at them as she stood back up. *Seems as if there's still a fair bit of whimsy left inside me after all.* Briella placed the matchbook back within its resting place and closed the wooden lid.

"I told you that doddering fool would take the bait!" The booming voice of her eldest stepbrother, Henri, could be heard as he came through the double front doors.

Stomping in behind him, her other stepbrother, Hugo, boasted, "I never doubted he would! He's as simple as they get. You must admit that you are a persuasive fellow and he didn't stand a chance."

Briella didn't want to leave the quiet safety of the parlor, but their evening meal needed to be finished and she couldn't do that if she didn't actually make her way to the kitchen. Perhaps she could sneak by unnoticed? Shrugging her shoulders, she resolved herself to walk through the parlor and out of its door. She tried to creep along the wall, but a floorboard squeaked, giving her away. She scowled down at the offending board. *Of course, you would announce my presence,* she thought. *Now I shall never get away.*

"Can you believe what you're seeing, Hugo?" Henri sneered at Briella.

Hugo turned toward her with menace raging within his dark eyes. "Why if it isn't the largest *rat* that I've ever seen! *Don't we take out the vermin,* brother?"

"Indeed, we do, or at least we show it where it belongs." Henri stalked towards her and Briella wasn't sure which horrified her more. The fact that he was making his way toward her, or the muddy prints his large boots were leaving in his wake. She had already spent a good deal of the morning on her hands and knees with a bucket of water and rags from her dress, scrubbing the tiled floor until her fingers cramped and her back ached.

As Henri ceased his lumbering gait directly before her, Briella decided that he was the more pressing of matters and arranged her face into a mask of serenity. He stank of wine and horse manure and needed to shave his days-old beard. She knew his torment of her was only beginning and looked down at her slippered feet. *Pretend all will be well and that you have not a care in the world,* she told herself while she tried to slow the racing of her heart. *I will not show my fear.*

"Why are you out in the open, walking our halls, *you little worm*? Don't you have tasks that need to be seen to? Like perhaps preparing our dinner?" Henri leaned closer towards her as his dark, dirt-colored hair fell forward into his squinted, muddy brown eyes.

"Yes, why isn't dinner on the table?" Hugo demanded from a few steps away. "I'm famished." His small brown eyes, set in a face with mismatched features, were glaring at her.

Briella calmly answered, "I was just on my way to put the finishing touches upon your meal. The table is set. If you would care to adjourn to the dining room, I'll have dinner readied shortly." She didn't meet either set of eyes, knowing better than to ever look directly at them, for that only seemed to provoke and prolong their cruelty.

"See that that's exactly what you do, *little worm*," Henri grabbed her roughly by the forearm and sent her careening into a side table. She tried to catch herself, but it was to no avail. The burgundy vase upon the small wooden table teetered dangerously until it finally crashed onto the blue-tiled floor, shattering on impact. There was a cluster of glittering pieces that reflected the glowing light from the lit silver wall sconces. The broken shards taunted her from their resting place.

"How clumsy you are, little rat," Hugo heartily laughed, staring down at her.

Henri made a tsking noise. "Must you break everything in sight? You're quite the terror to your surroundings. Papa won't be pleased at all. I suggest you get right to cleaning up this mess. Being the considerate man that I am, I'll distract Papa. You now have one half hour to have dinner upon the table. Don't offer up anything burnt either."

Hugo came up behind Henri and clapped him upon the back as he smirked at Briella. "Oh, and one more thing. There seems to be an abundance of mud here in the entryway. Do clean that up as well. *After* we've had our dinner and *before* you've had yours."

The brothers sauntered off and didn't bother to look back. They were similar in stature and coloring. They even walked in the same lumbering manner. They were bullies and proud of that fact. Cruelty was all that they had to offer to the world.

Once Briella knew that she wouldn't be heard, she stomped her foot, well aware of where the glass shards were, and closed her eyes. Her side ached and she didn't doubt that it was already starting to bruise. It was just one more mark upon her person in a long history of abuse. Once Mama had passed, her stepfamily had never balked at showing Briella exactly how they felt about her. *Why must I earn their disdain?*

She wanted so much to have a home that she belonged to, not this dilapidated prison that she alone was responsible for, keeping all of its crumbling bits together.

Briella loved the chateau, but seeing it fall apart at its seams was heartbreaking and it had been years since it had felt like a home.

She longed to belong to someone, to have someone praise her hard work, someone to converse with and who would listen to her thoughts. Someone who would appreciate her. Most of all what she longed for was the comfort of a warm embrace. It had been so long since she'd last been touched lovingly by her mother, that she had almost forgotten what a kind touch felt like.

2

TREAT ME WITH RESPECT

Dinner began with cucumber soup, a light appetizer to cleanse the palate, and the main course, and it all smelled divine. Briella begged her empty stomach to not make its displeasure known as she served each member of her stepfamily, noting the intensity of their gazes as they watched her every action. She felt like chilled fingers were ascending and descending along her spine, so cold was the malice that resided within their watchful and judging eyes.

The men hadn't dressed formally for dinner and her stepbrothers hadn't bothered to change out of their muddy boots. She grimaced when she contemplated how much scrubbing awaited her when she was finally able to direct her attention to the carpet that lay beneath the table.

Briella was clearing the soup bowls from the long oval table when her stepfather leaned forward and flicked his bowl onto the floor. Briella watched the contents spill out onto the carpet as she felt her heart fill with dread. *This will not end well. What have I done to earn his ire now?*

Alerion grabbed her wrist in a punishing grasp. "I have

a question to ask you, my dear." His face held a menacing look, highlighted by the flickering candlelight from the silver candelabras.

Briella paused and waited for Alerion to continue, she wouldn't dare speak before he made his accusation. She tried to not let fear show upon her face.

"I've noticed that several things have gone missing. I know that I have neither gifted nor absconded with them and I have already asked my sons. There's only you left that can be held under suspicion. So, I'll ask, dear Briella, have you misplaced things while attending to your duties? Broken them perhaps? Or do we have a thief under this very roof?" Alerion's dark gaze was set firmly upon her face. *He longs to see me flinch under his harsh gaze.*

"I have noticed that things have been missing, but that is quite normal, is it not? We've lost a lot of things these past few years. Perhaps you sold them as you did the tapestries or Mama's jewels? I would never steal from you. I *swear* it." Briella's throat had gone dry by her bold speech. She kept her sight averted from the other eyes within the room, but she could feel her stepbrothers glaring at her.

"I wish I could believe you. I never sold the tapestries nor your mother's jewels. What a silly notion." Alerion scoffed as his sons guffawed from their seats.

Briella knew that he had sold the missing items. She came across the transaction as they were being carted away and Alerion jingled the coins that were firmly grasped within his hand. Her stepfather had turned away from her questions as the overloaded rickety cart made its way down their gravel driveway. It had been heartbreaking to see her family's history parted with when she knew that there would never be a way to reclaim it.

"What can I say to you that would prove my innocence?" whispered Briella.

"Dearest Briella, all I ask of you is the truth. Are you so willing to face punishment for a lie? You wound me, my dear. After all I've done for you. Sheltering you, providing for you. I've treated you as my very own, and you treat me with such *disrespect.*" His words caused Briella to finally look up at him.

His dark hickory-colored hair was groomed perfectly, not one hair daring to rebel against his wishes. He looked remarkably young for his age; it seemed avoiding work of any kind was an excellent way to retain one's youth. His black trousers were perfectly pressed, and his tailcoat was midnight blue and showing not one errant wrinkle. His Hessian boots were shined to perfection. It had taken her ages to polish them. Briella looked into his hazel eyes and felt her frustration breaking free. She knew she should take his accusations and appear meek and repentant, but she was tired and beyond caring.

"After *all* you've done for *me*? *Me,* who serves you? *Me,* who prepares all of your meals, who repairs your home? *Me,* who cleans late into the night, long after you've retired and who wakes before you to do it all over again? *Me,* who you never thank, who you mistreat like the very dirt beneath your booted feet? If you think I deserve your condemnation, then be done with it. Do your *worst* as you've never attempted to do your *best* where I am concerned." Tears were flowing from her cerulean eyes and falling onto the white lace tablecloth.

Her stepfather looked at her with rage simmering within his eyes. Not a muscle moved to show his displeasure. He was always in complete command of his emotions. It was frightening how he could remain so calm when storms raged within.

"You leave me no choice Briella. You're unmanageable. I think it is high time we found you a husband and rid you of your household responsibilities." He let her wrist go and leaned back into the wingback chair.

Revulsion passed over her pale face. "You'd sell me off to another? Who would take care of the chateau? *You?* There is no one else! You've let all the servants go."

Humming deeply, he brought his index finger over his chin and smiled coldly at her. "You're not irreplaceable, my dear. I've recently come into new funds. Would you like to know where they came from?"

Shaking her head incredulously, the words exploded forth. "From the missing things you've accused me of stealing!"

Alerion laughed. "You're wrong. I received an offer that I simply couldn't afford to refuse. *You* in exchange for funds. Bizarre, I know. Congratulations, Briella. You're to be wed within the week."

"You have no right! I don't belong to you," Briella replied vehemently.

"Oh, but you do. The moment I married your sweet mother, everything in the chateau became mine, including you. And your new husband will expect you to be a dutiful wife. Isn't it my place to prepare you?" Alerion sat forward and stood up, towering over her.

Briella began to return to her senses as fear crept into her being. Goosebumps pebbled her skin as her empty stomach knotted itself, threatening to make her sick upon the carpet.

She was to be married? Leave her home? She'd have rather been beaten or starved willingly than to ever be forced to leave the chateau that had been in her mother's family for centuries, no matter how it tore her heart apart or wore her body down. *Not like this*. The chateau was so deeply embedded into her blood.

Papa had rescued the chateau and her mother from dire straits by marriage and brought substantial wealth to pour back into the coffers. The funds came by way of an inheritance as Papa's parents had been titled. His family had scorned the match and so no introductions had ever been made between the two families. Briella didn't even know whether her father's family knew of his passing. While her father had lived, they had been gloriously happy and wanted for nothing, and he never seemed unhappy about not meeting with his absent family. Papa had loved the chateau with its rich history just as much as Mama had. Her father's heart had suddenly given out and taken him away from them. With his passing a huge piece of her own heart had never mended.

Briella never thought about marriage for herself. She was so unlovable, she'd been shown that every day in these recent passing years. No one had shown her kindness except the servants, but they were all gone now. No friends nor family that she knew of had ever stepped forward to claim her.

There had never been another that made her heart race, nor make her smile remain fixed upon her face. She had watched the true love flow between her parents as she grew older and lost them, and she resolved that she'd never allow her heart to be broken by love. Her place decidedly was here at the chateau.

"I won't marry. I refuse," she defiantly stated.

"Then, you leave me no choice." Alerion reached for her arm, cruelly hauling Briella to his side. He marched her out of the dining room, down the hall, past the entryway, and straight up the stairs to her attic bedroom as the sting of his fingers bit into her flesh. He turned the doorknob and thrust her inside where she fell heavily onto her knees. He gave her one last menacing glare and shut the door.

Briella heard the key turn the lock and all her hope disappeared. She could fight and be bested and manhandled at every turn, or she could simply give up and give in. She wasn't sure which option was the best for her as both had frightening consequences. She felt so weary as endless emotions all collided together. She exhausted herself further by letting loose a torrent of tears for all that she had lost and for a future that would separate her from all that she had ever known. She cried so much that her chest and eyes grew sore, matching her aching side from the earlier encounter with her stepbrother and her new blossoming bruises from her stepfather. Briella withdrew a handkerchief from her dress pocket and blew her nose.

Pulling herself up, she made her way to her lumpy mattress and moth-eaten bedding. Briella didn't bother to undress or cleanse her face. Sleep was claiming her as she laid down and pulled the thin coverlet around her thin form. She would welcome the escape that slumber would allow her.

Tomorrow, she would face her dilemma. Tomorrow, she would decide which person she wanted to be, the fighter or the survivor.

As she drifted off, she thought again of her Mama and lamented the day that Alerion appeared into their world. *What a monster he turned out to be.* For a very short while, all was right in her world. And then, Mama had become ill and everything changed. Briella never knew a harsh word or a harsher reprimand until her mother was laid to rest.

3

AM I WORTH SO MUCH?

Briella awoke early the next morning with the crowing of the rooster. She laid in her bed and let her thoughts run wild. What was she going to do? Perhaps she could run away? Was it possible that she would find someone kind who would offer to assist her? Did kindness still exist in the world? Or did that belong in fairytales too?

Tossing the coverlet aside, she threw her legs over the side of the mattress and stretched. She could still feel the indentations pressing into her skin from the lumpy mattress. Her body ached from the uncomfortable bed, but it was all that she had. Her injuries from the prior evening complained as she slowly and stiffly rose.

Walking to her small dresser, she bent forward to cup the chilled water to her face from the chipped pale blue basin. She bathed her face, neck, and her arms. She didn't bother changing her dress, as she only had two available at present. Drying herself, she stood and gazed into the rosewood framed looking-glass that hung on the dingy wall before her.

Briella looked like her mother a great deal, but there was much of her father mixed in as well. Seeing her reflection stare back at her from the looking-glass made her catch her breath. Her mother had been so lovely until the sickness came. She shared Mama's golden locks and cerulean blue eyes that were heavily lined with long, thick lashes that curled up at the edges. They each had delicate noses and lips that were full, with the lower lip being just a tad larger than the upper. Briella didn't think she was ugly. How could she be when she so clearly resembled her mother? But her stepbrothers delighted in pointing out quite regularly how vulgar her appearance was. Perhaps that was due to her attire more than her physical characteristics.

She sat upon a wooden chair that wobbled as one leg was shorter than the other. She had claimed it for herself from the burn pile. There were some nights that she lay in this dreary attic and longed for the warmth of a fire. That wish was almost enough to make her light one using her precious chair, though she had no fireplace within the room. It was the one piece of furniture that she could claim her own and made the cold nights bearable. For one who didn't even have a proper bed, this was luxurious.

She reached into a wicker basket that was placed near the chair and pulled her hairbrush from within. She took down her golden tresses and brushed them. When she felt her hair was tangle-free and shining, she twisted it and pinned it back atop the crown of her head, letting a few tendrils frame her face.

When Briella felt that she was ready to greet whatever this day would bring, she rose and walked the few steps to her door. Reaching her hand out, she grasped the knob and tried to turn it but it was still locked. She closed her eyes and leaned her head against the wooden door with its peeling paint. She was trapped and that was something she could hardly bear. Her breath hitched within her throat, drowning the scream that beckoned to burst free as she pulled herself away and turned. *I shall not give into my fear. I am safe. I am well.*

She padded over to the large window; its paint had long since flaked away and the curtains were discolored and brown with age. She hadn't bothered to close the curtains last night. It wasn't as if anyone could really see her so high up from the ground. Briella peered out of the yellowing panes as she pressed both palms to them. The morning light was still creeping across the pale blue sky that held puffy clouds that she wished she could reach out and touch. She looked out at the neglected landscape and bramble that needed to be discarded. Her chores never included the outside upkeep, except for the small patch of the kitchen garden that grew their food.

The trio of males who resided within the chateau were still in bed and she didn't know when they would awaken or if they would bother climbing the stairs to fetch her. They would need to eat their morning meal and she knew that they would never stoop so low as to prepare it for themselves.

Looking out to the vast lane that made up their gravel driveway, she spied in the distance a flurry of carriages and carts making their way toward the chateau. She stood silently as they slowly traveled to a stop in front of the grand double doors. She saw tied-down furniture, baskets of fruits and vegetables, and chests with golden filigree that glittered in the early morning light. There were several men and women who alighted from the carriages. They were dressed uniformly and Briella gasped. Was she worth so much to another being that they would offer up all of this for her hand in marriage? *How can this be?*

Briella could not view much more from her place before the window and began to pace the small attic back and forth. She wrung her hands and balled up her stained apron. It seemed that she had walked miles by the time she heard footsteps ascending the staircase and the latch spring from its resting place. Her door creaked as it swung open and the floorboards strained beneath her captor's weight. Taking a deep breath, she turned toward the door.

Alerion's face peered back at her from the space created by the door opening. He was dressed in court attire of a white muslin shirt, black waistcoat with gold thread, black trousers, polished black Hessian boots, and one cleverly knotted cravat. He was groomed to perfection; the perfect image of a country gentleman. His face was set in a mask of stone and his posture was stiff as he held out his hand to her. "Well come along, my dear. We don't have all day."

"Where are we going?" Briella inquired without taking his hand.

"May *I* remind you that I do not answer to *you*. Now, do as you're told and be a good girl. I have no wish to dawdle," he declared as he waggled his fingers at her.

Briella walked to the door and squeezed past him, not bothering to take his hand. She looked down at her slippered feet and waited for him to pass by her. Experience had taught her that putting up a fight would only lead her to injury and further humiliation. She was much too curious about what was to come to risk his displeasure.

Sighing in exasperation, Alerion turned and descended the staircase. He didn't wait to see if she followed. They stopped on the floor reserved for the family bedchambers and walked down the long corridor until they came to her old room. Opening the door, he looked expectantly down at her.

Briella looked back at him and walked into the room where she saw a maid dressed in all black, waiting with her hands folded together and her back ramrod straight.

Briella padded into the room and heard the door close. She gingerly approached the maid. "May I help you?"

"Oh no, mistress! It is I who am to serve you. Are you ready to bathe? I have had the water drawn and it's still warm." The maid smiled at her as she bowed.

"But why? Do you know what I am getting ready for?" Briella quirked a golden eyebrow.

"Why, to meet the Duke of course! He has sent me along with a gown and all the trimmings so that your introduction may take place this afternoon. Isn't that lovely?"

"Do you know anything about the Duke?" Briella chewed upon her lower lip.

"Oh, not much. It was his mother's household that I came from. I have been instructed as a ladies' maid and now am ready to serve. The bath awaits..." She waved a hand in the direction of the copper tub where wisps of steam rose to dance atop it.

Shrugging her shoulders, Briella thought that she might as well enjoy a bath that someone else had prepared for her. She could not remember the last time that someone had waited upon her. And hot water was such a luxurious comfort. She nodded her head and followed the maid to the warm water.

"What is your name?" asked Briella as she allowed the girl to assist her in undressing. If she could carry on a conversation perhaps she could forget that she was naked in front of a stranger.

"Maude, mistress." Maude held up her dress and

apron. "Shall I...?" She tried to hide her look of disgust, but Briella still caught the expression.

"It's quite all right, Maude. I know it looks terrible. I use it too... Work in the garden. Would you please have it cleaned and returned to my... room?" Briella stepped into the warm, soothing water, which glittered with purple crushed flowers. *This is heavenly.*

"Of course, mistress." Maude balled up the clothing and bowed. "I shall return soon and help wash your hair. Shall I stay to help you bathe first?"

"No need, thank you." Briella reached for the scented soap and cleaning cloth and began to clean herself as Maude exited the room. It felt luxurious to soak in a tub and she could feel the layers of grime melting off her skin. *How is it possible for my body to have so much dirt caked into it?* The thought repulsed her. *Have I carried such grime upon my skin these past years and never was aware of that fact?* Briella couldn't stop the shudder of disgust that ran through her body.

Once she was satisfied that every inch had been thoroughly scrubbed, she leaned her head back and rested it against the cool surface of the copper tub. Briella had taken care of her bruises with a gentler touch and was glad of the fact that, though Maude must have taken notice of them, she didn't question how or why they had appeared.

She looked around her room as memories assaulted her. After Mama had died, her stepfather would enter her bedchamber and toss her clothing, dolls, and any other possessions upon her bed and demand that she choose which ones she was to part with. Briella had been unwilling to give up her dolls, which remained her only source of comfort, so she offered up her beautiful dresses. Then as the nights passed on she bid her trinkets farewell too. One by one, she watched as her things were gathered up and taken away until only a few of her beloved books and dolls remained. She had never questioned where her belongings had been whisked away to. She had just accepted that Alerion's actions were what they were and there was nothing she could do to stop him.

Briella remembered the night that Alerion had burst into this chamber and had dragged her from the safety of her bed by grabbing onto her braided hair and yanking upon it. He had informed her that she was no longer a member of the family and would need to earn her living. That had been the night that she first slept in the attic room. She blinked her eyes shut and took deep breaths; she didn't want to remember so many things at once. It was too much for her battered heart to feel when for so long she had forced herself to feel nothing at all.

4

DARE TO DREAM, BRIELLA

Briella stood beside her stepfather in the parlor, feeling like an imposter. Dressed and primped and smelling of the best perfume, she looked like a member of the family that she should have always been. She was a born lady of the house, but had never been allowed to take her place within it nor Society. Briella was a titled lady and had never claimed her status within the Court. Her hair was arranged in a mass of cascading curls that were gathered at the crown of her head and flowed down her neck to rest upon her bare left shoulder. Maude had used many pins to keep her locks in place. She wore a pale blue dress that had exquisite silver threading with delicate flowers all along its hem. It was like a dream. She had never worn a corset nor such exquisite underthings. Maude had taken a stone of some sort and vigorously attacked the calluses that marred her work-weary hands and pushed back her cuticles, buffing her nails until they shone. Briella looked exactly like how she remembered her mother. It made her extremely nervous and she worried that the Duke's first sight of her would be her retching upon his boots.

"Stop fidgeting," Alerion growled at her, giving her a look of censure.

She tried to breathe and think of pleasant things, but her mind would not be swayed.

There was a knock at the front door, followed by a creak and some gentlemanly pleasantries were exchanged. Then an older man with peppering gray hair and an impeccable dark suit was opening the parlor door and ushering in a gentleman behind him. "The Duke of Barclay is here to call upon you my lord," the older man bowed.

Briella found that she could not look up. She was so fearful of what her intended would look like. Her heart was racing and she was thankful for the gloves she wore that kept the sweat upon her hands hidden. What would his eyes say about him? What if he was worse than her stepfamily? She heard the tapping of a walking cane and then she saw polished Hessian boots halt before her as she lowered into a curtsey.

"My dear, I am pleased to finally be making this introduction. I had been given the misinformation that the line of Dubois was no more. Once I learned that Alerion had been keeping you a secret, I knew that it was my duty to offer for you. Our marriage will join two elite lineages and our children would carry such regal blood that their future and that of their children would secure their places within Society, forevermore." The Duke's voice was high-pitched but well cultured.

Briella took his offered hand, which was large and encased in a white glove, as she rose from her curtsey. She looked up at the man through hooded lashes and her heart ceased to beat for a moment.

The Duke was quite portly and the top of her head

barely reached his nose. She wasn't tall, so he was quite short. His beady eyes were a chocolate color and his hair was a copper shade that didn't at all compliment his ruddy skin that was covered in a sheen of sweat. He rather reminded her of a character in a story that she used to know long ago.

"Pleased to make your acquaintance, Your Grace," Briella said and smiled at him before stepping back a space. She took in his vibrant-colored clothing. His tailcoat was a very bright green and his trousers were a shade lighter. His cravat was tied in a complicated arrangement and the white lace was stiff around the folds of his double chin. But she had to say that friendliness filled his rich eyes and kind expression.

"Delighted!" the Duke chirped at her.

Alerion cleared his throat and addressed their guest, "Would you care to sit, Your Grace?" He waved his hand toward the two wingback chairs with burgundy cushions that were situated near the fireplace.

The Duke briefly looked over at the chairs and nodded his copper head. A curl flopped forward into his eye and he reached up to readjust it. "Of course!"

Briella followed after the men and, once the Duke had managed to comfortably sit, sat down upon the burgundy padding that topped the settee which was not situated so near the fireplace. He had seemed ill at ease and she wondered if the chair was comfortable for him. She arranged her skirts and folded her gloved hands across her lap.

After Alerion took his seat, the Duke spoke. "Has everything been to your liking, Lady Dubois?" he looked at her and smiled with a toothy grin.

"Indeed, thank you." Briella felt at a loss as to what she should say next. She had never been addressed with her title before, it was a shock. "Was your journey here pleasant?"

"It was! My coach is large enough. Its structure is very fine and the bumps along the road are hardly noticeable. Thank you for inquiring." The Duke had yet to take his eye from her.

"Yes, well, perhaps we can discuss the nuptial plans? When shall the ceremony take place?" Alerion was drumming his long fingers against the armrest of his chair, showing his impatience.

"I don't see why we should wait. Would tomorrow suit you?" The Duke continued to gaze at Briella and not her stepfather who asked the question.

"I think that would be the finest choice, Your Grace," Alerion replied and bowed his head toward the other man.

"Splendid! I could not help but notice what a fine form you possess, my lady. We shall, of course, have no trouble raising six or seven little sons, just as strapping as I. Perhaps, a few daughters as well," the Duke inclined his head to her.

Barking out a laugh, Alerion said, "My goodness, you are quite the industrious fellow."

"I find putting forth expectations at the first is always the best way to proceed. Wouldn't you agree, my lady?" He tried to wink at her, but ended up giving her one slow blink instead.

Briella swallowed and nodded her head. She didn't quite know what to say. It wasn't that the Duke repulsed her, he truly was not the worst that could have been forced upon her. She didn't find him attractive, and perhaps that would give her cause later to be recalcitrant. Despite his latest speech, he possessed kind eyes and she wanted to trust that he would treat her as a lady and not as a servant. There was a little niggling at the back of her mind telling her, very insistently, that he was not all that he seemed. *He has secrets lurking within his chocolate eyes.*

"If you'll excuse me, Your Grace, I have some business to attend to that simply can't be put aside any longer." Alerion rose and Briella felt her eyes grow larger with dismay. True, she didn't trust her stepfather, but it was not proper to be left alone with a man that was not yet her husband. Before she could make a protest, he was out of the door with it closing behind him.

"Well, that was abrupt. He's not very sociable is he?" the Duke squinted at her.

"No, I am afraid not." Briella drew her delicate brows together and blew out a breath.

"It doesn't matter. Now, we can really get to know each other." He went to rise from his chair but found that it was stuck to his backside. He tried to shake it off as Briella tried to hide her gasp. She didn't know if she should offer her aid and when she went to rise, he held out his palm toward her and she stayed where she was. *Oh my!*

Trying not to look at him, Briella gazed at the wall painting to her left. She pretended to be studying it when she was really looking from the corner of her vision to gauge his progress. He had sat back down and was rocking to and fro. He lunged forward and crawled with his hands until he took a great groaning breath that freed him from the offensively small chair. If his complexion had been red before, it was even more so, now. He somehow managed to gain his footing and Briella turned to look at him again. The Duke ran a meaty hand through his copper locks and straightened his cravat and tailcoat, then he sauntered toward her. Seeing that he meant to sit next to her, Briella scrambled with her skirts to scoot as far over as she could.

"Well then," he began. "This is much more cozy. Tell

me, my lady, have you ever traveled by sea?" He raised his bushy copper eyebrows as he sat heavily down next to her. Then he pointed to the seascape that he thought she had been staring intently upon. He withdrew a kerchief from his inner coat pocket and dabbled at the accumulated sweat that glistened upon his face.

"No. I haven't had the pleasure before," Briella replied.

"You really should! The fresh oysters are divine, the best to be had. In my earlier days, I used to go about with my friend who was a carpenter by trade. I've never been rude to the lower classes," he sniffed. "But we've long since parted ways."

"Oh, how sad for you both. You must miss him," Briella sympathetically appraised him.

"Indeed, but he's not in a position to visit and I cannot gain entrance to where he is. So, it's only fond memories that I have to content myself with. Tell me, do you ever wish that things were different?" He gave her a significant look, but she could not figure out what his look was trying to convey.

"How do you mean?" she blinked.

"Well, that your life was on a different course?"

"Well, sometimes. But wishing never made a difference. Magic only exists in stories." Briella looked off toward the crackling fire.

"You truly believe that drivel, don't you?" He placed his large index finger below her chin and turned her head toward him.

"Yes, I believe in the here and now and I grew out of believing that the fairy stories were real. Do you believe in magic, Your Grace?" she wrinkled her nose at him.

"Of course. What do we have in this life if not magic? Wishing for your dreams and daydreaming isn't a waste of time. It's the magic of living and allowing ourselves to dream that makes what seems impossible attainable. Life is rather colorless and dull when one only looks to the here and now. Dreaming made kings and queens and great inventions possible. That's where you can find the traces of magic-all around you." Briella was once again struck by the idea that his eyes hinted at hidden secrets and undiscovered mysteries.

"But that's not actual magic. How could it be?" she smiled at him wistfully. Briella found herself wishing that she could envision the world the way he described it. *It must be wondrous to believe in such things.*

"Ah, I see, you want to believe, but you've lost your sense of wonder," he smiled at her regretfully.

"I have lost many things in my life. Perhaps, I've simply outgrown my use for magic. I cannot say. I only know that magic is not something that I have experienced in such a long time. Does that bother you?"

"I find that it does, for if you cannot believe in the impossible, how will you ever discover *who* you are?" He raised a copper brow at her.

"I know who I am, Your Grace. I am the orphaned stepdaughter that no one wanted. I grew up before I should have and life became all too real. I haven't known genuine kindness in far too long. But… for you, I think that I shall try to rediscover magical ways." She smoothed the imaginary wrinkles from her dress and said no more. She wasn't sure how to feel about an adult believing in magic.

"Would you honor a request?"

"It depends on what the request is. Is it practical? Will it harm me or another?" she inquired as she tilted her head to the side.

"Tonight, just before the sun goes to sleep, look out of a window and make a wish. Wish for magic to reveal itself to you, for it to guide you to your destiny. But you must sincerely make this wish with *all* of your heart." He looked so serious with a frown marring his face.

"You wish for me to make a wish. For magic that could lead me to my destiny? But I already know my destiny. Is it not with you?" Her delicate brows furrowed.

"Only your wish will answer that question, my lady. Humor me with this request. This is all I will ever ask of you."

"Very well, I shall honor your request. But..." she trailed off not wanting to make promises she did not intend to keep.

"Do not let doubt creep in, for that is the surest way to kill a dream. And you have such beautiful dreams to dream." He rose easily from the settee and reached for her hand. He kissed the back of her knuckles and bowed over her hand. "I'll bid you adieu until we meet again, whether that day is tomorrow or sometime hereafter. Fly away with your dreams, Briella, you have such wondrous things awaiting you." He returned her hand to her lap and grabbed up his walking cane before making his way out of the parlor and toward his awaiting carriage.

5

BIP AND BOP

Briella felt ridiculous, yet here she stood, before her bedchamber window, waiting for the wishing star to appear. After the Duke departed, her stepfather returned and told her to retire to her childhood room for the remainder of the day. She suspected that he simply didn't want to be bothered by her presence. Not wanting to suffer his company either, it wasn't a hardship to withdraw from his presence.

Maude served her dinner from a silver tray in her room. The food was delicious with rich flavors from spices that she'd long forgotten the taste of. None of the items had been grown from the kitchen garden.

She didn't know what to do. It had been so long since she had leisure time to herself. Briella hadn't bothered to change from her afternoon dress, she saw no sense in it as she didn't think she would be going anywhere, and it was the loveliest thing she had worn in such a long time. So, she lounged around and tried to read, but all of the books were fairytales and after her promise, she couldn't bring herself to read them. *This was all so ridiculous*. And yet, if wishes and dreams could change her destiny for the better, who was she to disregard her promise? She had been no one of importance when she rose that morning. *What a strange twist this day has taken.*

Twilight bloomed upon the horizon, melting the sky into a pot of blacks and blues speckled with stars. Black outlines of birds flew home to their nests after another day's work. Watching until the sky turned ebony, Briella easily located the wishing star. It was the brightest beacon in the darkened sky. She took a deep breath, squared her shoulders, and closed her eyes, then opened them again and said aloud, "I wish to follow my destiny to know where I belong. I wish to believe in the beauty of wishes and dreaming whimsically, and I wish that magic would fill my heart once again." She believed in her wish with every part of her and, for a brief moment, felt something pulling deeply within herself. She waited, and when nothing happened her shoulders drooped. "It was all silly anyway. Believing in fairytales and what-ifs." Briella walked to her bed and sat wearily down upon it. She felt a sudden gust of air enter the room.

"Well, this is quite the bedchamber. Tell me, do you still play with these dolls?" a feminine voice questioned from the direction of the window.

Giving a yelp, Briella fell from her spot atop the bed straight to the floor as she let out an *oomph.*

"This isn't quite going the way I had envisioned," exclaimed the woman with blue gossamer wings that peeked out from her dark blue robe. Briella couldn't see her hair, and she thought that maybe she didn't want to, since the little details that she did spy were enough to keep her heart beating wildly.

"I'm sorry to disappoint you, whoever you are," Briella

spoke as she picked herself up from the floor, shaking out her voluminous dress.

"Why, my dear, I am your fairy godmother! Now, let's not delay, you must be made ready to go to the ball." She pulled a long silver wand from within her cloak and twirled it around in a circle. White glitter flew from the wand's tip and lit up the room with many shooting stars that hung suspended upon the ceiling and walls.

"A ball? Oh, I'm not going to a ball." Briella shook her head and closed her mouth, which had been hanging open. *What was happening? Surely not the work of my wish? How could that be?*

"Excuse me? What's that you say? Did you not wish upon *my* star that you wanted to embrace *your* destiny? Well, that's *me*! And here I stand, ready to bip and bop you along your way." The woman put her other hand upon her hip and looked at Briella expectantly.

"So, a ball is my destiny?" Briella waved her hand in the air.

"Precisely. Or, rather, attending that ball is! Come along and let me get a good look at you, let's see what magic we need to employ to get you shimmering." Snapping her fingers, she pointed to the floor before her.

Briella walked to the beautiful lady. "What may I call you?"

"Oh, I go by so many names. Perhaps, you should just call me Fairy Godmother? It does have a certain ring to it. Now, you are lovely, my darling. There really isn't much that I need to correct. *Hmmmm*." Fairy Godmother walked around Briella a few times in a full circle. "A change of dress and slippers, glass slippers! Oh yes, indeed, and let's add some jewels to your hair after we let it down, of course. Your lovely golden tresses should flow freely tonight."

"Isn't that rather crude and unrefined?" Briella bit her bottom lip nervously.

"Not where I'll be sending you. Now, close your eyes. This works better when you cannot see." Fairy Godmother clapped her hands together.

Briella closed her eyes even though she was feeling very trepidatious. *Could magic be reversed?* She felt sparks and tickles all along her body. She felt her hair untwist and her dress shift. She inhaled sharply when she felt cold glass upon her feet. *Oh my goodness!*

"Almost finished. Now… open your eyes! This is where the fun begins!" Fairy Godmother twirled her silver wand again.

Briella saw blue glitter swirling around her and when it settled it lay all over her clothing, and the exposed skin that she could see.

"Walk over to the looking-glass and really take in the full effect!" Fairy Godmother gave her a push in her lower back.

When Briella stood before the gilded looking-glass, she gasped. "Is this a glamour?"

"Nonsense. This is the *you,* that you were always meant to be. I just gave you a little nudge in the right direction." Fairy Godmother tilted her head to the side, her teal-colored eyes appraising her work.

"This is real, isn't it?" Briella raised her delicate eyebrows as she took her eyes away from her own reflected image and looked to the reflection of the fairy behind her.

"It's all as real as I am." Fairy Godmother nodded at her.

"But that's what worries me. I think I am dreaming and this has all been made up in my mind. I mean, magic and fairies and dresses that look like this." She looked at her image again.

Her dress was a stunning cerulean blue that perfectly matched the shade of her expressive eyes. There was a middle panel that had a twisted vine pattern that was edged in a sumptuous golden flowered lace that also decorated the neck. There was a wide golden lace ribbon that encircled the dress just below her bosom. The most striking of all was the tiny silver stars that adorned the ball gown. The flickering stars seemed to disappear and reappear at their own will. Her arms were covered just up to her puffed sleeves in a silver lace that allowed her skin to peek through from beneath them. Her golden-colored hair was loose and flowing down her back in cascading curls that seemed to sparkle as well. There were jewels attached to her hair in random places that shimmered and sparkled no matter what direction she turned her head. She looked down and stuck out one foot from beneath the hem of her gown. Upon it was a glass slipper that glittered in the magical lighting. It seemed as if galaxies were spinning within the glass in a riot of color. She gasped as her heart beat erratically at the wonder she was arrayed in. *I can't believe what my eyes are seeing. Everything is so beautiful and I don't know quite what to do with myself.*

"I know. My best work. I do love the little details. Nothing makes a girl feel more glorious than having the world at her feet." Fairy Godmother smirked at Briella through the looking-glass.

"But it's not really the world I'm wearing upon my feet, is it?" Briella turned to face her.

"Not exactly. But all the same, do be careful. Magic is only as good as the one it's created for. Make sure that you're standing under the beams of the full moon when the clock strikes the hour of midnight. This will only last until then, and you'll be whisked back to this chateau once the spell has broken." Fairy Godmother smiled benevolently at her.

"I shall do all that you say. I want to thank you for this kindness. If I wake and find that this was all a beautiful dream, it's one that I shall never forget." Briella smiled back at her.

"You might be surprised by this evening. Just follow all the rules that you've been taught in those fairytales and all shall be as it is destined to be. Come along now, darling. We're wasting a perfectly good evening." Fairy Godmother strolled back to the window and with a wave of her wand, all of the stars that were lighting the room flew to her, back into the wand, leaving only the chamber as it had once been. With a roaring fire and lit candles to cast shadows upon the chamber, Briella could hardly believe what had just occurred.

Fairy Godmother crooked her index finger at Briella, beckoning her to join her and Briella obliged.

"Off you go. Simply close your eyes and let yourself be carried away. If it helps, imagine that you're in a carriage with four white horses driving you to a night that you'll never forget." Fairy Godmother watched as she closed her eyes.

Briella felt the floor beneath her drop away. Her body was light, as though she was being carried on the wind. She wasn't dizzy, but she did feel like she had lost all sense of direction. She didn't want to open her eyes and fall, so she kept them tightly closed until she felt herself slowly descending downward. The ground beneath her was solid so she poked one of her slippered feet from beneath her gown and extended it to tap upon the ground. When she was satisfied that she wasn't going to fall to her death, she opened her eyes.

She was looking down at the stoneway before her as she blew out a breath. She was safe. She raised her gaze and looked before her. Her eyes found a burgundy runner, which led up a set of midnight dark stairs. She cast her gaze higher and, as she did, she saw twisted dark turrets reaching up to the darkly purple sky, which was filled with many stars twinkling brightly. It was an odd contrast, the brightness of the sky and the blackness of the inky turrets. *What sort of beings reside within this twisted structure that is surely a castle? It looks very ominous.*

Taking a moment to scan the landscape surrounding the twisted castle, she noticed that there were woods with many tall trees with trunks that were as dark and twisted as the inky castle. The entire scene was shrouded with a floating mist giving everything an ethereal glow. She didn't hear any sounds of wildlife nor insects, but that could have been due to the lateness of the hour, or the scarcity of protection that the forest offered. *I wonder what lays behind the castle, but it is much too large to see around from where I am standing.*

She thought she imagined a pair of glowing scarlet eyes alight within the darkness of the forest, but when she turned back to look again, there was nothing there. But she still felt as if something was watching her every move. She suspected that beasts waited within those shadows for their next meal, and she did not want to linger too much longer out in the evening air. *I have had enough of beasts to last me a lifetime.*

Briella put one glass slippered foot in front of the other and, reaching down to gather the hem of her glittering gown, she slowly ascended the stairs. Even the twisted railing was inky black. The stairs twisted until she was brought before two gigantic doors that looked as if they were made from granite. She had seen no one since she was whisked away, and that gave her pause. Should she enter through the doors or descend the stairs to wait out her evening? Chills began to pebble her skin. She felt as if she was being watched. Briella looked to the side of one massive door and saw a gargoyle staring down at her. At first, she thought that it was a statue, but the more she met its menacing gaze, the more uncertain she felt. It was an enormous thing with a horned head and long tapered claws that dug into its perch. It was when one furry eyebrow raised at her, that she had made her decision. Briella felt sure that if her destiny was to die this evening, then nothing could cease the course of that, she might as well venture forth even if death awaited her. *I do so long to see what awaits me within those castle walls. It's almost as if some unknown force is beckoning me forth.*

Deciding that she would be safer within this strange castle than standing stupidly outside of it, she lifted a silver-gloved hand to grasp onto the dark knocker that was shaped like a rose in full bloom. Briella hit it against the door three times. The door swung open, and yet, she saw no one on the other side. Was this castle bewitched? An enchanted castle sounded much better to her wild imagination than a haunted one. Briella stepped into the entryway and watched the door close behind her.

6

THIS CANNOT BE REAL

Dim lighting illuminated the entryway giving shadowed views of gilded, black-framed looking-glasses that lined the walls. Carved roses trailed along the dark frames. The stones lining the walkway were a polished black that gleamed in the low lighting. A chandelier hung from the middle point of the high raised ceiling which was black and glittered. The candles that it held were scarlet. Briella could see the wax dripping onto the base that held each candle, it gathered there but did not trickle downwards.

There were strains of mesmerizing music that greeted Briella's ears once the door shut firmly behind her. The melody's notes were eerily welcoming, and Briella felt compelled to seek out the source. Without a soul in sight, she wandered down the corridor and stopped before a room that held conversations and the enchanting music that drew her in. There were no doors, just an archway to pass through that was decorated in black thorns. She couldn't fathom how anyone would not want to give their full attention to the notes being played by what sounded like a small orchestra. Why, it made her want to spin and twirl and forget all her troubles.

Once she reached the entrance, she peered into the room and forgot how to breathe. Dancing, standing, and conversing were beings that she had never seen before. There was a brown rabbit head attached to a human body, garbed in a glittering golden gown that shone like the sun itself. The skirts swished and swayed during a dance with a gentleman in a deep maroon suit, his frog feet bare for all to see. There were many different animals in their full form, wearing clothing and acting as if nothing was amiss. The word "faeries" came to mind as she watched the creatures engage in various activities, but their eyes, lips, tails, and pointed ears gave them an otherworldly beauty that would always make them stand out to her. Their hair and fur varied shades, from blue to green to orange, pink and purple, as did their eye color. There seemed to be at least one defining feature about each that was inescapable as being from the Fae race. *How is this possible?*

Briella looked toward the refreshment tables that lined the long inky black wall off to the side. There were blue crabs with their pincers serving up what looked very much like quiche, while tiny flying faeries were pouring dark wine into fluted glasses that shimmered in the light of the candles that adorned the tables, walls, and floors. When Briella looked up, she spied some cream-colored candles floating all by themselves in the air. Magic was very much at work here, and it was both thrilling and terrifying to behold. *This is absolutely astonishing. I must be dreaming but how my dreams could conjure this up, I have no idea.*

She looked down at her glass-encased foot, tapping

along in time with the music, before frowning and taking a deep breath. She slowly exhaled and blinked before she felt another compulsory urge to gather up her hem and throw herself amongst the dancers. But to lose herself in the crush would not do. Briella reined in her unruly feelings. She did not want to draw attention to her presence for she was not yet ready to meet those who frolicked within.

Turning her attention back to the ballroom, Briella wondered if these were glamours that she was seeing, but all the same, decided that it wasn't a room that she wanted to venture into, no matter how much she longed to join in the communal merriment. There were rules where the Fae were involved, and she wished that she could recall even one of them from her story books. The idea of this entire affair, basking in the presence of faeries, was ridiculous. Had she bumped her head? But then, she thought of Fairy Godmother and how very real that had all been. She'd been touched by the being, looked upon her, and had even held a conversation with her. *That was real, wasn't it?*

Briella looked once more upon the inviting chamber and its inhabitants and noticed the ugliest ebony throne that sat before the room. Its arms were rigid and twisted. Its legs, though also warped, ended in three perfectly clawed tips. And seated upon the monstrosity was a male. Perhaps, it was their King? Resting atop his head, was one glorious black crown, and though it was perfectly still, it glittered. It was split into three sections that all came together at its black jewel-covered base. The middle section stood higher than the sides and inset in the midst of that, rested a withered rose. The entire crown was magnificent.

She gazed at the features below that hauntingly

beautiful crown. Blond hair that looked as if it was tied behind the neck shone in the candlelight. She couldn't quite make out his eye color, but his aristocratic nose was straight. She noted the shape of his lips and how they were turned down into a most unpleasant scowl. Feeling her mouth go dry her heart began to race. She had heard of sensual lips before, but Briella had never understood what that meant until she gazed upon his mouth. She wondered what kissing him would be like and then grew bewildered wondering where that errant thought came from. She pushed the ridiculous thought away.

The monarch wore a midnight blue suit with a white shirt and a black cravat, black Hessians encased his feet, which were crossed at his ankles. He looked fearsome and wonderful, and Briella vowed to do her best to escape his notice, lest she incur his wrath. How handsome he was even with his somber, cantankerous mood. Briella felt drawn to him and she was not certain how to act with this shocking discovery. She had a craving to run her fingers through his golden tresses and shook herself internally. A giggle slipped past her lips and she quickly threw her hand up to her mouth to silence it. What nonsensical thoughts she was having! She felt like someone was watching her. When she looked toward the throne again, it was empty. Briella was surprised to feel disappointed as a knot formed within her stomach. *Where has the beautiful faerie gone?*

Briella began to step away from the elaborate ballroom when she heard a voice coming from just behind her. Halting her steps, she listened. She could almost make out the words asking, *"Who are you?"* followed by *"How curious her presence is."*

She could see no one, but thought that tonight maybe even guests could make themselves invisible. After all, wasn't anything possible in a land with faeries? She gathered her courage and straightened her posture as she turned to walk further down the corridor and away from the ballroom. She wouldn't think of faeries as kissable beings from this moment on.

Every few twists of the corridor she traveled, a lone gargoyle stood sentry. Their watchful gazes rested upon her, but they must not have deemed her a threat because her course was never deterred.

Briella soon spied another room with dark, ornate wooden benches and black potted plants that were twisted and dead; she had no idea what they were but decided that she might as well visit this room. She could collect whatever she saw along the way to add to her discoveries. Briella treaded softly into the room, noting the old, black wallpaper with withered roses on it every few inches. The thought occurred to her that if she reached out to touch the roses, they'd be textured, like they were molded into the walls. She marveled at their elegance.

Briella turned, taking in the full scope of the room. On either side were huge oil paintings of figures who wore crowns and jewels. Some had very animalesque parts, but most did not. Some looked very human, and some had that one defining Fae quality that set them apart. Underneath each portrait hung a small black plaque with names and titles etched in golden lettering.

Realizing that these were the kings and queens and even possibly their children, she couldn't help the curiosity that drew her to gaze at each one. What other human wouldn't claim such an opportunity? Some of their names were vastly different from what she was used to. There was a Faebert, a Faenella, and even a Faeweil. She saw that there were no last names given, just a first, along with the dates of their rule. Some were dated back to the beginning of time, but those beings clearly had very animal-like traits.

She walked to the other side of the room where the portraits seemed more modern in their execution and coloring.

"Yes, little one. Venture this way. For you have a very unexpected surprise awaiting," purred that same voice from earlier.

"Who's there?" Briella scanned the room.

"A friend, perhaps, if you wish it. I'm certainly not a foe." The voice was masculine and had a feline trill. If cats could talk, she imagined they would sound just like him. But this was the land of Fae and anything was possible, she reminded herself. Perhaps, it really was a talking cat.

"Why are you hiding?" she asked.

"Because, it's so much more entertaining," he purred.

"Fine. Keep your secrets. I'm used to being the laughing stock," Briella calmly replied.

"I don't wish to laugh at your expense. I simply want to watch your discoveries."

Ignoring the voice, Briella continued her perusal of the portraits. When she arrived at the face next to the last, she gasped. She could not believe her eyes and wondered why she hadn't fainted; her shock was so great.

"You bear his likeness, you realize? Same graceful mannerisms, and though you must resemble your mother, it's in your bones. The same magical traces reside," the voice remarked, much closer this time.

"I do not understand. How can my father be…" She looked down at the plaque underneath his portrait which read, *Marcel, Prince of Faerie of the Spring Court*.

"You've come home, dearest Briella, and we've all been waiting for you. Your destiny awaits."

"But I can't be part Fae. My father did not have a single

Fae quality. I don't have any either. This is ridiculous! *You're* ridiculous! I'm not wasting another moment in this obscene castle!" Briella bent down and reached for the hem of the ball gown, before she turned on her glass heel and fled the room.

7

REMEMBERING THE FORGOTTEN

Briella ran straight for the closed front doors located in the castle entryway as if she were being chased. Her racing thoughts kept perfect time with her heartbeat as unwanted feelings assaulted her sense. The two massive doors towered before her like fierce sentinels and wouldn't open. *Trapped, how I hate this feeling!* She frantically banged upon them with her gloved fists and pleaded; still, they remained stoically shut. She was locked inside. *Forever trapped…* She wanted to laugh, to cry, to mourn. She wanted to break something, anything, to wake from this horrible nightmare. She wasn't a faerie, not even half of one. And yet, she had seen her father's face in that room. Briella let her hands fall to her sides as she faced the doors in thought.

She didn't know what to think, or how to feel. Frustration began to fill her being, eclipsing all of her other emotions. She'd been an empty vessel for so long and did not belong anywhere except for her chateau. She had forced so many memories to the forgotten places within her mind, that it was easier to believe she was beneath everyone, rather than cling to ghosts of what *love* was like. And she had been loved. She'd been treasured, once upon a time.

Briella recalled her father's voice from her memory. It had been masculine but musical. He used to sing in his baritone voice and it was enchanting, like living within a dream. She remembered that when he sang, she'd see colors or images, like flowers, float through the air. *Had that been real? Was that his Fae ability?* Mama had said that he could sway an army with his voice, and it was nearly impossible to say no to any request that he made.

A sinking feeling weighed heavily in Briella's stomach as everything clicked into place. She had loved him fiercely. He could easily have been of Fae descent. He was charming and handsome and quick-witted. He could turn the mundane into the extraordinary. She swallowed against the tightening in her throat. *How can this be? What does this mean for me?*

Deciding that she couldn't stand in the entryway the rest of the evening, she took a deep breath and calmed herself. It wouldn't do her any good to continue panicking and trying to understand things that her mind was not yet ready to embrace. If she truly was part faerie, she had nothing to fear in meeting her fate. Besides, what torture could they enact that her stepfamily had not? She had been degraded and mistreated and even hated. She could do this. She could walk amongst the Fae and, for one night, dream that she belonged. She could try.

Briella tread back toward the ballroom, wondering if the reason why she had been able to resist the alluring notes of the music was because she had called upon her Fae heritage. Perhaps the Fae side of her could not be compelled as easily as her human half could? *Didn't humans always end up in various states of trouble in the stories?*

Briella wracked her brain trying to recall the tales, but they seemed to be too distant in her past: they were like mere whispers that floated on the wind, nothing tangible that she could cling to. Elusive and far away…

How she longed to belong to something or someone again. To have a destiny grander than scrubbing floors and feeding ungrateful beasts. If this was her destiny, then she had flown to it and should embrace it, never mind her reservations.

At home, she was a pest, an unwanted, unlovable thing. Could she be more here? Could her tender heart learn to once more reach for dreams that weren't yet dreamed? Could she grasp enough happiness in one night to keep her warm for the rest of her life? There was only one way to find out.

Placing one tentative glass heel in front of the other, she entered the ballroom. She was greeted by a tiny faerie with red, glittering wings and hair that matched. Her dress looked like red rose petals that had been plucked straight from the bush and stitched upon her delicate form. She flew right toward Briella and stopped an inch from her face.

"What are you?" The tiny faerie squeaked, staring at her with suspicion marked upon her tiny face.

"Do you mean to ask me who I am, instead?"

"No. I precisely asked you *what* you are. It matters not *who* you are," she stated with a huff and crossed her tiny bare arms.

"Oh, well then, I am… Well, I'm not inclined at present to tell you." Briella tried to duck her head and take a step under the floating being.

The faerie immediately flew down to still her movements. "You're rather rude. I like you. How faetastical! I've decided to befriend you. My name is Fleur and I am a sprite." She came closer to Briella's face and with her tiny fist, bopped her upon the nose.

"Oh!" Briella exclaimed as she scrunched her nose. She felt a tiny tingling at the spot where she had been touched. It was more of a distraction, a curious feeling.

"Now, unnamed friend, let's get you dancing and have an entertaining evening!" Fleur reached out and grabbed onto one of Briella's golden ringlets and pulled. The sudden action alarmed Briella.

"Must you tug so forcefully? I do not desire to have the hair ripped from my head!" Briella called out as she rushed her steps to keep up with the determined faerie.

Fleur gave a musical giggle. "Nothing a little Fae magic couldn't fix. But since you're my new friend, I shall let you go."

Briella did not bother to respond to her new vexatious acquaintance. She followed her hair until it was dropped and then looked at where she stood. A tiny blue crab was blinking its large black eyes peering up at her in a suspicious manner. She thought she spied a scowl upon its features, but it was hard to be certain.

"Well, what is it that you want? I don't get paid to be stared at," the tiny crustacean inquired in an accent new to Briella's ears. When Briella only looked at him some more, he focused his gaze onto Fleur and said, "She's simple, then? Is that it? Have you befriended a simple human? It's the faerie wine you're after, I'd bet my right pincer."

"How perceptive, you are, Sebastian. She does seem lacking in her wits, but nothing that a night here won't soon cure." Fleur held out her hand for two flute glasses of dark liquid. Sebastian gave them to her and nodded to the throne.

"He seems to have wandered off. He does that far too

often. When I served my king, he never left his own galas. It's rude," Sebastian huffed.

"It must be much more fun to wander off than to sit and watch the entertainment happen all around you." Fleur handed one of the flute glasses to Briella, who cautiously took it. How either the tiny faerie or crab managed its weight was a mystery to her.

Briella watched the candlelight glittering within the glass as she turned it in one direction and then another. The rainbow of colors was mesmerizing. She brought the glass to her nose and inhaled the aroma of fruit and spices. *It smells delectable.*

When her gaze wandered to the room's other inhabitants, she concluded that, while they were dancing and laughing, they also seemed wary. How could such a thing be possible in a decadent setting like this? She felt gooseflesh rise along her arms under her glittering gloves at the almost menacing undertone floating along in the air. There was an undercurrent of unrest, perhaps even maliciousness. *Perhaps I am not as safe here and I had hoped afterall…*

"Listen here, human. You had better listen to me and *not* drink that. Terrible things happen to ill-behaved young ladies who do not listen. I won't be around for much longer this evening and as we're now acquainted, it's my duty to look after you." Sebastian glared at her tersely, "*Don't* drink that."

"I, thank you for your concern. It's kind of you," Briella smiled down at him.

"Don't mistake intelligence with *kindness*. I only can advise you, and from past experience, people often do *exactly* what I warn them against."

"Oh, in that case, I shall take your advice into

consideration. Thank you." Briella saluted him with the goblet.

"Don't you dare listen to him, Unnamed! He only wants to spoil our fun!" Fleur shrieked as she shook her tiny fist at him.

"Bah," Sebastian waved his claw. "You want to keep her. You'll say anything!"

"Well, what's wrong with that? It's been ages since anyone new visited. Besides, have you considered that she might be the *'you-know-who'* that we've been *you-know-what* for?" Fleur's sapphire eyes squinted at the crab.

"Ah, no actually. And for good reason. It's best not to get our hopes up. Anyway, what can a *human* really do?"

"What can't a human do?! Mark my words, my little crabby friend, grand things are happening!" Fleur clapped her tiny hands with glee around her glass and some of its contents spilled over its sides. The wetness didn't seem to bother her at all.

"Excuse me, but do I want to know what you mean?" Briella looked from one to the other. She was used to being talked about but still felt it rude to completely be ignored.

"Nope!" Fleur exclaimed as she once again leaned down to pick up a lock of Briella's hair and tugged her away from the table.

Briella rushed to keep up with the tiny menace. She followed until her hair was dropped again and stood before the handsome Faerie King. He towered over her; she had to look up to meet his stormy eyes. Her head only came to the middle of his chest. She swallowed when she met his gaze and wanted to immediately run away. He was fierce and impressive and so unearthly beautiful. *What must he think of me?*

"Your Majesty," Fleur bowed and pinched Briella's arm to get her attention so that she too would show the proper respect. It dawned upon Briella with sudden clarity that she was standing before the Faerie King of the Spring Court. She quickly reasoned that if her father had been a prince of the Spring Court, then that must be the Court in which she now found herself.

Briella quickly curtsied and blinked as she rose to once again meet his gaze. She didn't dare speak as she was swept up and away into the mossy depths of his extraordinary eyes. She was absolutely mesmerized. *Eternity could pass and I would be content to wither and age, just to keep my gaze locked with his.* There was a curious warmth in her stomach and a thrill was blossoming in her heart. She felt as if he held closely guarded secrets and, if she were patient enough, perhaps one day, they'd come spilling out.

"Who is she, Fleur?" the Faerie King demanded. He wore a frown and for some strange reason, that only seemed to make him more appealing to Briella.

"A very dear friend. We are practically inseparable."

"Indeed. May I remind you of the rules? We do not cater to humans and their ilk and she has no place here," he sneered at Briella. Her cheeks heated, taking on a blush as Briella fought back against her blooming retort. Her fingers curled at her sides as the King's words played over and over in her head.

Human.

Ilk.

No place here.

Was it not her father's face that hung upon the portrait gallery's wall? She had just as much right to be here as any other faerie; just as much right as he did.

"But it's only for tonight Your Majesty," Fleur protested, bowing her head. Briella closed her eyes and sucked in a deep breath, bringing herself back to the situation at hand.

"See that is exactly how things unfold. We've too much to attend to without the inconvenience of more unwanted guests," he stated as he briskly stormed away.

Briella watched him as he once again sat upon his inky throne. He did not look at her again, and her brow furrowed. If she really was part faerie, why didn't anyone seem to sense it about her? Did she not have a place here after all? It was true that she didn't want to stay forever, but she wanted to belong in at least one world. And now that she knew the truth of her parentage, she didn't wholly belong to one place or the other. Her thoughts made her come to the realization she truly did desire to belong to this unimaginable world if they would allow her to stay even for just a little while longer. *But it isn't up to me. What is it about me that causes such disdain in others?*

Quickly, Fleur flew into her line of vision. "Pay no attention to King Grumpy. He's always like that. Well, he used to be much more impossible, now he's quite almost tolerable." She crossed her arms across her small chest and frowned for a brief moment, pouting at the King as the orchestra struck up a new melody.

Briella's eyes glistened as she recognized the tune. It had been the melody that her father had hummed to lull her to slumber each evening. *Papa tucked the pale pink coverlet under Briella's chin and placed a gentle kiss upon her forehead. She smiled up at him with all of the love that she felt.* I am safe and loved and all is right with my world.

"And now to chase the sweet dreams that await you, my little precious daughter." Papa began to hum.

Swirling stardust of purples, pinks and blues floated along the air. They changed to individual shapes of flowers and tiny animals. From one shape to another, they formed just to disappear and reform as another brilliant configuration. The ceiling was alight with the enchanting sparks and Briella was delighted to witness such a sight. This was one of her favorite things that Papa could do. With the music of the melody her body began to relax.

Feeling sleep pulling her into the realm of dreams, Briella yawned. "Papa, you will keep the monsters of this world away, won't you?"

"But of course, my dear little Poppet. You never need worry when Papa is near. Now close your eyes and listen to my song."

Briella blinked and she made herself concentrate on the here and now. She had forgotten the wonders of the magic that dwelled within their chateau for as long as Papa had lived. *How could I let myself forget such a thing?*

Realizing that Fleur was addressing her, Briella tucked the memory away.

"Let's dance! Oh, I see the perfect partner for you!" Instead of pulling her along by her tresses, Fleur grabbed her puffed sleeve and guided her over to the wall where a faerie with the head of a goat was conversing with a faerie who had dark blue hair and a black tail that stuck proudly out behind his back. The horns that aligned on either side of his temples were ebony and curled just at their edges.

Briella thought that he was stunning, but feared that her tiny faerie friend would foist her off upon the goat-headed one. *And I do not know if I can manage a dance held in the arms of such a creature. He's frightening and I don't know if I would be able to stop staring at his strangeness. I would hate to cause offense and embarrass myself.*

Both males were regally dressed in black trousers and fitted tailcoats with gold thread. There didn't seem to be much padding on either faerie's frame except for that which was their own solid form.

Seeing the pair before them, the men bowed and this

time Briella was quick to dip into a curtsey. When she rose back up, the attractive horned faerie was looking at her curiously.

"Shall we dance Godfrey?" Fleur held out her arm to the goat-headed male.

“It would be my pleasure.” Godfrey allowed Fleur to grab onto his index finger and lead him to where other couples were dancing.

Briella watched the odd pair as they swayed to the music. She felt relieved that she would not be partnered with him. Fleur simply held onto his finger as he whirled them about and if one didn't know better, it might look as if her partner danced alone.

The floating candles were still casting their glow onto the objects below them and making everything appear magical. The hanging vines that clung to the inky dark walls were thorny and twisted, and from the glow cast upon them they appeared menacing. There were various metallic-colored bubbles that floated from a corner. The effect was breathtakingly beautiful. *Otherworldly to be sure.*

Looking before her, Briella noticed that there was a portly faerie stumbling toward her with bushy, magenta eyebrows and hair. She quickly held out her hand, holding onto the fluted glass to stop his progress. He grabbed the glass from her, smiled with vicious pointed teeth, and was once again stumbling around the room. While Briella had never seen a shark before, he very much reminded her of one with the sharp smile he had cast her way.

“Would you care to dance with me?” The attractive faerie she'd been left with spoke beside her. Up close his dark blue hair and ebony horns shimmered in the candlelight. *He is breathtakingly beautiful.*

Briella gave her full attention to him, then took his offered bare hand and let him lead her into the crush of bodies that were twirling in every direction. She gasped when she caught sight of the floor they were standing upon. It looked like smooth blocks of ice with red roses frozen inside. They were perfectly preserved and, given the decor of the room and even that of the twisted castle, they looked out of place. She could feel her eyes widen as her breath hitched. *Another stunning feature that does not quite fit in with the inky blackness. How remarkable!*

Seeing the surprise upon her face, her dance partner said, "There is untold beauty everywhere. 'Tis often in the least likely of places to be discovered. But it's there." He brought his left arm around her waist and positioned the hand he'd been holding to the proper pose for the dance.

"I'll look forward to seeing what else I shall discover tonight." Briella easily followed his lead as they glided back and forth.

"May I learn your name, fair lady?"

"It's Briella. Am I to learn your name in return?"

"*Tsk,* has no one warned you of the danger that one's true name can cause? Never give your true name to a faerie. We can and likely will use it to cause you endless grief. It makes glamouring you so much easier." The faerie's lips quirked into a wicked grin revealing perfectly white straight teeth that spread across his handsome face. Briella's stomach knotted; a pond of dread swirled deep within her. She met his gaze, noting the menace that lurked in the dark pools of his eyes as they held her captive.

For a moment Briella's heart forgot how to beat. Then she simply laughed as her stomach twisted with nerves. What else was she to do?

"Don't believe me, little one? Maybe I can demonstrate this lesson for you," he whispered, leaning in close to her ear. They kept dancing, twirling around the other couples on the floor, but his gaze on hers never faltered. His eyes were intent on proving his point. Briella felt her mind cloud with a light, buzzing sensation that caused her to blink, breaking whatever connection her partner held over her. She took a deep breath and cleared her throat, feeling the intrusion flit away. He remained silent, only his lips pulled into a frown as he whirled them around. When the song ceased, he led her back to the spot where they had met. He shook his head. "Holly berries?" he asked.

"Whatever do you mean?"

"I can't spy any on your person. Perhaps you've hidden them?" He peered at the top of her gown along her bust, shook his head, and snapped his fingers. "I know! You've strung them around your leg?" Making to grab her dress, he bent over, but Briella quickly smacked his hand away.

"How dare you!" she hissed.

"I'm deeply intrigued." He straightened as he gripped his chin with one hand while the other hand supported his elbow.

"I don't care." Briella pushed past him and weaved her way to the other side of the room. He didn't try to follow. Relief washed over Briella. *Faeries can be the absolute worst creatures!* The sound of her dance partner's harsh laughter rang in her ears, floating along in the air.

What nonsensical whimsy! What nerve! A perfect stranger trying to take liberties and delighting in her fright. This was not something that she'd ever willingly let happen, and the reminder of her cruel stepfamily was most unpleasant. Wishing it was midnight and that she was back at the chateau, as safe as she had ever been, Briella grabbed a cracker with some sort of paste on top of it from an enchanted floating tray that was just passing by and took a bite. She gagged as she tried to swallow the bitter food, and reached for a glass from the now, crabless table.

She drank the entire flute before she could process the significance of her actions. When the foul taste had abated, she threw her hand over her mouth and gave a muffled cry. For, she had just done the one thing that she knew she should never do. She ate the faerie food and drank the faerie wine.

8

LIBRARY: A PLACE OF DREAMS

Briella waited for someone to notice what she'd just done. She waited for someone to either jeer or cheer her actions. She waited for a different feeling to creep into her being, to twist her insides up, or for some force to ground her heels in place so that she'd be forever forced to dwell in the land of faeries. But when nothing happened, she let out a sigh that turned into a giggle.

Oh dear, perhaps the wine was getting to her. She felt euphoria sweep over her senses and didn't quite know what to do with herself. She felt like spinning in her place, or perhaps, grabbing a partner and really enjoying herself. She couldn't care less if she danced herself to death. She remembered a cautionary tale of a girl who danced under the full moon with a faerie, and though she tired and thirsted she couldn't stop her feet from dancing. The poor girl danced until she fell over dead. Briella didn't wish to meet the same fate.

She felt her foot tapping to the delightful scales of the music. What was done was done. *Oh well!* Hearing a clock strike, Briella counted the chimes. There were twelve signaling the lateness of the hour. It was midnight and she wasn't standing under the moon. How was she to know what the time was? There had been no way for her to have kept track of it. She shrugged and swayed in place. If Fairy Godmother wanted her to return to the chateau, she'd have to come find her. Briella didn't think she'd make it too far, as the room began to spin. She had never had wine before and doubted she'd ever even so much as sniff at it again. She stayed where she was and let her cares and worries drift away. *Everything is so lovely. Why was I so frightened before?*

Briella had been swaying for who knew how long when Fleur flew up to hover before her nose. She lifted her hand to wave the offending creature away, but Fleur wouldn't be discouraged.

"Is Fleur even your real name? Your true name?" Briella blurted out.

"Why no, you silly girl. Why would you ask that?" Fleur looked at her with furrowed brows.

Briella only giggled in reply.

"You drank the faerie wine!" Fleur exclaimed, clapping her tiny hands together, "What faetastically wonderful news! I knew you wouldn't disappoint me. Now, we'll be friends forever or until your wrinkly body falls over."

Not knowing what to say, Briella stayed silent. She took a step toward the large French doors, located off of the sidewall, and pushed one of the heavy doors open.

Fresh air greeted Briella as she walked out onto the terrace that was decorated with a little round table and matching chairs and various potted plants. Twisted plants grew here and there, wrapping their vines around anything within their reach. Briella took in a deep breath, trying to calm her rioting nerves, and let out a sigh before looking up. The pink moon was directly overhead and the stars were glowing with a teal hue. Briella grasped onto the twisted railing and held on tightly, not wanting to lose her balance and plunge to her death. The hold that the wine had upon her was waning. From this height and angle of the castle, she had a better view of the twisted turrets. One looked as if it leaned so far out, it could tumble over at any moment. *Why is everything so twisted here? The surroundings as well as the beings?*

Again, she took a deep breath and tried to calm her unrelenting nerves. Closing her eyes, Briella thought about the chateau and wishes and about magical nights and all that she had learned in one short evening. Her life was changing in momentous ways, and she felt powerless to alter her present course. That shouldn't have been anything new to her, she'd felt that exact same way for years. But here, she wanted more. She desired to matter and not be brushed aside. She longed to live in the twisted castle and learn everything that she could about her family and heritage. She had so many impossible questions that needed answers, and if magic dwelled within her veins, she would need to get a handle on it as quickly as possible. *I don't wish to be the cause of a calamity. And I certainly don't wish to harm another.*

Fleur flew up beside her and patted her ear. "You've had a tiring evening. You mustn't be sad. There's too much misery within these walls. You need to rise above that and seek out your destiny."

"Destiny? Why does everyone keep saying that word to me? How am I meant to follow a path that I cannot perceive? What if I make mistakes?" Briella opened her eyes and turned her head to look at the tiny faerie.

"We all make mistakes. Anyone who doesn't hasn't really lived. It's learning to embrace your past and all the faulty parts of yourself that really grows a being. Stretch,

Unnamed! Reach for the stars and don't stop, ever. You're so much more than you've ever been." Fleur looked at her and blinked, then gave a hearty laugh as she fluttered back into the ballroom.

Briella watched her go, wondering at the strangeness that possessed the tiny faerie, and turned back toward the stars. She wanted to believe, in what she wasn't yet certain. But she wanted to dream and *truly* live. This was her chance to be more, and she would take it and grasp onto it with arms outstretched and with an open heart.

She looked down toward the castle grounds. There was a bubbling fountain with a statue of a beast who also possessed the features of a man. She couldn't quite make out all of its features. Water spouted up between the creature's hands, which were curved together as if holding onto the water. Perhaps he was meant to stop the flow of water? *You can no more stop the flow of the water than I can my destiny.*

The pale pink moon shone brightly up above her in the darkly purple sky. Its light allowed her to view much of the land before her. Looking beyond the rows of withered rose bushes she noticed the forest. And Briella spied the pair of glowing eyes and shivered as she wondered if they belonged to the same being who had watched her upon her arrival. She was uncertain whether the being meant to endanger her, but she meant to stay far away from it.

Turning away from the forest and the haunting eyes, Briella walked back to the doors and turned the handle to once again enter the ball.

She weaved her way through the dancing pairs and toward the entry, leaving the ballroom and its guests behind her. Briella walked along the corridor and passed by many rooms without looking to see what they contained, passing stationary gargoyles whose eyes seemed always upon her. When she couldn't take another weary step, she stopped at the end of the corridor where a black granite door stood before her. She took a deep breath and held it until she turned the door handle, pushing it open.

Her breath rushed out as she entered the room and pushed the door closed with her body as she leaned her weight against it. Briella simply stood there and looked around the chamber. There were rows of books that reached up to the vaulted ceiling and lined the walls. There were dark carpets along the ebony stone floor. A huge unlit fireplace was situated within the middle of the room that could be accessed from either side, and dark pillows were placed before it where one could lounge while reading. But it was the books that thrilled Briella the most. There were so many! She spied a cozy corner where a settee was situated next to a small table where a lamp was lit. It looked like Heaven. If she could have tried to describe her perfect room, this would have surpassed her imaginings.

There were dozens of floating silver stars along the vaulted ceiling which was topped with a glass dome that allowed the moonlight to shine down upon the library. It was magical the sight took her breath away. She wanted to curl up upon the settee and read every single book, no matter its contents. They were lovely and such a treasure to discover. Briella briefly wondered if this was a room allowed to all or reserved for the King. She didn't want to be barred from this beautiful sanctuary. *Here I could happily hide away from all my troubles.*

Leaning away from the door and stepping silently further into the chamber, she walked to the first shelf and lovingly touched the spines of the books with her fingertips. When she discovered that she could read the titles which weren't written in some Fae language, she brought a hand up to her mouth to stifle her expression of glee. *This is marvelous! I can barely contain my excitement.*

From a little way down the wall, she heard movement. She stepped away from the shelf and peered toward the noise. The Faerie King of the Spring Court looked at her as he snapped his book closed. His body faced toward the shelf while his head was turned toward her. He replaced the book to its space upon the shelf, then turned his body to face her as he crossed his arms over his large, impressive chest.

"What are *you* doing here?" he growled out.

"I-" she stammered, not certain how to meet his ire.

"You what? This is my personal room. No one dares to venture into my domain," the King frowned at her.

For some odd reason, she felt compelled to walk the short distance to stand before him. But it wasn't as if any magic had been used upon her. She couldn't make sense of the feeling. Briella only knew that she wanted to be nearer to him and to feel his warmth. She should have been frightened by him, and yet, that's not what she was feeling at all. It wasn't hatred that met her stare, she'd seen plenty of that residing in her stepfamily's eyes. Curiosity was alight within his mossy green gaze.

"Do you have no sense of self-preservation?" He curled a dark blond brow at her.

"Apparently not, Your Majesty," she replied, shrugging her shoulders.

"It's customary to bow before your King."

Briella curtsied hurriedly before him. "Are you my King?"

"It would appear so. You drank the wine, did you not? Sebastian isn't really attending to his duties well enough."

"Oh, he's not to blame. He did caution me. I didn't

mean to drink or eat anything. I had an unnerving dance partner, and wasn't thinking clearly until I realized what I had done. Can it be revoked?" Briella winced at the hopefulness in her voice.

"I am afraid not. The real question is, what am *I* to do with *you* now that you're here?" He clasped his hands behind his back and began pacing before her. A lock of his blond hair fell forward into his face and he threw his head back to dislodge it. There was an odd tug on Briella's heartstrings at the boyish gesture. How was it that so fearsome a King could do something so endearing? He was scowling when he stopped before her. "What skills do you have? Can you cook? Garden? Nurse the ill?"

Briella took a moment before answering. *I do not wish to be stuck here doing the drudgery work. I'm tired of working myself to exhaustion.* "I can sew."

"Really?" He looked her up and down and stroked his chin with his hand. A glimmer of hope blossomed within her chest.

"Oh yes!" Briella enthused.

"I think you'll do quite well then. We could use a skilled seamstress," the King replied before turning on his heel. Without a word, he took off toward the library door. Reaching down, Briella gathered her skirts into her grip and ran after him.

"Your Majesty!" Briella felt panic squeeze her heart.

"What?" He ground out with an impatient clenching of his jaw as she continued along the corridor, not bothering to slow his pace for her.

"I believe that there's been a misunderstanding."

They turned right and then began to descend a grand twisted staircase. There were black wall sconces hung every few feet along the walls and a thick burgundy runner laid upon the stairs.

"You can sew?"

"Yes, but..." Briella was just keeping pace behind him. She had to watch her feet so that she wouldn't lose her footing upon the twisted stairs that turned in odd directions.

"You will be our seamstress. That will be your post from now on. Now, no more questions, if you please."

Furrowing her brows together and biting her lip, she kept silent as they finally reached the floor again. The last thing she wanted to do was displease him. There was a set of doors and the King led her to one at the very end of the hall. It was no surprise that in every direction that she looked there was nothing but inky darkness. Even the landscapes that hung in their ebony frames along the walls were darkened to a point that Briella could barely make out what they depicted. *What a depressing and oppressive atmosphere.*

He motioned to the black door and nodded. "These will be your chambers. I'll have someone bring you all the necessary equipment that you'll need that cannot be found within. Settle in, I'm sure you will be quite busy."

"Thank you, Your Majesty. May I ask you a question?"

He nodded. Briella looked up at the King's crown, studying it as she searched for her words. How did it sit so elegantly upon his head? Her eyes lowered and she looked into his arresting mossy green gaze. He wasn't scowling and didn't seem impatient with her, like when they'd first met. She wondered what had changed, but that wasn't the most pressing concern at present.

"Is this castle under an enchantment?"

The King stiffened. Now, he was scowling at her. "What would make you wonder that?"

Briella straightened her posture, breaking eye contact as she looked down the hallway. "Everything. From the inky blackness dripping from every corner and crevice, to the forest which seems menacing, to the beings here who were celebrating, but who did not seem to be really happy. Even you, you seemed dreadfully bored tonight. It's the only explanation that makes sense. And now, here I am."

Leaning against the door frame, he folded his arms across his chest. "And here you are."

"That's not an answer."

"It's the only answer that I can give you."

Huffing out a breath, Briella just stood there. Frustration was making her careless. Her position was precarious and she needed to better guard her feelings.

"Look around yourself, see what you can discover." The Faerie King uncrossed his arms and opened the door.

Briella took one last look at him and walked into the chamber. She heard the click of the door closing and turned around in a panic. Briella rushed back to the door and wrenched it open. It wasn't locked and she hadn't been trapped. She peered out into the hallway, but didn't see the King. It was as if he'd vanished in a wisp of smoke.

Turning back and closing her door, she turned the lock. It was curious, she supposed, to lock out others, when she had spent years being locked in. Tears sprang to her eyes, threatening to spill down her cheeks and Briella fought back her emotions. She wasn't a prisoner anymore. And while she wasn't free to do exactly as she wished, this existence, this beautiful freedom, was better than anything she had ever had. She wouldn't let oppressive thoughts of doom and gloom overshadow her anymore. This was her new reality, and she would simply do her best. She would oblige the King, but she would seek out her own answers. She couldn't wait to discover what great mystery hung around the next corner. If she could help, why not endeavor to do so?

9

NAKED TALKING MICE...

Briella padded further into her bedchamber and let out her breath in a rush of air. She felt the frustration leave her body as she made her way over to the window. Black drapes hid her view. In the black wooden cabinet beside the window, Briella found a simple nightgown to wear to bed, and it was easily the most lovely one she had ever worn. The cabinet was an exquisite piece of work that stood upon four clawed feet that might have once boasted brass rosettes for decoration. After changing into the nightgown, she hung up her ball gown and stowed away all of her magically created pieces into the cabinet. The gown and glass slippers were just as charming as when they had been magicked upon her person. She had taken a moment to touch the material of her gown and smile. She briefly wondered what Fairy Godmother was doing, and if she knew whether Briella had returned home or not. She hoped there would be no consequences for not returning as instructed, and as she closed the cabinet door, exhaustion settled deeper into

Briella. She washed her face and hands in a little room off to the side of the chamber's entrance.

The water closet was in a separate room, something that was both unseen and unheard of by Briella. There was an indoor spigot that produced water at one's own will with just a turn of its handle, a curious chamber pot attached to a porcelain chair, which one sat upon as purple water flowed continually within it. There had even been a smaller room with dark tile and another spigot that came from above. She assumed that this area was for bathing and intended to try it out the next morning.

The ebony fireplace which had been lit when she entered was large with carved roses and twisting vines creeping along its marbled edges. Situated not too far away from the blaze was the bed which was the focal point of the entire room. It was a massive four-poster affair with various blankets and the bed hangings looked as if they were stitched directly onto the bed frame. Once she had climbed under the coverlet and settled in, she felt like a princess. The mattress was not lumpy, instead it was soft and luxurious. It was a place to build the most fanciful dreams and the most peaceful of slumbers. Briella hadn't bothered seeing what else made up her chamber, but she knew that there was another room attached to her bedchamber and she assumed it was where she was to attend to her seamstress duties. It was not long before her dreams carried her away.

BRIELLA STRETCHED AS SHE AWOKE THE NEXT MORNING. As she did so, recollections of all that had taken place within the past few hours rushed to her mind. She was in the Spring Court and had no way in which to return to her beloved chateau. Briella had some amount of safety surrounding her and didn't want to leave this land just yet. There was still so much for her to discover. To her surprise she realized that the bruises previously marring her body had disappeared and she suspected that the magic Fairy Godmother had used upon her had completely healed her.

Tossing her coverlet aside, Briella climbed down from the massive bed. She clambered over to the fireplace, wondering how the flames were still so high. It was curious how the flames burned with a mossy glow, reminding her of a certain set of eyes that belonged to a face that did not smile. Perhaps, the fire was enchanted like many other things in this castle seemed to be.

She stood for a moment, watching the flames lick at the charred wood, and wondered when her panic would ensue. She was not a seamstress. *And here it is,* Briella thought as her hands came up to either side of her face as she leaned forward. Her breathing became haggard as her pulse sped up. Twisting knots took root deep within her stomach. What was she going to do? She could sew, that was not a lie, but her level of skill was nowhere near accomplished to that of actually being a seamstress. *What am I going to do? I am in so much trouble.* Briella felt her pulse ratchet up as her breathing rapidly increased.

Running away was an option. Wasn't it? She could always fake it. *Why yes, Lady Fae, your dress is supposed to fall away from your frame while you walk. It's quite the fashion, you know. Yes, Mr. Rabbit Head, your trousers are actually meant to have see-through seams. Yes, yes, the tailcoat is supposed to have mismatched sleeve lengths. What a nightmare.* Did they behead here? Was that an appropriate punishment for liars? Perhaps, they would take her fingers as punishment. She really did not want to face the King again, but there was a chance that she would run into him. Though she could handle most mistreatment, she did not desire to face the displeasure of a king. For some odd reason she wanted him to esteem her, to grow to like her; to value her as a member of his Court. She didn't suppose that was likely to happen if she produced unusable goods.

She was kneeling before the fireplace, sweeping the ashes from its hearth, when her stepbrother, Hugo, found her in the kitchen. He leaned over her and pushed her into the ashes as his laughter rang out. "Now you shall be the Lady of the Ashes!" Briella's face was covered in cinders as were her hands as she struggled not to inhale the powdery residue. "Perhaps we shall rename her, Cinder Ella!" her other stepbrother, Henri, called out from the kitchen's entryway. Their laughter had carried them from the room. The jeering voices of her stepfamily leered their way into her thoughts and she felt their words pelting her like stones. *"Unfit" "Unwanted" "Ugly" "Unlovable" "Rat" "Vermin" "Worm" "Trash"* they repeated in her mind. Briella brought her hands up to cup her ears, but her movement had no effect stopping the flow of the words assaulting her.

"Hello, there. Perhaps, if you want a friend or two to confide in, we may assist you?" a smallish female voice called out.

Briella whirled around in place as her hands fell from the sides of her face, searching for whom the voice belonged to. She could see no other being within the room. Briella scratched her head, her eyes growing wide as a thought dawned on her. *Am I going mad?*

"Down here, by the chair, Mistress of the Seam."

Looking down, Briella spied a trio of brown mice who were looking up at her. She blinked in amazement.

"You reckon she's daft?" inquired one of the tiny mice in a squeaky male voice.

And that's when Briella shrieked and ran toward her bed and, reaching it, she flung herself onto it. *Talking mice?* Feeling frightened, as she had never encountered animals that could speak to her, Briella tried to reason with herself that having rodents addressing her was quite normal and not some sort of panic-induced hallucination. *And yet… last night there had in fact been talking animals that I conversed with. Because in the realm of the Fae all was possible, wasn't it?*

"Shhhh. She can hear you!" admonished the same female voice.

Briella peeked out through her fingers, shielding her eyes. "What can I assist you with?"

"It's us who are meant to be assisting you," replied the female mouse.

"But we can't very well do that if she's going to forever run away. I can't decide whether I want to be amused or horrified at her lack of manners." The male mouse lifted his nose in the air.

Here, Briella felt conflicted. She didn't want to be rude or to cause offense. Yes, she had seen mice before. She had even talked to them, mostly coaxing them to go away. But never had she conversed with them. Taking a moment, Briella supposed that they were also Fae and that there must be a difference between them and the dirty house mice that she was accustomed to. Knowing that she was making a terrible impression, she tried to calm her racing heart by slowing her breathing and attempting to relax her tightly wound body.

"*Pfft*. She must be frightened. The poor dear. We won't harm you," cooed the female mouse. "You need not be afraid."

Briella took a deep breath and slowly climbed down from her bed. She crept back to the wingback chair and knelt down. "I am so sorry if I offended you. I was caught by surprise and, after all that I saw last night, I really should not be surprised by your presence. Forgive me?"

Nodding her head, the female mouse approached her. "It's a pleasure, Mistress of the Seam. We were tasked with assisting you today. What shall we do to help?"

"I'm not quite sure. You are Fae, yes?"

"That we are! You do know the differences between Seelie and Unseelie, I hope?" The male mouse twitched his whiskers.

"I'm afraid not," Briella admitted.

"Oh!" He rubbed his small paws together. "Well, the Seelie faeries tend to stick in human-like forms, neglecting their animal-like qualities. They prefer refinement and the finer things to be found in polite Society. They are elegant and refined and *utterly* boring. Can't stand to be around them for too long. Now, the Unseelie faeries, such as myself, prefer to be wild. We like our animal form and the freedom that comes with that. We don't like humans *at all*. We have often been accused of malice towards humans and causing them harm. But show me a Seelie that hasn't glamoured or tricked a human in some manner. In that aspect, we tend to stick together. The Seelie made a pact to stop causing utter destruction amongst the human race long ago. They have even gone so far as to influence their culture and that has resulted with great works of art and literature; far surpassing that which the vile creatures should have been capable of if left to themselves. And going so far as to share inventions to make their utterly useless lives more enjoyable. *Ick*. Now, the Unseelie would delight in nothing more than enslaving the human race and breeding you to fill our bellies..."

"That is quite enough, Jacques! You know we don't think that way any longer. Pay him no heed, my dear." The female mouse gazed up at Briella with an imploring look upon her mousy features.

"If you are Unseelie, why are you residing here? Is this not a Seelie court?" Briella gave the trio a patient smile. This was an excellent opportunity to glean as much information about the castle and its inhabitants as she could.

"Oh, it is. One year long ago, we were invited for a Faecrenzial Spring Equinox celebration which celebrates the passage of Spring, and its importance to renewing life, and we have stayed ever since. Most Courts you'll find are consistent with both Seelie and Unseelie." The female mouse smiled.

"Unwillingly," Jacques muttered, crossing his furry brown arms.

"Hush. My name is Pernella, Mistress. You have my word that no one will be eating anyone," she looked pointedly at Jacques. "And we are happy to be of service to you."

"Thank you, I appreciate that. I wonder how you can remain in your Unseelie form and ignore your instincts." Briella arched a golden brow at the trio.

"Oh, it's been so long now that it's quite easy to behave. The King made a proclamation that any Unseelie residing within the Spring Court would have to conform to the laws of his Court. It's strictly upheld."

"And we like our heads right where they are." Jacques agreed grumpily.

"Perhaps you can tell me why almost every being seems unhappy here. Is there something that I should know so that I may keep my head right where it belongs?" Briella looked from one mouse to another.

Smiling at her with a great showing of many perfectly

pointed teeth Jacques said, "There isn't much one can say."

"*Ah ha*. So, there is something afoot and no one can tell me what that is. I wonder why?" Briella rose and paced the length of the room pondering all that she knew. Perhaps it was an enchantment or a curse? Something was ominous and she meant to puzzle it out.

Pernella wrung her little brown mousy paws. "It's best to just let things be. Better to think about the here and now. And right now, we are tasked with assisting you, so let's assist you. Shall I send Jacques to fetch your breakfast tray?"

"Uhm, no. That's quite all right. I suppose I should see the room I'm meant to be working in and see what supplies I'll need." Briella tried to keep the grimace from her face. It was one thing to face mice in her bedchamber, and quite another thing to have one bring her food. She didn't want to think about who had prepared the food last night, even if she had only had one disgusting cracker. Little mousy paws touching her food was something that would take her time to become accustomed to. Plus, there was the whole issue of them possibly craving human flesh, and that was a whole 'nother topic that she'd like to never think about again.

"Right, well I suppose you'll want to dress first before we begin for the day?" Pernella looked at Briella with bright black eyes.

"Excellent idea. I shall do that at once. I will need a dress to change into. Do you suppose you can help me locate one?"

"But of course. You only need to think it, and one shall appear in your closet." Pernella ran to the cabinet and stood on her hind legs to paw at it.

"If one can just appear, why do you need a seamstress?"

"Well, they have to come from somewhere. We can't just pull them from the air. Someone has to create them, or you have to be in possession of an enchanted cabinet, which this happens to be, I don't know where it gathers the clothing from…" Pernella trailed off.

"Hmmm. So, one could just ask this closet for whatever one needs?" Briella had an idea that she could just have the closet produce the clothing that she would need to create. Was it an endless supply? Would she be walking around in another's clothing?

Pernella thoughtfully tapped her chin with her paw. "I suppose so."

Nodding her head with a smile gracing her face, Briella walked to the cabinet and concentrated on envisioning a morning gown in pale pink with darker ribbons and cream lace accents. She also thought of matching slippers and a matching poke bonnet just in case she was able to venture out of doors. When she opened the cabinet door Briella saw tiny sparkling silver stars that accompanied the magical enchantment. Her clothing was awaiting her and so she pulled everything out and held them to her chest. Then she walked to her water closet to begin her day, but first, it was time to find out how one bathed under the spigot in the little black tiled room.

10

WE'RE ALL MAD HERE

"This is where you'll find the ribbons and lace. They're very fine, are they not?" Pernella watched as Briella closed the drawer.

"Very fine, indeed. I haven't seen such sumptuous lace in ages. Where are the scissors and needles stored?"

"Over here, they've been kept in this basket since the last Mistress was here."

Looking through the basket's contents, Briella ideally inquired, "What happened to the last one?"

"Ogre or troll, no one really knows." Pernella shrugged her shoulders and stroked her tail.

"Do you mean that she met with ill tidings?" Briella felt her eyes widen.

"You could say that. But it was a long time ago, before I ever came here. The silly creature was roaming the woods seeking out enchanted spider web. No faerie of sound judgment would ever venture so far into those woods. There are beasts and vile beings who eat flesh and who call the trees their home."

"How perfectly dreadful!" And it was. Briella swallowed the lump that formed within her throat and made a vow that she would never enter those woods. *Nothing was worth the agony of being eaten.*

"It was, but it was such a long time ago. Faeries tend to have long lives, excellent memories, and eternally embrace grudges." Pernella preened her whiskers while watching Briella curiously.

Briella changed the subject back to safer grounds. "Well then, who has been creating the clothing?"

"Well, I believe that a great deal of it is all just a glamour. Some faeries are more accomplished in that particular art. They could very well be wearing rags and it would take a very knowledgeable being to see through their glamour. We only get fabrics once in a while and with no one willing to take up the needle… and why would anyone bother when they can glamour or strike a bargain for one?" Pernella twitched her whiskers.

Briella inspected the various bolts of fabrics that were curiously not the color black. But when she thought about it, last night at the ball, there had been colorful clothing. So perhaps the curse or enchantment only applied to ordinary things? No, that couldn't be correct, because if so, then they would be able to verbalize what it was that kept them all so morose. She ran her hands over a very beautiful shade of red before turning back to survey the room.

She had been pleased to discover that, while they were in the lower level of the castle, there were many windows to allow the sunshine in. True, the windows were all situated up high, toward the ceiling, but she would count her blessings as they presented themselves. The light cast its glow upon the large wooden table that was arranged in the center of the room where specks of glittering dust danced along the air. There were four body forms arranged in formation off to the side of the table against the longest wall on which to arrange the clothing. Briella took a moment to look at the dust particles that floated upon the air. For not being used, these rooms had all been very tidy and clean.

There were a few black chests that were located in the room's corners, housing buttons and bits of decoration. There were fans and laces, and all manner of things that any seamstress would be thankful to be in possession of. *I wonder if I could simply throw some of these items into the enchanted cabinet and ask it to create something…*

The floor was black stone and cold. The fireplace, though not as large as the one in her bedchamber, was lit and doing a fantastic job of heating the room. Another thing to be thankful for. She was not accustomed to having a fire lit for her comfort alone.

There was a bench that sat in front of the wooden table, and while it did not look comfortable, Briella supposed she could do her sewing in the rocking chair by the fire.

All things considered, it was a very adequate room and functional, and she was happy to have a place that she could be Mistress of, even if her domain only consisted of two chambers. Even if she was to continually have uninvited guests and would have to become familiar with the presence of others, Briella felt content and that was a feeling that she did not know how to process.

There was a loud crashing coming from the hallway and Briella wondered what manner of mischief was afoot. She briskly walked to the door and threw it open, as she quickly leapt to the side of the doorway. The other two mice were racing toward the entrance with their arms loaded with goods. A light-colored cat with lime green stripes chased after them. Briella watched, her eyes wide, as the mice dropped their tiny baskets. They climbed the table legs to safely perch upon the edge of it. She watched them grab their chests, trying to regain their breath. Jacques leaned over to peer down at the tabby cat, whose tail was twitching back and forth.

"What is happening? I thought that eating each other was forbidden?" Briella questioned the mice.

"Yes, well please feel free to remind Mr. Nasty McNasty of that fact." Jacques huffed out a breath.

"Spoilsport. I only wanted a bit of fun. I wasn't going to chew on you, just a few little licks. It's not my fault that I'm stuck here. I have much better things to do and more entertaining places to be," purred a familiar voice.

Briella tapped her chin with her pointer finger and instantly realized to whom the voice belonged. "So you are the mysterious voice."

Turning his bright bottle green gaze upon Briella, the cat gave a sly grin. "Guilty as charged. You, my dear, are a breath of fresh air. I haven't been so entertained in years, not since I left my lands to venture here for the Faecrenzial. What a disaster that became."

Stepping closer to the cat, Briella knelt down. "Can you discuss with me what you know? Is this castle cursed or enchanted?"

"Alas, I find that I cannot. My lips are sealed. It's frustrating, you know, to constantly be on the verge of speaking to only have the words whisked away."

"Where are the lands that you mentioned? Where do you come from?"

"In a land out of time, one that you've never heard of. I used to think that there was no place run quite as mad as home, but I see the same madness starting to plague this castle. Each day we all grow a little more mad here, and it's *so* delightful. For if you stay long enough, and you will, you too shall feel the icy fingers of madness creep into your soul. And then, the fun shall really begin. Oh! How we'll laugh and dance. And how the tea and cakes will flow… just like *home*." The grin that crept onto the cat's face frightened Briella. He really did seem mad with his mouthful of pointed teeth. His smile seemed to overpower every other feature upon his feline face.

Shaking her fist and addressing the cat from her perch upon the fireplace hearth, Pernella scolded, "You're terrible, that's what you are. You're crueler than any Unseelie I've ever come across, and that is saying a lot!"

"*Psh*. Compliments will get you nowhere, mouse." The cat brought his front right paw up to his face and proceeded to bathe himself.

Rising from the stone floor and hugging her arms to herself, Briella didn't know what to say or do. She didn't like the idea of going insane, but she supposed that it was better than being cursed, or perchance that was the curse?

Without warning, Briella's chamber door flew open, banging into the wall and nearly leaving a hole. Everyone jumped, except the cat, and in flew Fleur, who landed upon the table. "Here you all are! I've been searching for hours. I see that you are entertaining Unnamed, how very rude to exclude your best friend." Folding her tiny arms, she glared up at Briella with her fierce sapphire eyes ablaze.

"I apologize, I didn't mean to exclude you, Fleur." Briella tried to soothe her friend.

"Well, at least I am here now. And it's a very good thing that I am. I'm not sure that you understand the company in which you are in. Cheshire isn't so terrible, but these mice have been known to cause a ruckus. Did the little bossy male one try to eat you?"

"I think there was mention of it, but I don't recall an exact threat."

"There had better not be! Unnamed is under my protection and you shall feel my wrath if any harm befalls her," Fleur stated as she eyed each creature.

"Stop your silly posturing. We were directed by King Ezekiel to assist her. He was quite adamant that no harm should come to her," Pernella pointedly told her.

King Ezekiel, that is his name? It suits him, Briella decided.

Turning to Briella, Fleur looked at her thoughtfully. "How did you end up here?"

Briella felt all eyes upon her, she straightened her posture, folded her hands together, and said, "Well, I went for a stroll and came to a room that I entered and discovered a library containing so many wondrous books. I was caught completely unaware as the Faerie King came upon me and demanded to know what I was doing there. He inquired about what skills I possessed and decided that I should be the seamstress. I followed him here, and here I've been ever since."

"King Ezekiel of The Spring Court gave you a position and brought *you* all the way down here?" Fleur questioned with an incredulous tone of voice.

"Yesss..." Briella had not known that his name was Ezekiel. She had done her best to push thoughts of him and his beautiful face away. *And those kissable lips.*

All of the room's occupants were staring at her with a mixture of confusion.

"Curiouser and curiouser," Cheshire began to purr loudly.

"How very faemazing! I am all astonishment." Fleur danced around in the air. "His Majesty is not known for being kind or even taking the time to be bothered with mundane chores."

"It was late," Briella offered.

"Doesn't matter, Mistress. It's wholly out of character for our King to go out of his way," Jacques declared.

Clapping her tiny hands together, Fleur spoke to Briella, "Well, *I* serve King Ezekiel directly, and he never does anything without just cause. So, he must suspect something that we do not. He has bid me to invite you to the Court this afternoon."

Not knowing what the proper response was to this invitation, Briella simply smiled.

"We have some time before you need to dress for Court." Pernella got down to the business at hand. "How would you direct us to help you settle in?"

"I did have one thought, but it's not very pressing and I don't want to cause offense," Briella hedged.

"What is it?" Jacques grumbled.

"Do you suppose that we could fashion some clothing for you? At least, some trousers and a dress for Pernella? Would that be too demanding?"

Jacques rubbed his face with a paw. "What next? I expect you'll be wanting us to wear tiny gloves to sweep the floor?"

"It was silly of me. I do apologize. I shall get used to your nudity. It's only the thought of your little bodies climbing all over every surface unclothed is a bit much for me at present." Briella gave them an imploring gaze.

"I don't suppose you mean me, my dear?" Cheshire purred.

"Oh, not at all."

"There's a double standard here. Why does he get to run around naked and it's us that concern you? He's much bigger as is his anatomy," Jacques complained with a frown.

"Well, Cheshire isn't assisting me, is he? I imagine that he'll soon be off doing whatever it is that he does. And you'll be here with me. Honestly, I could use the practice and your size makes for, well, perfect practice size." Briella smiled and beamed at him.

"Makes sense to me," smirked Cheshire. "I never do anything industrious if I can circumvent it."

"It's settled! Let's clothe the mice and go to Court. What a faetastic first day for you!" Fleur chirped.

Pernella busied herself measuring their sizes while Fleur helped Briella pick out fabrics for their clothing. Cheshire found the whole affair entertaining, and so, he stayed curled up upon the rocking chair to supervise. The third mouse, who was finally introduced as Gustavious, was picking out tiny seed pearls to use for buttons.

Eventually, Briella sat down on the bench before the long table and traced a pattern before she began to cut it out. So far, she thought that things were going very well. Perhaps this wasn't going to be a complete disaster. When it came time to start sewing the pieces for Pernella's tiny dress together, she found that the needle was too large, so she located another and began again. At first, her stitches were perfectly placed, but somewhere along the way, they began to pucker the fabric. By the time she had added the sleeves, she noted that one had decidedly more volume than the other. One was up higher as well. Briella swallowed and closed her eyes. This was a *disaster*. If she could not manage to create one small dress, then this whole endeavor was doomed. She added the buttons, which she could not align correctly, and set the finished dress aside. She felt herself sinking into the depths of despair. *I am doomed.*

Excitedly, Pernella picked up the dress and whirled it around. She quickly lowered it over her head, and put her arms through the puff sleeves, and tried to pull it evenly down to her ankles. But it would not obey. Looking down at her body, Pernella looked befuddled.

"Is it supposed to be like this? All wonky and willy-nilly? I admit to not being an expert as I've never before worn clothing, but it's not quite right, is it?"

Fleur flew over and landed beside Pernella and frowned. "It's really unique. It's a work of art."

"It looks like something that the cat threw up," Jacques commented from his place at the end of the table.

"He's not wrong. I once ate a bird and brought it back up and it looked a fair amount better than that. My apologies, my dear." Cheshire grinned at her.

Covering her flushing face with her hands, Briella agreed. "It does look frightful. What am I going to do?"

"Have you ever sewn before?" Pernella asked, as she furrowed her dark brow.

"Yes! Many times as I have explained to the King. But never from scratch. I am an excellent mender, though. The King shushed me before I could be detailed about my abilities," Briella lowered her hands from her face.

"Well, I can sew. And with time, I could teach you," Gustavious offered.

"When did you learn to do that?" Jacques asked with incredulity in his squeaky voice.

Bristling, Gustavious said, "You don't know everything about me!"

Jacques threw up his paws. "Touché."

Fleur patted Briella on the cheek. "All will be as it's meant to be. Never fear. It's time to prepare you for Court!"

Briella had a sinking feeling that she would prove to be an utter disaster at Court as well. She didn't want to attend

Court even though her curiosity was high as to what Court was like. In the mortal world, she had been a titled lady, but she'd never been treated like one. But here everything was different. She had even acquired friends, and to her, that was the most valuable gift she could have ever been bestowed with.

11

A COURT OF FAERIE FLOSS

Since she had never attended Court, Briella wasn't sure what to envision even with the detailed descriptions given by her friend. It took three attempts before Briella finally produced a dress from the enchanted cabinet which met with Fleur's approval. Finally though, the dress had found favor with Fleur. It was gold and boasted puffed sleeves and a darker golden ribbon gathered just below her bosom. Along the hem were golden blossoms, which were raised several inches outwards from the material. It was stunning.

Reaching into the cabinet, she retrieved her glass slippers. Briella swept her hair into a knot at the base of her neck with just a few select strands hanging down along the sides of her face that curled to her shoulders. *I wonder how I shall compare with all of the other perfect faeries? Would I stand apart from the audience in an offensive manner?*

When Briella stood before the gilded black framed looking-glass, she was speechless. She looked lovely and wondered if anyone would admire her. She felt like each time she gazed into a looking-glass, she looked less human and more Fae. Perhaps, that was part of her hidden faerie heritage blossoming. Was it a trick of the light or were her features changing? Pushing those thoughts away, she turned away from the looking-glass. She had not let herself think of her father and did not want to have her thoughts scattered when she needed to present her best self.

She wouldn't be wearing gloves, and it made her arms feel bare. It was not an accessory that most faeries bothered to don, and she figured that trying to blend in was a very good idea.

Briella watched on with amazement as the tiny fairy closed her eyes and breathed out heavily. Fleur used a glamour to change her dress into an effect that reminded Briella of vivid purple iris petals. Fleur's dress began to shimmer as it turned colors and style. Opening her eyes, she gathered her red hair and pinned it up onto the crown of her head, leaving tiny ringlets loose along the sides of her face.

"Now that we are ready to meet the Court, there are a few rules that I must advise you of. First, never address the King, or anyone, for that matter. Wait to be spoken to, and do not under any circumstances, make eye contact with another being. Remember that this castle is overflowing with too many aimless Fae creatures, and the amount of mischief and entertainment to be found at your expense is immense. Second, remember who *you* are. Do not behave as if you are beneath another. Third, you are human and are extremely breakable. Hide if someone should attempt to kill anyone else. It does happen sometimes, you know. Under the table makes a safe exit way, use its path. Be polite, but do not grovel if something unfortunate should occur." Fleur nodded at her and waited for her to say something in return.

"Oh, is that all?"

"Is that not enough?"

"Oh, no, it's quite enough. Must I attend?" Briella entreated her new friend.

"Absolutely! It would be a great insult to one and all, if the newest inhabitant did not attend. Everyone is curious about your presence. It's best to meet them in a controlled setting."

Briella nodded and pulled open her bedchamber door, waving for Fleur to exit before her. They made their way to the stairs and ascended two floors until they came to a grand entryway, which was very different from the one she had ventured through last evening. It was decorated in landscapes and their vibrant colors looked very distinct against the inky blackness all around. There were pedestals and decorative vases rested upon them. But the vases were empty. *Perchance, nothing of beauty grows within the gardens?*

Soon, they came to stand before two large granite doors that had wilted roses carved into them. The doors opened as two uniformed guards, dressed in black with black helmets and black swords secured to their waists, bowed their heads toward the ladies. Their presence took Briella by surprise as it was the first time she had seen any guards. The gargoyles were scattered amongst the shadows in the corridors and within the chambers.

Fleur flew straight into the room and Briella followed at a more sedate pace. She looked up at the ceiling, which was domed like the library had been. There was a massive hanging chandelier in the center of the ceiling, which was lit with many black candles that dripped wax onto the bottom of the structure, but never seemed to fall to the black marbled floor. There were more floating candles which seemed to always be employed. It took an abundance of candlelight scattered about the chamber to keep the harsh dark shadows at bay.

Along the walls were stained glass windows that depicted growling beasts, a beautiful cloaked being, and one figure upon its knees. Another window held a broken crown, and another was of twisted vines and roses. The most intriguing images of all were the gargoyles that flew in various poses, descending from pink clouds. Did they depict the details regarding the mystery that plagued the castle? She wanted to wander closer and inspect them, but now was not the time.

The focal point of the room was a raised dais, which was swathed in black silk that hung down in heavy curtains. Placed upon the dais was a throne that looked as if it was created from twisted branches. The four clawed feet were pointed. Upon the throne, sat the King. He was regally attired in many layers of black. The same inky crown rested atop his blond head and his mossy green eyes held a guarded look. Was this what he looked like naturally? *He is just as handsome as I remembered, perhaps even more so.*

To either side of the dais sat two enormous gargoyles. They stared straight into the gathered Fae, unblinking, while only their chests moved, rising and falling as they breathed. No one seemed to pay them attention, and so, Briella let her breath whoosh from her lungs. They were not the same pair that had stood sentry at the double front doors the prior night of the ball, but they had many of the same common features. And yet, there were enough differences marking them as distinct beings. Colorations and textures of their fur were the obvious signs that they differed one from another.

Briella stepped toward the shadowed wall where she could still see the proceedings but was safely obscured from most of the room. Tables laden with decadent food, and what looked like a chocolate waterfall flowing into a punch bowl, were situated across from her. The many faeries in attendance stood all around with their attention riveted upon the Faerie King. Fleur flew up to the dais and flapped her wings as she hung suspended in the air next to her monarch. The chamber contained no other chairs except for the massive throne.

Two faeries, one of which was part horse, were arguing about something to do with a well, while the King was listening with his hands clasped before him. It seemed as if they would never cease arguing.

King Ezekiel finally threw up his right hand in a demand for silence. "Enough!" he bellowed as his furious gaze settled upon the two squabbling faeries.

The two men bowed and quickly silenced themselves. The King whispered with Fleur who was busy nodding at him. They conversed for a few more moments, and then the King addressed the crowd.

"I find that you both are equally at fault. We must try to get along. If you cannot agree to a schedule, perhaps, I shall be forced to intervene further, and simply take the land away from each of you. I am sure that there are others who would be willing to claim your small properties. I'll not tolerate this constant bickering," King Ezekiel replied firmly. The two faeries bowed before him and scampered away into the crowd behind them.

A man who could barely keep his tailcoat buttoned approached the throne. His hair was the color of brass and his defining feature seemed to be his brass mustache which resembled the ticking hands of a grandfather clock. In an austere voice, he called out for Lady Elise and Lady Chloe to step forward and curtsey before the King. The two females were stunning, clad in beautiful dresses that caught the light and shimmered.

Addressing the first lady, the Faerie King inquired, "What is your grievance?"

Lady Elise had brunette hair that was twisted upon her head and tiny seed pearls were threaded throughout it. There were two cinnamon horns along either side of her head that were mostly hidden by the height of her hair. She ran her hands down the front of her purple dress and stepped forward. "Your Majesty, *Lady* Chloe glamoured herself to look like me and stole a kiss from *my* husband."

"Lies." Lady Chloe stated as she folded her arms across her chest. Her blue gown was decorated with sumptuous lace edging at its neck and hem. Hair that flowed loosely down her back was the color of ripe strawberries, matching the tuft that poked out from under the back of her dress. *That must be her Fae trait, the tail.*

The King switched his gaze to Lady Chloe and glared at her. "*You* will remain silent until spoken to."

Lady Chloe meekly bowed her head.

A male faerie just as equally beautiful stepped forward and bowed before King Ezekiel. "May I speak, Your Majesty?"

"Only if you have further insight into this matter," the King spoke in an irritated voice.

"Of course, Your Majesty. I am Lord Ollie, whom the Ladies are speaking about. What my wife Lady Elise states is true. I thought I was in an impassioned embrace with her, and once our lips met, I knew that she was not my wife. I am not in the habit of kissing other beings and was quite mortified to be placed in such a position. I began to shout at the glamoured faerie and my real wife came rushing into our bedchamber. She grabbed a vase and threw it at the imposter's head who dodged the blow and quickly fled out through the balcony."

"I see. And if you did not know for certain who you were kissing, why do you make the accusation against your sister-in-law?" King Ezekiel's brows furrowed.

"She is forever causing us grief, Your Majesty," began Lady Elise. "And the next day when I confronted her about her trickery, she simply laughed in my face and walked away."

The King stroked his chin with his fingers and then leaned forward from his throne. "Lady Chloe, what do you think is a proper punishment for such an action?"

Lady Chloe stepped forward and smiled prettily. "Why, no punishment, Your Majesty. 'Tis true I glamoured myself to look like my sister, but really no harm was truly done, excepting to Lord Ollie's pride. Who is rather a terrible kisser, I must confess. My poor sister." Here she looked at Lady Elise with a cruel twist of her lips. "I should not be punished for enduring his assault."

Lord Ollie began choking on air with his dark eyes widening. "*I* did not assault you! You vile creature. My kisses are perfectly adequate."

"Indeed they are, my love!" Lady Elise rubbed her hand across her husband's back.

"Lady Elise, what do you think is a proper punishment?" the Faerie King inquired.

"Imprisonment! Let the nasty faerie rot." Lady Elise spoke with a bitter tone lacing her words.

Lady Chloe began to cackle and the Court seemed to

grow listless as they began to whisper amongst themselves. Fleur rose into the air and blew a tiny trumpet which silenced the chamber. *Where had Fleur retrieved the trumpet from? Perhaps it was glamoured?*

"Very well, *Ladies*. I offer a solution. Lady Chloe will offer her services to the royal laundry wing for the span of three months' time. A fitting punishment, I think, for employing dirty schemes against relations," the Faerie King decreed.

Both ladies seemed unsatisfied with the decree but bowed before their monarch, nonetheless. They backed away into the throng of their peers with Lord Ollie closely following his wife.

When movement jarred the crowd, Briella craned her neck to see what the fuss was about. She spied a trio of emerald-hued goblins wearing trousers who were pushing each other around impishly. They were employing their fists upon each other while the beings surrounding them tried to give them space. One of the castle guards rushed in to calm them. *I suppose that this behavior must be common,* Briella thought as the Court proceedings continued on.

And so it went, for the course of another two hours, with petty claims while nothing life-threatening happened. Briella found her attention wandering and looked over at the food table. She had skipped breakfast that morning and ate a sparse few grapes and some cheese that Fleur had placed before her as they dressed for Court. No one paid any attention to the food, and so Briella suspected that it was not an acceptable thing to partake of until the audience with the King had concluded.

The same male faerie who seemed to be an important servant to the Faerie King, came before the gathered again and announced that the audience for today was concluded, and they were free to make merry. The crowd started to pair off and the room grew loud with a frenzy of voices. Briella watched as the faeries partook of the feast set out before them. Whilst they dipped cups into the chocolate fountain and drank, she looked on. Briella wanted to fill her empty stomach, but was afraid to draw attention to herself. She had been relatively obscure since she entered the throne room and wanted to remain so.

Briella turned toward the throne again and saw King Ezekiel rise. He met her stare and started toward her when a male faerie stepped into his path, bowing before him. Briella watched as the King glared at him and the faerie paled, seeming to apologize as he backed away. He nearly tripped over his own feet in his haste to withdraw from sight.

Briella's brows drew together, and she brought her bottom lip between her straight teeth. She hadn't seen a temper from the King, and he didn't unnecessarily punish any of his subjects. Why did he command such fear? Yes, he had meted out punishments, but they were adequately sentenced. And Heaven help her, if she had to sit through an entire afternoon of ridiculous fodder and be responsible for an entire kingdom, she might have been tempted to show her displeasure as well.

The Faerie King halted his stride before her and Briella quickly curtsied.

"Are you enjoying your first encounter with Court?" King Ezekiel asked, awaiting her answer.

"I'm not quite certain how I should answer that, Your Majesty."

"Truthfully?"

"Ah, well, it's all very surreal to me. I still feel as if I'm in a dream and I'll wake and everything else will dull after this," Briella replied honestly.

"Interesting."

"Why is everyone frightened to incur your displeasure?"

Raising a blond brow, he said, "Because when the occasion calls for it, I can be quite a beast. But then, one who rules over the unruly must be so. Weakness would not do."

Not knowing what to say in response, she remained silent. *I certainly do not wish to incur his displeasure.*

"Have you tried our Faerie Floss yet? It's quite delicious."

"No, Your Majesty. What is it like?"

"It's like devouring a cloud. It's pure sugar, and what I imagine happiness to taste like. It grants you a feeling of euphoria for quite a few minutes after you've consumed it." He motioned for her to walk beside him.

They stopped before the food table, and he reached for a cone that held the magical treat. Unsure whether she really wanted to take a bite, she hesitated.

"It's quite harmless, I assure you." King Ezekiel looked at her sincerely.

Briella quirked a single brow. "And when a faerie says it's harmless, can you really believe it to be so?"

"Touché. You have my word as a ruler that no harm will come to you," he said as he held out the Faerie Floss to her.

Briella took it and pinched off a small amount of the purple-colored fluff. She put it into her mouth and gave a sound of enjoyment. After it melted in her mouth, she smiled at him. "It's marvelous! It's Christmas morning and it's a warm embrace from a loved one. It's like finding home when you've forgotten your way." She did feel euphoric and had to make her mouth cease its uttering of words. She held the treat out toward him, but he shook his head.

"I never indulge where eyes can bear witness. It wouldn't do for the euphoria to overtake me. Who knows what mischief I'd lead the Court upon. No one would ever forget it either. Fae are long-lived with excellent memories," he explained.

"And they need a fierce ruler."

He nodded.

Flying up between them, Fleur huffed, "The Autumn Ambassador is ordering about the staff again and they've threatened to poison him."

King Ezekiel scoffed, "It would be a service to the entire castle if they did."

"Indeed. He always makes me want to get a little stabby. Shall we let them have their way?"

"No, we'd just end up with another spy and who knows how horrid they'd be." The King turned his attention to Briella and said, "It's been a pleasure," before turning on his heel and briskly walking away.

"Well, enjoying yourself, Unnamed?" Fleur inquired as she swiped a tiny handful of the purple Faerie Floss.

Briella watched the King for a moment. She blinked before replying, "So far, and it's been very tame."

Laughing uproariously, Fleur nodded. "Let's make haste and visit the pond. We'll feed some of this to the fish."

"Won't you be missed?"

Shaking her head, Fleur grabbed Briella's puffed sleeve and pulled her along past the other faeries and out the door. "Sometimes I'm ill-suited to be an advisor, I'm not exceptionally diplomatic and I do enjoy making mischief. But then there are times when I want to be free and I'm even more chaotic. Have you ever felt like your whole existence resided within a box?"

"I have. And you feel as if you can't quite catch your

breath? Like if you don't find that freedom, you'll lose yourself completely? I'm not certain, but I think I'm finally starting to find myself. I never realized how lost I was." Briella paused for a moment before continuing, "I hope I never get tucked inside that box again."

12

TRUE LOVE'S KISS

The pond was located in the middle of the solarium, which was a room with glass walls which allowed for sunlight or moonlight to enter. There were no other living things within the room except for the fish. The pots were all empty and the gardening tools sat forgotten beside a small black cabinet that stood alongside the wall. The glass walls allowed a view of the garden, which was indeed nothing more than bramble and bushes. Night had completely fallen and pink clouds were decorating the darker purple sky. The bright light of the pink moon lit up the sky above them. The twinkling teal stars were breathtaking and every few minutes they spied a shooting star. Briella did not waste her time making wishes, for she truly didn't know what to wish for. She supposed that her innermost desire was to discover what had taken place in the Spring Court, and whether it was by curse or enchantment. She believed that a curse would be much harder to break than an enchantment, but she couldn't be certain. Her knowledge of such matters was severely lacking.

Briella watched as Fleur threw pieces of the Faerie Floss to the koi goldfish. While it was a mischievous thing to do, it didn't harm the fish. They seemed to swim a little faster and some leapt up from the water in search of more of the treat. Briella supposed it was also a little dangerous for Fleur as some of the fish were larger than she. Briella didn't know what she'd do if one leapt from the water and swallowed her tiny friend whole. Stars twinkled on the surface of the brilliant blue pond as orange, red, and black goldfish swam beneath the surface. Briella watched, mesmerized by the fish, and found herself lost in thought.

The euphoria had fled from Briella's mind after the King had left her side. It was curious to be singled out within the crush of the Court by King Ezekiel, and Briella wasn't sure if it was a compliment or dangerous to be honored as such. From what she had been told by her new friends, the King wasn't very sociable.

It took longer for Fleur to cease with her giggles of glee. They were both silent now that the fish had eaten the last of the Faerie Floss. It was growing late yet Briella had no idea what the time was.

"I'm famished. We should go to the kitchen and liberate some dinner." Fleur rose into the air.

"Is that allowed?" Briella asked, worried that they might break some unspoken rule. *Was stealing food from the kitchen a crime?*

"But of course. I am, after all, vital to the running of this castle. They wouldn't dare turn me away!"

Briella followed her tiny friend down a twisted staircase and was greeted by the aroma of marvelous food as they neared the kitchen. Briella was pleasantly surprised that even though Fleur was in an excited state that she did not pull upon her hair, nor her clothing. Fleur did, however, keep looking behind her to be sure that

Briella was indeed following her. It was progress in their friendship and Briella could not help but smile. A few more steps and they entered the large room. There were an innumerous amount of faeries scattering around doing various tasks. There were pastry chefs busy creating decadent desserts and chefs mixing soups and different varieties of meats being spun on roasters. The kitchen was warm in part due to its many fires, but also because of the many floating candles, which were more than necessary in the doom and gloom that the ever-present darkness created.

They went into the pantry, and from the larder Fleur took croissants, roasted beef, and some sort of bluish berry that resembled a strawberry in size and shape. Briella spied a basket and grabbed it to tuck their dinner away inside. On their route from the pantry, Fleur flew off toward a massive wooden table laden with chocolate desserts. Briella also noticed an abundance of Faerie Floss and hoped that Fleur would not choose that for she had had enough of the fluff. When Fleur returned to her side, she held some sort of chocolate pie and winked at Briella.

"You're going to love True Love's Kiss! It's absolutely faetabulous!" Fleur enthused as she placed it into the basket that Briella held.

"True Love's Kiss? What exactly is that?"

"You will have to be patient and see!" Fleur chirped before she flew out of the kitchen. Briella rushed to keep up with the tiny being.

Briella padded down the hallway and together they descended the twisty staircase and soon came upon the seamstress's quarters. They entered the workroom and greeted the mice that were busy sewing different bits of material together.

Briella set the basket down upon the worktable and

turned to look at Jacques, who was fashioning a glove. The stitches were neat and the length was impressive for one so little. She then walked to the head of the table and watched as Pernella sat diligently sewing some lace to cream-colored fabric. Gustavious was watching her progress and giving her directions every once in a while, and to this Pernella would nod her head.

Gustavious looked up at Briella and gave a toothy grin, which moved his whiskers high upon his brown hairy face. "They're quick learners! I am so pleased with their progress. We'll soon have an array of beautiful garments."

Briella clasped her hands to her chest and exclaimed, "I am so thankful for you! For each of you. Thank you all for being so willing to assist me." She turned to make eye contact with each mouse.

"I think you'll be happy that while they were practicing I was creating clothing for us. I think you'll be pleased, Mistress of the Seam," Gustavious assured her.

"That is faetastic! Thank you so very much for all your diligent work." Briella was quickly learning the faeisms that Fleur seemed to toss out freely. *When in Faerie, one must be ever adapting.*

"Best take a break, my fellow tiny beings!" Fleur announced. "We stopped by the kitchen and have quite the sumptuous feast."

At her words, the three mice put their work away. Jacques pushed a spool of red thread toward the basket and sat atop it. Pernella brought a small box over and perched upon it, while Gustavious sat down between them and folded his small paws.

Briella reached into the basket and first produced the croissants. She broke one into three pieces, and then withdrew the roasted beef and handed each a chunk.

Fleur held up a pitcher of what Briella thought must be

lemonade and poured tiny cups for each of the mice and herself. Briella found large buttons and laid them down as plates. The mice immediately set their dinner down onto their large plates.

Briella went into her bedchamber and located the cup and plate that Fleur had delivered along with grapes and cheese earlier in the day, and brought them out to make use of for herself. While she was not over her aversion to sharing a table with vermin, she was trying her best to rethink her feelings on the matter and enjoy the friendship so readily offered to her. If she had had talking mice at home, would her days and nights have been more bearable?

As they began the meal, the mice began to explain what they had been learning while she was away at Court, which was mainly mastering neat stitches and the sewing on of buttons. When they had finished their late dinner, Fleur flew up to the basket and retrieved the chocolate pie to *'Oohs'* of the mice. Gustavious patted his large stomach and Jacques rubbed his hands together.

"What is so special about this pie?" Briella inquired and raised one of her golden brows.

"It's not just any pie, Unnamed! This pie is enchanted and with your first bite, you'll start to see visions of your true love. The more you eat, the more detailed the visions become!" Fleur exclaimed.

"How many times have you eaten it and had these visions?" Briella curiously asked.

"Oh, a few times..." Fleur trailed off, staring into the distance with a wistful expression on her face. Briella cleared her throat, watching as the small faerie shook her head and came back to the present.

"After all those bites, you have not yet met your true love?"

"No. Not yet, but I have a very good idea of what he looks like. I just haven't met him yet, because I suspect that he resides in another Court."

"Do you never visit the other Courts?" Briella cocked her head to the side.

"No. Not in many years. None of us venture far from the castle," answered Fleur as she looked down at her hands. "But when I do come face to face with him, I will immediately know that he is my true love. I shall never want to leave his side; it will all be so faetastically romantic once we lock gazes."

"I saw my true love, once." Gustavious's face held a dreamy look. "I was standing on the territory line of here and the Winter Court and she was sitting by Lake Winterestes running a brush through her golden hair. And it was the same as in my True Love's Kiss visions."

"Blonde hair? What mouse has blonde hair?" Jacques demanded in a boisterous tone of voice.

"I never said she was a mouse. She was a lady faerie." Gustavious sniffed in an offended manner.

"A lady? How would that ever work, my friend?" Jacques's brow furrowed.

"I would have to become Seelie, and for her, I would. I would grow wings and fly to the moon to gather stardust if she desired it."

"True Love's Kiss is quite powerful," agreed Pernella in a serious tone.

"Certainly, and what else do we have to look forward to in this long life? Love is worth giving up some things if you're gaining more in the process." Gustavious glanced at each of them.

"You are insane. I do not want love if it requires me to change. Bah," Jacques waved his furry paw in the air and then turned his back upon them.

"You're just sensitive to the fact that you don't have any idea who your true love is. Let's not delay any longer, I cannot wait for Unnamed to take her first bite!" Fleur cut a piece and excitedly handed it to Briella.

Briella took her plate and then remembered that there were no utensils nearby. She shrugged her shoulders and looked at her friends. Picking up the dessert, she took a bite. The flavor was rich like a mousse and sweet like the Faerie Floss had been, making her moan. She blinked her eyes, and then before her she saw a figure. She heard the appreciative sounds of the others enjoying their slices of pie. She took another bite and tried to enjoy the merriment the others were having. Her skepticism was rearing its head. But she took another bite and the figure turned toward her and seemed to return her gaze. She could just make out golden hair. After another bite, she started to be able to discern that he had mossy green eyes. Those eyes were accompanied by a deep frown. With another bite, she saw a tail with a tuft of white hair upon its end. Briella wanted to laugh at the ridiculousness of the whole affair. She didn't want to think of who this figure resembled because it was a ludicrous idea. It couldn't be the Faerie King Ezekiel, because she had never seen a tail trailing along behind him like it was now. She let a giggle escape.

"And what is so hilarious?" Boomed a voice very much like the King's.

Startled, Briella let out a small squeak, which she quickly covered with a hand.

King Ezekiel stared back awaiting her response, but soon grew impatient and asked, "What have you been up to, little halfling?"

"Halfling? You know what I am?" Briella covered the gasp she made with her hand again, then she turned to her friends, but they weren't in the room with her any longer.

"I do. I knew from the first moment that I saw you."

"But how?" she spluttered, removing her hand from her face.

"It's magic that lives in you, it calls to me. I can scarcely ignore it, even now, when we are chambers apart. In the same room, your blood dances along the very air that I breathe. Your magic is the first thing that greets me upon waking, and the last thing I feel before dreams carry me away. And what dreams do I dream? Ask me," he commanded.

Shaking her head, Briella couldn't find the words to use. She feared what discoveries were yet to be made, especially where he was concerned.

"I command you to ask me."

"What dreams do you dream?"

"I dream of a little girl. I dream of a chateau far away in another world. I dream that unkind things are happening, and I am powerless to do anything to make them stop. I dream of a woman who could change everything, but I can't help her discover who she is. That is the dilemma that my dreams try to solve." King Ezekiel sighed and rubbed a hand through his golden locks. It was her first view of his head without his crown. Even his hair was perfect, though she had always known that it was. But the way the light softly touched it, giving it life as the highlights glimmered, threatened to steal her breath away.

"How frustrating for you," Briella said breathlessly. *I shall not give into where my wild imaginings want to take me. My heart can't allow such a thing.*

"It is. It's not a habit that I like to practice. And yet, you do not ask the next logical question."

"I don't think that I really want to."

He made a sound half like a laugh and half like a groan.

"I have no wish to irritate you," Briella hurriedly confessed. She only ever had the desire to see him pleased and content. Was happiness too far of a stretch for him? Was he capable of spending minutes a day with a smile upon his handsome face? She longed to unearth those answers.

King Ezekiel started to become fuzzy and he sighed, "I assume you consumed some sort of enchanted food?"

"True Love's Kiss," Briella admitted as she swallowed the last bite. It wasn't a large enough piece to bring him back completely, but he did linger on.

His brow quirked as he said, "Interesting…"

"Why is it interesting?"

"Do you realize what the enchanted pie does?"

A thought occurred to Briella. "How long have you been dreaming of your mystery girl and chateau?"

"Ages. But you don't readily answer my questions, little one."

"Is this real? Or just a vision? Are you really here?" Briella asked in a quiet voice that neared a whisper.

"I am as real as you wish me to be. I would advise you to seek me out. Perhaps the library would be an ideal meeting spot. I often retire there after a long day. But you'll need to sleep soon. So, seek me out another night. Sleep sweetly, Briella," he said as he disappeared entirely.

Blinking, Briella began to see her friends appear one by one within the room. She took a deep breath. She suddenly felt tired and in need of a good night's slumber. Had the vision been real? She had not understood that it would be real. Maybe it was just how the vision worked?

Flying up to float in front of her face, Fleur clasped her hands. "Who did you see?"

"I can't be certain," was Briella's reply. She did not want to reveal who it was because she wasn't at all certain what it meant for her. *My destiny, my future lies within this castle and now with a King? Impossible in so many different ways. This cannot be real!*

Briella watched as the mice all began to chatter amongst themselves in their squeaky voices. Fleur gave her a questioning look before shrugging and joining the mice.

Blinking her tired eyes again, Briella bid her friends a restful sleep and wandered into her bedchamber when a thought halted her steps completely. *The Faerie King knows my name!*

13

THE TROUBLE WITH INSEAMS

When Briella entered the workroom the next morning, she was greeted cheerily by the mice who were all dressed in their new clothing. Pernella twirled around and exclaimed about how much she loved the new dress. It fit her perfectly, with the hem ending at her ankles, and the color of pale pink suited her black eyes and brown furry body perfectly. Jacques grumbled, but showed off his black trousers which his long tail could stick out from. Gustavious was also wearing trousers, but his were a midnight blue and he even had a white shirt with tiny pearl buttons sewed onto it. He looked dashing for a mouse. Briella clapped her hands and declared how lovely they each looked, before walking over to her workstation.

She busied herself with learning how to cut out dress patterns with the large silver shears while Gustavious instructed her. He seemed to be pleased that at least this she could do very well.

The morning turned into the afternoon, and still they worked, learning how to become proper little tailors. They stopped for lunch which was delivered by a castle servant who had a large elephant trunk and tusks that protruded from his human-like face. The rest of his body was normal, as far as she could discern. He wore the livery of the castle which was black. *Do not stare,* Briella begged herself. *True, I have never seen all of the animals which reside here, but I must not make a cake out of myself. I shall soon become accustomed to this world. I hope…*

When it became time for the evening meal, the mice scurried off to join their friends, so Briella straightened up the workroom. She examined each piece that the mice had created and her heart swelled with joy. They were doing this for her, regardless of being ordered by the King. They could have given away her plight and been done with her and their assignment. But they did not. They befriended her and made her feel welcome and it made her feel valued and wanted and that brought tears to her eyes. She was valuable and worth something, and when the voices and words of her stepfamily wanted to crowd into her thoughts, she would remember the kindness she had found from the smallest of creatures, and carry them with her no matter what lay ahead.

There was some leftover cheese and bread from their luncheon, so Briella took the plate with her to her bedchamber and tucked herself into the wingback chair by the fireplace. She never saw anyone light or attend to the fire, nor had she seen anyone cleaning, but her room was always pristine. She was tidy by nature and then by demand, but she did not have access to cleaning supplies, so she had not dusted nor mopped. She had seen maids bustling about within the castle, so they must have been very silent and quick when seeing to their tasks.

It had been an eventful few days, to say the least. She was still waiting to wake up and find herself in her lumpy bed. She would be filled with sorrow to learn that this was all a dream and she would dreadfully miss this world. She might even mourn a set of mossy green eyes, but she did not want to dwell upon thoughts of *him*. She was being a coward in not seeking him out. She was embarrassed by her vision and, if he had truly been there, what were his thoughts? She was mortified when she thought that he might think her silly. His opinion mattered to her, though she did not want it to. She wanted to be free from the scathing remarks or pitying looks of others. He would pity her, a halfling with no family and a horrible past. She was pathetic. But to see him view her as such, would be soul-crushing.

Briella ate her meal and then readied herself for bed. It was still early but, as her eyelids grew weary and drooped, her thoughts drifted to the morning and she couldn't wait to greet it. Climbing into her four-postered bed, Briella tucked the coverlet around herself and laid back, shutting her eyes as sleep consumed her.

When Briella rose the next morning, she quickly bathed and asked the enchanted cabinet for a proper morning gown of pale blue and matching slippers. Adorning the dress was a large darker blue ribbon that gathered just below the bosom and tiny white flowers were sewn all along the material. The pale blue slippers had the same tiny flower print upon them. She skipped the gloves as no other being seemed to wear them, except for on formal occasions, which this was not. Briella had never felt more beautiful than she had in the past few days. It was astounding what proper hygiene and beautiful attire could do for one.

Waiting for her were her trio of assistants, who were busying themselves with drinking from little teacups. The aroma of hot chocolate greeted her and Briella smiled as she closed the door and joined them. She sat on the bench and drank from her teacup, releasing a sigh. This was a treat, one that she had long been denied, as it was too expensive to waste upon a mere servant. They sat in comfortable silence.

The chamber door banged open, surprising Briella and her assistants. In rushed a very tall faerie male, who otherwise looked normal, except for his fingers that ended in clawed tips.

"You are the Mistress of the Seam?" he asked with a booming voice. Briella rose from the bench and approached him. Smoothing out the imaginary wrinkles in her day dress, she looked up.

"Yes, how may I be of service to you?"

"I require trousers and a fitted tailcoat. They need to be ready by the end of the week and fashioned from brilliant colors from your best material. I must look exceptional. Can you make that happen?" He peered down at her imperiously from his higher height.

Looking over at Gustavious, who nodded at her, she addressed the faerie. "I assure you that it can be done. Perhaps some measurements are needed for us to begin?"

Gustavious nodded and ran to fetch the measuring tape. The faerie removed his tailcoat and walked before the fireplace. He stood with his back facing the room. Briella took the measuring tape from Gustavious and walked to stand before the haughty faerie.

Briella looked over at her mousy instructor who rubbed up and down his hairy arm. Understanding dawned upon Briella and she measured out the faerie's arm length. She called the measurement out to Pernella, who was busily scribbling notes. Next, Gustavious crept behind Jacques and encircled his chest. Briella mimicked his action, measuring out the faerie's chest. She also thought to take his waist measurements, which would be appropriate, then called those measurements out as well. Glancing back to Gustavious, she watched as he knelt before Jacques and pointed from his ankle up to his hip. Jacques folded his arms across his chest as he rolled his black eyes.

So, Briella knelt before the faerie and took the measurement. After she called out the number, she looked at the male mice who were arguing. Jacques was trying to push Gustavious away from him. She frowned, trying to make sense of what she was to measure next. She was peering intently at them from the side of the faerie's long leg, which she had clasped onto.

"I don't mean to be rude, but I am in a rush. Do you think you could finish this soon? I believe next you need to measure my inseam," the impatient faerie said in a bored tone.

"Oh, of course! The inseam..." Briella agreed as she once again looked at the mice. Pernella had set down her notes and had Jacques in a headlock, while Gustavious quickly caught her eye and motioned to the area inside of the leg. How had the faerie not taken notice of the squeaky outburst? *Oh my Heavens...* Briella quickly squeezed her eyes shut. She could do this. She would do this.

As quickly as she could, she brought the tape measure up to the faerie's inseam and called out the measurement. Briella rose quickly and walked over to the table where the mice were all gathered. They looked as though they hadn't moved an inch. But as she looked between her team, she thought that Gustavious's eye was swelling. Her heart gave a lurch. He was hurt because of her. *I have no idea how to be a seamstress and now he is hurt because of my ineptness. I should have thought ahead and learned the proper measurement areas.*

"Very good, I shall be by at the appointed time to collect and pay for my clothing. No trickery or enchantment sewed into them, if you please," the faerie made the demand as he quickly exited the room.

Briella let out a huge breath and rounded on the mice. "Gustavious! Your eye! I am so sorry!"

"'Twas not your fault, Mistress. It was *his*!" Gustavious pointed at Jacques.

Bristling, Jacques huffed, "Don't touch my inseam again, and we won't have a repeat performance."

The two glared at each other for a few moments before Pernella said, "*Tsk*. We should not have to repeat this experience again. Briella is a quick study, and she now knows what to measure. You two are worse than children!" She turned to Briella, "Now, let's get to choosing fabric and Gustavious can direct us from there!"

"You can hardly place the blame upon me. We are, after all, Unseelie and our baser instincts cannot be kept at bay forever. A little bloodshed always puts a spring into the step," Jacques replied with a malicious smirk.

"There's always the fact of the ever-present madness that grips the mind. Once it settles in, there is no amount of goodwill that can banish it away." Gustavious looked thoughtfully at his companions.

Pernella just shook her head at them and made a shooing motion with her tiny mousy paws.

Briella thought about the madness that they referred to and had an unsettling feeling creep into her stomach. She did not know what she would do if such madness took hold of her. In truth, she did not want to think about the possibility, and so she pushed it away.

They spent the next few hours choosing fabrics and designing the clothing. Briella found that every time she tried to sew neat stitches, no matter how carefully she paid attention, she always puckered the fabric. She was exasperated with herself. They took a long lunch break and went back to their creations.

When it was time for dinner, Fleur flew into the room and announced, "I am so tired! All day long, it's *'Fleur do this, Fleur do that.'* Who does he think he is?"

"The King of the Spring Court." Jacques offered, to which Fleur just rolled her eyes.

"King Ezekiel," Gustavious stated.

"Yes, I know!" Fleur groaned. "But must he be so needy?"

"Perhaps it's the pressure of the job, the weight of his large crown? I'd be cranky to have to carry that load around all the time," Gustavious said thoughtfully.

Waving her fingers at the mice, Fleur directed her attention to Briella and spoke, "You and I are having dinner in the atrium and no one else is invited. I've sent the menu to the kitchen and if we don't make ready, we will be late."

"Oh," answered Briella as she looked over at Gustavious, who made a shooing motion with his hands. She smiled and said, "Thank you all for everything!"

"'Tis our pleasure to be of service," Gustavious said as he bowed toward her.

Fleur took ahold of Briella's sleeve and tugged it toward her bedchamber door. They left the mice and entered the other room, and after inquiring what she should wear to their meal, Fleur told her to request a simple dinner gown from the enchanted cabinet.

Stepping up to the cabinet, Briella thought for a moment and then asked, "May I please have a muslin dinner gown with embroidered silk flowers and vines that line the hem with satin slippers to match?" Briella took a deep breath and then opened the cabinet's door to see the sparkling silver stars signaling that her wish had come true. She reached inside and gathered up the dinner dress, undergarments, and slippers to match.

Once she had donned the cream gown and slippers, she styled her golden tresses atop her head and left a few ringlets to line either side of her face and neck. Briella walked to the fireplace where the hot iron was waiting for her use. Gingerly picking it up and padding back over to the corner where the dressing table was located, she brought the hot iron back to rest upon a tray. Once she sat upon the padded bench, she carefully picked up the hot iron and wound her loose hair over the curling instrument. When Briella had curled the hair on either side of her face, long golden curls hung down. The effect was quite fetching. Through the looking-glass, she smiled at herself. Fleur rose from the back of the brush that she had been sitting upon and took flight. They had not conversed as Briella had readied herself because Fleur seemed lost in her own thoughts.

Rising, Briella hurried her steps as they ascended one set of stairs and walked through the corridor. They took a left turn that she had never taken before, and within a few more steps they had entered through to the atrium. The room was barren besides a single wooden table and a chair that sat in the middle. Upon the table sat one larger plate and a smaller table and chair. When they approached, she could see a shimmering flute of faerie wine and a smaller glass of water meant for her. Fleur had her own version in miniature size placed before her spot.

As they sat down for their meal, Fleur began to whine about her day again.

"Can you believe that he ordered me to break up a dispute and then shouted at me that I took too long? I mean *hello to you*, Your Majesty, I am only a few inches tall and they were massive. It takes a large presence to stop two trolls from tearing each other apart. And do not get me started on the foul odors expelling from their drooly mouths." Fleur took her index finger and shoved it into her mouth and made a gagging sound.

"He can't be all bad. He must value you very much to rely upon you so heavily," Briella told her friend.

Sitting up straighter in her tiny chair, Fleur exclaimed, "Yes, he must. I am irreplaceable and a great help! But you know, he is still a tyrant. You have not yet met his wrath! He can be a terrible bully."

"How do you mean?" Briella frowned, "What sort of things has he done?"

"Oh, well, he expects everyone to cower before him. He has always been very demanding and impatient, and when he was younger, it was so much worse."

"It sounds as though he's improved."

Fleur nodded, biting her lower lip, "I suppose so. It was a gradual change. He's stopped being so selfish, though he is still gruff and uncaring. However, he doesn't shout as he used to."

Silence lingered between the two of them, each lost in their own thoughts as they finished their meal. Briella looked out of the glass atrium walls, fixing her attention upon the woods. Her skin prickled, forming goosebumps as a pair of glowing eyes watched from the trees. Her memory brought her back to the night of the ball. She had seen glowing eyes then, as well. Was this the same creature? Were there various monsters roaming the woods? She released a sigh, relieved that she was in the safe confines of the castle walls. The creature, whatever it was, couldn't reach her.

When Briella looked up, she saw a few faeries in garish masks entering the atrium. They fanned out and each sought a corner of the barren room to inspect. Briella had an uneasy feeling in response to their presence, her stomach became unsettled, and she felt like icy fingers were trailing up and down her spine. She wondered if she was indeed safer within the castle walls after all. It was then that Fleur leaned forward and quietly insisted that it was time to leave. Fleur placed her silk napkin upon her plate and pushed her chair backwards.

"Briella, you will come with me," a voice commanded into her mind. She quickly scanned the room, checking to see if the speaker was amongst them. She quickly deduced that they were not as none had their focused attention upon her.

"Now, Briella. I am waiting."

Briella looked to Fleur, who was flying toward her when one of the faeries leapt forward and grabbed Fleur by her tiny wings. *They must have moved with increased faerie speed!*

Briella reached out her arm to attempt to rescue her friend, but her arms were pulled roughly behind her back. A foul-smelling rag reminiscent of rotten faerie fruit was shoved into her mouth and tied behind her head. The last thing that she saw was Fleur being thrown into a wine glass that was then upturned onto the table, trapping her friend. Darkness flooded her vision as a horrid smell infiltrated her nose; it was then that Briella knew a sack had been thrust over her head.

14

INTO THE WOODS

Briella tried to fight back. She was desperate to rescue Fleur, and though she had been a victim many times before, she would not willingly succumb to her abductor's wishes. Briella kicked and tripped and even let herself fall down, until she was hoisted up onto a brawny shoulder. Her dinner threatened to make a reappearance, and so, she ceased all of her movements and bided her time. The air was brisk on Briella's calves and the sounds of nature grew louder in her ears as trepidation awoke within her. She hoped that she was not being taken into the woods, but that hope was dashed with the sound of branches snapping by the unsteady gait with which her captor lumbered.

Time ceased to exist and soon Briella was lowered onto the forest floor. Her back smacked against a tree and the bark bit into her delicate shoulders and back. She winced, despite her vow that she would show no weakness. Her stockings felt as if they were torn as a cold substance that could have been blood or mud or perhaps both soaked into them, making her skin chill. Somewhere along the way she had lost a shoe, and she was glad that she had not worn her glass slippers. *But perhaps such thoughts don't matter? This faerie means to harm me. I must keep my wits about me.*

Her captor whisked the sack from her head, dislodging her pinned hair, which tumbled her locks around her shoulders. She was certain that a few long tresses were now attached to the sack. Briella blinked, allowing her eyes a moment to adjust before shifting her gaze up to her kidnapper. Recognition flashed through her memory as he leaned toward her. He was the rude faerie that she'd danced with at the ball. His handsome face held a sinister sneer, and his dark eyes observed her with menace. She took a moment to sit up and straighten her shoulders, despite moving closer toward him. She felt a sticky wetness adhering to her dress, but ignored it to face her foe. She had suffered far worse injuries, she could withstand a few cuts. She would never again cower in fear.

"Here we are, dear Briella. I did warn you about gifting my kind with your true name. All forests have wolves, you know." He stroked his chin. "Now, let's play a game, shall we? I'll give you a command and you'll try your best to fight against it! I command you to kiss me," her horned captor spoke compellingly.

She felt a small nudge to do as he bid, more like an annoying itch, but it was easily ignored. Briella just stared at him, defiantly.

"Hidden holly berries again? Just what is it that keeps you from obeying my will?" he mused. "Or perhaps, you are more than you seem?" He quickly stood and reached for her arm, wrenching her up to stand before him. Cruel eyes searched her body, making her spine more rigid. Letting her arm go, he walked around her with his dark tail twitching behind him. Briella felt the weight of his unwavering stare but resisted moving. *"What are you?"*

"I don't know what you mean," Briella said as calmly as she could. She swallowed, knowing full well that she'd just lied. But she needed to be careful. This faerie could cause her a great deal of harm if she didn't tread lightly. She'd select every word with care, at least, until she could get out of the woods and away from her tormentor.

"Don't play coy with me! I am not one to be disregarded. I will find a crack in your will, and when I do, you will bow to my every whim."

"You very well may. But at what price to your own soul?"

Her captor gave a harsh laugh; spittle flew onto her face. Briella's lips formed into a thin line as she fought against the lurch in her stomach and the sting of bile rising up her throat. She closed her eyes, cringing, before realizing that she'd just made her first mistake. The faerie moved so fast that she hadn't had a moment to register what was happening. His hand whizzed through the air, thundering as it made impact with her face. Briella's knees buckled beneath her as she fell onto the forest floor. Tears sprang to her eyes and heat flowed into her cheek in the spot where his hand had struck her. She whimpered as the tears flowed down her cheeks. He leaned down, towering over her, and shouted insults her way, but she could not understand his words. Briella shook her head, trying to clear the ringing in her ears.

A scream rang through the trees causing nearby birds to take flight. Briella stiffened, attempting to make out the noise, and sat alert. There was a crash, followed by a few muffled voices. Briella's eyes widened and her heart sped up in her chest. Before her stood King Ezekiel, dangling her abductor high above his head with his outstretched arm, while he held onto the cravat at her captor's throat. The faerie was choking as his booted feet kicked the air around him. Briella blinked, stunned at the sight. She gave her head another shake and the ringing cleared from her head.

"*You* dare to touch *her*? That which is *mine*! You vile, rubbish, disgrace! You shame the Seelie race!" the Faerie King shouted into the purpling face before him.

Briella suddenly felt terror grip her heart as her pulse increased even more and her breathing became erratic. She was trembling and afraid at this version of the King. She had never seen him in such a violent rage, and this was the behavior that the gossips had accused him of. His face was twisted with fury as he shook his prey. Uncertain what would happen next, Briella scooted backward along the forest floor, and though twigs snagged at her hair and jagged bits tore through her palms, she still moved away from the frightening scene playing out before her. Everything in her was screaming at her to avoid this situation at all costs. Past memories were assaulting her senses, and she could not distinguish between the abuse of her stepfamily and that which the King was executing. When she backed into a larger tree and could go no further, she drew her knees up against her chest and tucked her head and arms into the cocoon. She rocked back and forth. Before her closed eyes, moments of pain and abuse flickered through her mind and they were overwhelming her. She heard shouted slurs and felt past injuries just as she had when they had been inflicted upon her. She didn't know up from down, left from right. All that consumed her was fear.

Briella didn't know how long she stayed as she was. It could have been minutes, hours, or days. She startled when a hand rested upon her bent head, and she instantly burst into sobs, begging him not to harm her. She felt hands applying pressure to her forearms, then memories of her stepfather were shaking her, gently. *No*. That was not correct, he had never been gentle with her.

"Briella, look at me," begged King Ezekiel.

She took a breath, but could not stop the sobs that were consuming her. Uncurling her body slowly and bringing her head up to look, she saw that it was not as her ears had told her; her stepfather was far away, and it was the King who was touching her, entreating her to meet his eyes. Eyes that were no longer filled with anger, but now held a tenderness that she had never seen reside within the mossy depths. She could not make sense of why he was crouched before her.

"You are safe, that I promise you," he spoke softly to her. He reached out and carefully stroked her jaw; his gaze settled on her cheek, which she felt swelling.

Swallowing, she took deep breaths and viewed him through her teary vision. *I am safe*. She was not back at the chateau, and no one was striking her. Her abductor was not before her tormenting her any longer either. Wiping the tears with the backs of her hands, she heard the King gasp. She stiffened back, slowing her sobs, and lowered her hands. Her eyes widened as she looked to the King, awaiting his next response.

Ever so gently, King Ezekiel grasped onto her wrist and turned her palm toward him, bringing it up and closer to his face for his inspection. His gaze turned thunderous again. Briella flinched, trying to pull her hand back to herself. After another fierce tug, he freed her wrist and took the other, repeating the action. Briella let him look at her hand as he brought the other one up to peer at. Her palms were bloody and bits of debris clung to her tender skin. In the back of her mind, she realized that she was in pain, but the spots were all over her body and it was hard to distinguish which was her worst injury.

"You have wounds," he stated matter-of-factly. "They must be tended to. We should return directly," his smooth voice soothed something buried deep within her heart.

"You said my name. You've said it twice now," she told him as she looked into his beautiful mossy green eyes. It was the only thing her mind could focus on to try to forget the pain that wracked her body.

He nodded. "So I have."

"But how did you come to learn it?"

"Now is not the time to discuss this. You need to have your wounds cleaned and you need to get warm; you won't stop shaking."

The King wrapped his arms around her back and she winced, crying out. The anguished tears started to flow again. She knew that she was in real danger of fainting away from the blinding flashes of pain that were wracking her body and threatening to drown her.

The King slowly leaned her forward and peered at her back. He snarled, which startled her, and she jerked which only exacerbated the pain. The King made a soothing sound and leaned forward to place a delicate kiss upon her forehead. The tension fled from Briella's body as the gentleness of his action filled her with peace and something else that was entirely foreign to her. She was much too distracted and weary to try to puzzle out exactly what that something else happened to be.

Attempting to carefully lift Briella once again, he placed his arm under her legs where her knees bent, and the other he wrapped around her waist. When she didn't cry out in agony, he rose while tucking her against his chest. He smelled of cut grass and rain showers; there was even a hint of charcoal. It was a curious blend, but perhaps for the Faerie King of the Spring Court, it made perfect sense. These were all comforting aromas that she would always associate with him forevermore.

They continued on in silence under the moonlight, without the use of faerie speed. Briella wasn't sure which would be worse, the jostling of the movement of slowly traversing the ground, or the rushing movements of speed to end this journey. *He is being so careful with me, I feel as if he treasures me. But that can't be?*

The tears had run their course as numbness crept into Briella's being. She was glad that for now, the pain was not present. She raised her head to see where they were.

"Do not look," the King requested.

There was a longing in Briella to defy his words. She had been told all of her life what she could and couldn't do, and she wasn't about to take orders now, not even from a King. She opened her eyes and glanced behind them. Her faerie captor was bent backward over a tree trunk. Her breath hitched in her lungs as she fought against the urge to cry out. Her fingers flew over her mouth.

Sighing heavily, King Ezekiel told her, "He's not dead, though he may wish for that fate once he wakes to a prison cell. Every day more are banished there, and the air is oppressive with rot and decay."

"Why are so many there?"

"It's the only place they can exist without harming others. There is a darkness that pervades my Court. I cannot stop it, and I've watched the best descend into the clutches of madness, and nothing can release its tightening hold."

"What brought all of this about? Is it a curse? It sounds as if it were." Feeling his eyes upon her, she looked up at him. With a grim set of his lips, he shook his head at her warily but did not answer.

It wasn't long before they reached the castle and entered through a side entrance that was guarded by two faerie guards and one fierce gargoyle. The gargoyle showing his disdain glared at them all equally.

"There is a mad one out in the woods. Bring him to the prison, at once," the King ordered the males who bowed and jogged out to do as bid, while the gargoyle stayed rooted upon its perch seeming to judge every action that was taking place before it.

Briella lowered her head back to King Ezekiel's chest and squeezed her eyes tightly shut. She felt drowsy and let her mind wander.

Briella felt herself being lowered and she was careful to keep only her side touching the furniture, for she surmised that would be the most comfortable position in which to recline. Slowly she opened her eyes and noticed that he had gingerly placed her onto a chaise. She watched as the King pulled upon a bellpull. They remained staring at each other until a knock sounded on the door.

Once King Ezekiel had ordered bandages, antiseptic, and called for the castle physician, he removed his tailcoat. It was stained with blood along its sleeves and front. He loosened his ruined cravat and tossed it onto a wingback chair. Then he walked over to a beverage cart where he poured out faerie wine into two small goblets. When he walked back over to the chaise, he handed one of the goblets to Briella.

"You might as well drink. I don't imagine that any of the care you'll receive tonight will be pleasant, as some of the wounds look to be healing. You still need them to be cleaned."

Throwing back her head and drinking deeply from the

goblet, she closed her eyes. When Briella opened them again, he had moved over toward the fireplace and she watched the glittering light dance within his goblet as he drank.

Briella gazed around the inky black room with comfortable furniture. There were two wingback chairs with clawed feet and a small desk. The fireplace seemed to be the focal point of the room with its drooping roses. *This must be a sitting room.* There were faded portraits of Spring along the walls. One was of a garden with rioting colors and a burbling fountain that reminded her of the outside of this castle. Another was of flowering trees with small animals and birds encircling them. The last one was of a couple who wore royal robes and each had a crown upon their head. They reminded her of the King with their magnificent eyes and blond hair, but then, all of the faeries were beautiful to behold. Each portrait had to be studied carefully as the oppressive darkness had bled the colors together and added hidden depth within its shadows.

Briella gasped as she tried to sit up. King Ezekiel turned around and was swiftly at her side.

"You must rest."

"I forgot! Fleur was trapped! Oh, you must find her! If anything happens to her, I will never forgive myself!" Briella exclaimed as fear gripped her heart and she began to tremble.

"I shall send my guard to her aid at once. You need not fear." His eyes held her gaze for a moment before he made his way to the door, opening it.

King Ezekiel summoned another servant and ordered his guard to locate Fleur and see that she was safe. He wanted a healer to examine her to see if she had any injuries and wanted to be informed the moment that she was located. Sitting down in one of the wingback chairs, she could tell that he was tense by the set of his shoulders and the hardening of his eyes. They sat amidst a very heavy silence.

Before long, another knock reached their ears and the door silently opened to reveal a slightly older male faerie. He approached the King, who met him halfway into the room, and they began to speak in whispers. They both walked to the chaise and looked down upon her. She met their stares as the physician set his black bag down and addressed her.

"I am the Court Physician, Dr. Grant, never fear, we shall soon have you right as rain. Now dear one, let's get a good look at these wounds," he said as he bent down to peer at her back. He *tsked* and picked up each of her palms to examine them, inquiring if she had any other injuries.

"I think my stockings are torn from falling and then scrambling away," Briella admitted.

The physician nodded before moving to check her legs. Carefully, while trying to respect her modesty, the physician drew up her hem and remarked, "Oh yes, there are a lot of scratches here as well. None very deep."

When she met King Ezekiel's eye, his jaw was clenched. She had the desire to both flee from the intensity of his heated gaze, and also to reach out and try to soothe his concern away. She had certainly endured worse before, and when she voiced that thought he growled.

"If only I could hunt them down, those vile men, those entrusted with your care, I would wipe their entire existence away," he seethed. When she flinched at his words, his brows drew together and he lowered himself toward her, resting his forehead against her. "Sweet girl, don't you understand that I would do anything for you?" he whispered. "You don't yet understand, but you will."

15

UNDERSTANDING THE IMPOSSIBLE

The physician tried to take care with his movements while tending to Briella's wounds, but anytime she would moan or cry out, King Ezekiel would demand that he use more care. His voice held a frightening tone, but she was not alarmed. The King stayed by her side the entire time, sitting upon the rug next to the chaise to oversee every action made by Doctor Grant. Briella felt secure with him being so close to her, and his words of affection kept replaying over and over within her mind. She kept turning them rightside up and upside down. She finally made herself believe that, since he was her King, in his eyes she was just another being under his protection, and that what he expressed to her was what any sovereign would feel about a subject of his. *No more and no less.*

While the physician was cleansing her back, there was a rapping upon the door and the King quickly tread over to it and pulled it open. He spoke to someone that she could not see. Closing the door, he strode back toward her and said, "Fleur is safe. One of her wings was torn, but it is being mended and she will be well soon. Do not worry, she will need to rest, but she will heal."

With a half smile, Briella replied, "I'm thankful that she has been found. I'm so distraught that she is suffering because of me."

"Fleur would not have wanted to let you go without a fight. You are on her mind frequently. She considers you her friend. Please rest," he pleaded with sincerity that was reflected not only in his tone of voice but within his shining eyes as well.

"'Tis a curious thing, your healing is more advanced than a mere mortal, and yet, it isn't quite that of which a Fae is capable of possessing," the physician told her and then thoughtfully added, "Perchance there is Fae blood that courses through your veins?"

Briella immediately thought of her father, but kept silent. She still was not sure if such information would be helpful to her survival within the Spring Court or would hinder her more.

It was King Ezekiel who spoke, "What nonsense. If she were Fae blooded, or even half, I above all would know."

"Of course, Your Majesty," he was quick to state as he rubbed one hand down his chest. "Well there, now, I believe that I have finished. Time will work wonders and you should rest." He turned his attention to the King. "Shall I ring for a footman to escort her back to her chambers?"

Frowning, the King answered tersely with a *'no'* and then with a haughty command mentioned that Doctor Grant was dismissed.

Briella watched as the physician bowed and backed out from the sitting room. Watching the door close behind him, she turned back toward the chaise and tried to sit up.

The King immediately assisted her in getting situated and brought a black blanket to rest over her shoulders.

Hedging her words, but really desiring to know, she inquired, "Would you know if I possessed Fae blood?"

"Yes and you do," he replied. "I smelled it as soon as you entered my line of sight. It's not something that any but the most powerful of faeries can determine. So, your secret is safe with me, little one."

"At the ball, you mean? When you first saw me?"

"When first I saw you, yes," he answered as he avoided her eyes.

Briella thought about her vision when she had consumed the decadent dessert, True Love's Kiss. Had he truly been aware of her existence long before she ever arrived in his lands? She wanted to be more direct in her line of questioning, but she felt like a coward when she could not make the words form upon her tongue. He had been so gentle with her; he had rescued her and brought her to safety, making no demands whatsoever upon her. She fidgeted where she sat.

"You will not ask me the questions that are burning behind your lovely blue eyes," he smirked at her, leaning his head toward her so that they made eye contact.

"I am no one, and certainly lowly enough to know I should not question my King."

"No, I think not. I believe that you are stalling, but for what purpose, I cannot say."

Taking a moment, she finally gained the courage to seek the truth. "The other night…"

"Yes?" he patiently replied.

"Fleur introduced me to True Love's Kiss. And I thought that I saw someone and was wondering how reliable the visions are."

"Ah. I hear that they are fairly accurate. Did you

glimpse a tall, dark, handsome faerie? Perhaps he had more Unseelie qualities than you wished to see? Maybe he bore the head of a toad or hoofed feet? Or maybe you spied *a tail*?"

Briella looked at him and gasped.

"Am I correct? Did you find him repulsive?" he inquired quietly as he averted his gaze.

Finding her voice she said, "I did not find any fault with him, only the vision. I believe it was flawed."

"How so?" he questioned as he once again cast his eyes upon her.

"What I beheld is an impossibility. It simply can't be real."

The King stroked her injured cheek with one long tapered index finger. "You may find that things in Faerie are far more real than anywhere else. We do not view the world as humans do. We feast, and we dance, and we love without fear and embrace our destiny. If we can look around us long enough to gain wisdom, it can be found. Even in the most unlikely of places. We do not sneer at love. We live as we do all things, with wild abandon."

"That sounds impossible to me."

There was a weary smile that curled upon the King's lips. "What did your heart tell you about the vision?"

"That it was real, but the impractical part was that it seemed as if I held a conversation with the male. And if it was supposed to be a vision, how would that be possible? Would he be pulled into the vision with me?" Briella asked, twisting her hands together.

"Not normally, no. But the more powerful the faerie, the more attuned to you he would be, and the more likely that the magic in this world could make the impossible a reality."

"I did not say he was a faerie."

King Ezekiel smirked at her and said, "You did not have to tell me a thing."

Briella stood up as quickly as she could with her body still aching. The movement sapped what little strength she still possessed and breathlessly blurted out, "It's late. I should let you retire. I feel as if I could sleep for a week." She let the black blanket crumple to the floor as it fell from her shoulders. The emotions swirling within her were too much for her to process and time was what she needed to gain perspective. *Time and to be alone.*

Without waiting for his reply, she hurried her steps to the door making her body heed her command to keep going. Before her hand could wrap around the handle, he was there opening the door for her. She still could not look at him. Briella walked by him and smelled the aroma of cut grass, rain showers, and charcoal again. She closed her eyes tightly and then opened them as she continued walking down the straight hallway. The King was silently following her down the two flights of twisted stairs.

Soon, they stood before her bedchamber door and she knew that she had to say something to him. "Thank you for… everything." She would not look into his bright gaze, instead, she focused on a golden button attached to his waistcoat.

"No need to express your gratitude. I regret that I was not sooner at your side. This never should have happened. I apologize for the whole affair," he somberly remarked.

Looking up at him, she smiled and said, "Good night."

He leaned toward her and opened the door saying, "Slumber sweetly, Briella. Dream of everything that makes you happy." Briella's heart warmed within her chest. *He says such sweet things to me that my heart practically overflows with feelings that I don't know quite what to do with. If only I could evoke such sincere emotions within him. How might he look at me then?*

Nodding at the King, she tiredly entered her bedchamber. Looking over her shoulder, she watched him close the heavy door. She padded to her four-poster bed and sat wearily at the foot of it as her thoughts churned.

So, her vision had been real and he was her destiny. But was she his? Did destiny give different paths to the same fated pair? She was so unworthy of him and it pained her heart to admit that she really adored him. Though he had frightened her this evening, his anger had not been directed at her. He was furious that ill had befallen her. Yet, he had been merciful to her abductor, sparing his life.

Did she want to rule beside him in the Spring Court if such a thing were even possible? Could she ever measure up to a fate bigger than she? Bigger than she could ever imagine? Was it worth pursuing? And if he came to resent her, could she bear that too? Was it better to view the emotion swimming within his eyes, bask in that emotion in his arms, or forever separate herself from him? He did have very kissable lips that she longed to feel ardently pressed upon her own, but was that enough to see them through forever? There was still so much that she did not know about him, and about the world that she was now residing in. Would she be able to learn what she must in order to make the appropriate choices? *Would the overwhelming pull between them ever abate? And for Heaven's sake! What does this connection mean? For I know that he must feel its tug as well…*

If he wanted a future with her, could she deny them both? To lose her heart was a loss that she could not come back from. She had lost herself, her dignity, and her value over the years. Could she part with the one thing that still remained hers to give? Her heart wanted to soar from her chest and present itself to the Faerie King, craving to finally be treasured and to know what true love was like. Would she dare trust her heart over the reservations that her head kept reminding her of? Like the very real threat of looming madness and a curse that held everything in a vise and squeezed until all color bled from the land. That was a terrifying reality. Could she uncover the truths hidden within these cold stone walls? Did she really want to?

Yes, no matter what may come, she desired to free these people. If she could help, she wanted to. Everyone deserved a happily-ever-after, even those stuck in prison cells.

Briella wanted her life to matter.

16

SHOCKING DISCOVERIES

The next day was miserably spent in bed, and though Briella tried to sleep, she was still sore, making rest nearly impossible. She thought of the forest and how fortunate they all were to have escaped it before any beasts had appeared to devour them, especially ones with glowing scarlet eyes. What fortunate luck it was that the Faerie King had discovered her plight so quickly. Briella briefly wondered how he had managed to locate her so hastily. It was just one of many questions swirling around within her troubled mind.

Every time she closed her eyes, her mind would show her memories of her time with her captor, and that would lead her along a vast trove of recollections of abuse suffered at the hands of her stepfamily. It was counterproductive to rest. Her tortured mind was unyielding.

The mice visited her and kept her updated on the progress they were making upon their first order, informing her that Fleur was mostly healed. It was only by the order of the King that Fleur lingered within her chambers. They both needed time to recover. But Fleur was chomping at the bit to commiserate with her friend. Her mousy visitors came and went until tea time later that afternoon.

Occasionally, Briella's thoughts turned to the King. He had voiced such tender sentiment the prior evening. He had shown her kindness, a warmth of spirit. But there was a fierceness that resided within him, a violent force that she still shivered from even in the light of day. He was capable of great deeds just as easily as he was capable of rage. It was the malevolence that had caused her alarm, whether it was directed at her or not. She could not easily separate the duality of his personality that she had seen in others time and again; the anger of men entrusted with her wellbeing had taught her that monsters were real. The worst kind of monster was one who was wearing the skin of a human, for they were the most deceptive of all. But a faerie was a known danger, an ever-changing being. And yet, it was in the land of the Fae that she had experienced kindness and true happiness. Could she, should she, trust in the attention given to her by the King? He had seemed genuine in his concern for her. That was a puzzle for another day. Briella's mind was tired of mulling over the entire affair.

Briella had finally pulled herself out from under her coverlet and readied for the evening. Her bathing had taken longer, to her dismay. She was filthy from her evening trek through the woods. She was mortified at the idea of appearing so dirty before King Ezekiel. *But what could I have done differently?*

She arranged her hair atop the crown of her head and left golden ringlets hanging freely along either side of her face. Briella found it difficult to let the locks hang down uninhibited, as she had when she first walked into the castle. While she attended to her daily tasks within the castle, she preferred to style it up. While at the chateau, she had always had her hair up in a twist or simple knot. Any loose tendrils were easy prey to cruel fingers set upon causing her anguish and pain.

Briella padded over to the enchanted cabinet. "May I please have something with little frills or lace." She was satisfied when it produced a simple dinner gown in periwinkle silk. It was elegant and she felt unencumbered by ornamental decoration. Her body aches would have been made worse, having heavier material to contend with. Briella took little time to don her evening wear. Once she was readied, she made her way over toward the looking-glass to look for any discernable flaw.

"Settling in well enough I see," a familiar voice purred. Spinning from the full-length looking-glass, she turned to see Cheshire perched upon the end of her bed, watching her as his striped tail twitched back and forth.

"Cheshire! To what do I owe the pleasure of this visit?"

"I am simply confirming your presence within the castle. There are rumors flying quickly through the Court today, and they, my dear, all involve you and a certain royal one, and a midnight rendezvous."

Throwing her hands up against either side of her blushing face, Briella exclaimed, "What utter nonsense!"

"Hmmm, but then, why is your face as red as the Queen of the Lunar Court's prized roses?" Cheshire began to idly lick a paw.

Ignoring his question, she replied, "I had a spot of trouble last night and the King rescued me."

"Yes, I know, as does the entire castle. You're famous, my dear."

"Cheshire, what can you tell me about your time here?

About this curse?" She longed to change the topic of their conversation and did so as she came to sit beside him.

He twitched his ear at her and said, "What is there really to tell? You know how I came to be here. I wonder, have you asked the King your pressing questions?"

"He won't speak about it either, it's all taboo. Were the prior king and queen alive when you first arrived?"

"Of course, they only died a decade ago. They were stupid faeries, really. They made mistakes and we are all paying the price for them, still."

Drawing her brows together, she inquired, "How were they stupid? That seems unkind."

Making a feline sound of dismay, he answered, "It's not my fault. I see a spade and I call it a spade. They were good rulers, but where they failed affects us all. They were unfit *parents*. That, in itself, is the whole problem. Make of that what you will." Stretching, Cheshire rose and stalked to Briella's pillow where he settled himself.

"Make yourself comfortable, Cheshire," she scoffed.

"I always do. Where do you think I spend most of my day while you toil away?"

"Here?"

"Of course, my dear. Why waste the space?" He yawned and then closed his bottle green eyes, dismissing her. She was not sure whether she should be offended or not.

Briella finally just shrugged her shoulders and made her way through the twisted castle until she came upon Fleur's bedchamber. Stopping to peer at the tiny door, which was one of many tiny doors along an inky black wall, she tapped upon the appropriate black door using the nail of her index finger. The door opened to reveal Fleur, who was paler and hunched over with a bandage completely covering her left wing. When Briella caught sight of how poorly her friend looked, she gasped.

"'Tis not so terrible now. Last eve was a different matter, entirely. I am on the mend. I've been positively consumed with wondering how you fared," Fleur hurriedly told her.

"I am better. I didn't sleep much because the horrors kept repeating themselves. But I'm almost mended and that's cause for celebration for me, especially since you're improving too," Briella told her.

"The mice helped alleviate the worst of my concerns. It's absolutely *unfaely* to be ordered to stay locked within my chambers. I'm famished. Shall we make our way into the dining hall? You'll have to scoop me up and carry me. I'm useless with this infuriating wing." Fleur shook the shoulder that was attached to the injured wing.

"Of course, I shall." Briella reached down and gently scooped her tiny friend into her palms and straightened back to her full height. "I'm not hurting you?"

"Not at all." Fleur sat within the half circle of Briella's smooth palms and fluffed her purple dress skirt out. The petals chosen for her dress resembled tulips today.

The pair remained quiet as Briella made their way to the grand dining hall. The room was brightly lit with floating candles and the din of conversations and laughter met their ears. There stood a massive fireplace in the middle wall of the stone-walled room, decorated with blooming roses and the oppressive inky black that nearly hid all beauty from sight.

Briella felt a small nudge of trepidation at entering a room filled with so many of the Fae race. She did not want to distrust every being she came across. She was trying her best to leave behind her past of being so cautious when she entered a room, never knowing how her stepfamily would treat her. But now she had good reasons why she should remain vigilant, even here in the Spring Court. She knew better than to lump villainous intentions with the entirety of any race, but here she was so much less than the faeries were. She was much more *breakable* than they were.

Fleur pointed a tiny finger toward a table off to the side of the room, located next to the connecting door of the kitchen, and so, Briella made her way over to it. She did not want to be seen given the gossip running amuck. She wanted to remain hidden from sight. *A small measure of safety would do me immensely good.*

A waiter dressed in the black castle livery dashed before Briella and pulled out her chair. Briella sat and thanked him and he gave her a frown as he walked away. Remembering how unfashionable it was to show signs of appreciation, she internally cringed.

Carefully setting Fleur down upon the top of the butter dome, she inquired, "What shall we dine upon tonight?"

Fleur was about to answer when a silver cart stopped beside their table, and from its center Sebastian said, "Now, there is trouble. Why am I not surprised that *both of you* found danger?" He placed his pincers upon his blue hips.

"It's hardly our fault! We didn't ask to be the center of a faerie's madness." Fleur glared at the crab.

"Uhm hum. And I'm not a crustacean," Sebastian huffed as he turned to whisper into the ear of a pink lizard dressed in a green tailcoat. The lizard ran to retrieve a tiny wooden table and chair that were situated off to the side of the cart and rushed them over to Fleur. He arranged the table and chair facing Briella and helped Fleur into her seat. With a flourish of his clawed hand, Sebastian whipped a napkin open and dropped it across Fleur's lap. Fleur nodded at him, but remained silent.

"Try not to be the source of further upheaval. Just enjoy a fine dinner and then rest in your rooms this evening." Sebastian rocked his body upon his backfins.

"You bossy little creature!" Fleur screeched. Her delicate face had turned an alarming shade of ruby. Briella tried to soothe her with a look, but Fleur wasn't looking her way. She was glaring intently at the crab, when her face morphed into a smile. Her coloring began to fade.

"You know what? I'm famished. So, I'll order for Briella and myself, shall I?" Fleur smiled malevolently. When Sebastian nodded his consent, she continued, "Let's start with stringy lobster bisque. Then, I'd love a crab salad made of meaty chunks, followed by the largest broiled lobster tail you can find. Be sure to not forget to bring us those delightful crab puffs that Cheshire is always raving about. I don't know why, but I'm desiring a menu that snaps and pops tonight with lots of melted butter. And double that order."

Sebastian seemed to flinch with each additional word of the order until he became a paler hue of blue. Briella felt sympathy for him. *I do hope that he is not directly related to any of the crustaceans on the menu. What a horrid thought.*

Sebastian snapped his pincers and the silver cart whisked away. *An enchantment*! Briella watched the connecting door to the kitchen slam after it and looked back at Fleur.

"That was unkind." Briella frowned, turning her gaze to her friend.

Smiling wickedly at her, Fleur stated, *"Oh Unnamed,* didn't you know that we're all unkind here? Why, the madness and never-ending boredom are enough to drive all kindness from one's soul. That's why it's so very important to not provoke a faerie. We're teeming with creative ways to enact vile deeds."

A chill ran down Briella's spine at her friend's eerie words, causing her to shiver. She hadn't truly feared Fleur in days, and she had to remind herself that no matter how she'd come to view her as a friend, she was still a faerie and given to wild flights of fancy. She suspected that her friend would never seek to cause her harm, but when madness touched one's mind, who knew how much damage it could accomplish. Once upon a time, Briella had thought that she was safe with the others who were entrusted to care for her, and that had been a living nightmare. Never again would she view others through unworldly eyes.

Neither spoke until Sebastian returned with their soup. The lizard produced their bowls as the tiny crab looked on. Briella couldn't lift her eyes from her bowl, but she heard the pleased sounds Fleur made as she sipped her spoon's contents. Cringing, Briella took a sip. Her discomfort grew as the meal progressed. She was hungry, so she ate, but she hardly tasted what she put into her mouth. Waves of disgust rolled through her when she considered how indelicate it was to sup upon a creature much like the one who was serving you. She began to question her friendship with Fleur and she didn't like how this evening was turning out. The increasing discomfort made her want to flee into the night. *Perhaps there will always be sides to these beings that will frighten me.*

Ruminating over the dangers of this Faerie Court, she thought that she only had herself to rely upon. Here, she thought that she was making friends and carving a place for herself, but perhaps that wasn't what she was doing at all. Maybe she was just delaying her fate. If this madness was due to the curse, it was in her best interest to find a way to break it. Only then would she be truly safe.

17

OLD COMPANIONS

After dinner was concluded, the two parted ways at Fleur's chamber door. Fleur gave her a small soft smile before she entered and closed the door. Briella was at a loss to understand what, if anything, her demure smile had meant. She had really come to care about Fleur and she suspected that the tiny being returned her regard. Maybe an off night was simply to blame for Fleur's earlier behavior. Briella was more than ready to dismiss her friend's terrible mood; she wanted to see the best that she knew resided within the tiny faerie, though she would remain watchful. Perhaps Fleur's sprite nature led her to mischievousness and to sometimes veer into a path that was frightening to behold. *No one being could be truly all bad nor all good. Could they? There were so many differing shades to each unique personality.*

Instead of seeking the comfort of her own chambers, Briella retraced her steps until she stood before the King's closed library door. She hadn't been able to view his table from her side of the room at dinner, but she had caught conversations addressing his presence. Every so often, her ears would catch the mention of her name. Since she had done nothing wrong, she had held her head up high and pretended as if nothing was amiss. *Cheshire must be correct, perhaps the entire castle was gossiping about her and the King…*

Briella suspected that if she lingered long enough, the Faerie King would find her within his sanctuary. So she twisted the knob and entered his domain. *I hope that I may meet with him again, so that we may speak.* Softly, she padded across the carpet until she reached a wide wall of books. Randomly choosing one, she walked over to one of the reading nooks that were settled in every corner of the library and quietly sat down. Each snug area contained a padded bench with a throw pillow and a lamp that was resting atop a small table.

Drawing up her legs and bending her knees, she arranged her legs to her side and then fluffed her hem until she was satisfied that her pose was modest. Then, she opened the book and lost everything else to its pages.

"I'm pleased that you're making yourself comfortable," King Ezekiel crooned from behind her. Briella jumped and the book flew from her hands. Briefly, she wondered if she should rise and curtsey.

The King quickly retrieved the tome from the air before it could fall back down and harm either of them. He read the title and said, "Curious choice. I did not take you for a student of philosophy."

Briella cradled her face with her palms and exhaled slowly before answering, "I think the book chose me. I didn't know which book I had reached for. Something about it drew me toward it and isn't that the start to any worthwhile adventure? Having the book invite you to get lost within its pages. Maybe the book chooses its reader just as much as the reader chooses their book."

"You talk as if the books have feelings or a will of their

own, when it's the will of their author that they follow." King Ezekiel came and sat down beside her. He offered her the book back and she took it, settling it into her lap.

Wrinkling her brow, Briella said, "But just because they're staying true to themselves doesn't mean they don't possess their own unique magic as well. Everyone needs a guiding hand from time to time."

"Do *you* need a guiding hand?" His face was so close to hers that she could feel his warm breath against her cheek. The scent of cut grass, rain showers, and charcoal wafted from him, enveloping Briella.

"I think I need more than most, perhaps."

"Is that so?"

Barely breathing, her chest heaving, she answered breathlessly, "Yes."

He was erasing the distance between them to perchance kiss her. Briella's gaze fixed upon his lips as he drew nearer, more sure of what his drawing closer meant. *What if I disappoint him? And with all the beautiful beings that reside within his Court, his notice of me makes me feel as if I could take flight. But oh, the chance to have my first kiss shared with this handsome King, it's like a fairytale come true. It's everything I never knew that I craved.* Her pulse was racing with anticipation as everything else except for him disappeared from the room. The Faerie King was but a hair's breadth away from her lips, when a log in the fireplace before them shifted and cast mossy green embers upon the floor before their feet. The magical flames burned higher in their grate and hissed. The magic of the moment changed and Briella couldn't say whether she was disappointed or not. *Kissing him would have completely changed my whole world.* Briella blinked to clear her thoughts.

The King leapt up and stomped the glowing embers

underneath his booted feet. When he was satisfied, he blew out a deep breath and ran a long hand over his face. Then sitting back down, he leaned back. Raising his arms over his head to rest along the sides of his pointed ears, he clasped his large hands together as he slid down in his seat.

"It seems as if everything here has life. Even the magical fire," Briella said a bit fervently.

Smiling and angling his head toward her, the King quirked a brow and asked, "The books can have life, but the fire can't?"

"Did I say books have life? I suppose you could have thought so."

He reached toward her and wound a golden curl of her hair around his long tapered index finger. "Tell me a secret."

"I think my secrets are better left kept to myself, Your Majesty."

"Hmmm. For now perhaps, but one day soon, you will want to confide your innermost secrets, your *desires* to me." His gaze traveled from her eyes to her lips.

Briella tilted her head and said, "We shall see. Does that mean that you will confide in me as well?" *I have never flirted before and it's both exhilarating and frightening.*

The King smirked at her. "If that would please you."

Not certain what to say next, Briella thought of a secret she could share with a King of Faerie that wouldn't seem pathetic or just ridiculous, so she decided upon a safe topic. "When I was younger, before my parents passed away, I was gifted with a dog named Bruno. He was a bloodhound and so very sweet. He used to accompany me everywhere that I went, and he slept at the foot of my bed."

"And that's your secret?" Amusement was shining from his mossy gaze.

"Not quite. Be patient, I'm getting to the point. After my mother died, my stepfather gave him away to a farmer on our land, for a price of course. And even though he wasn't mine any longer, he'd come and visit me once a week while I worked in our kitchen garden. My secret is that even after I was forbidden from seeing him ever again, for a time, I still did." Briella felt his finger trace a tear down her cheek. *The gentleness that he possesses for me touches my heart; I also find it surprising that he could care so much for me.* She hadn't shed a tear for Bruno in such a long time, as she had willed her heart to not mourn him. The fact that an errant tear had appeared was very unsettling.

At first, when his visits had stopped, she had cried a great deal. One dreary day she was approached by the farmer who explained that Bruno had grown older and couldn't get around as well as he desired to any longer.

"Did he pass away?" King Ezekiel softly inquired.

Shaking her head, she replied, "I don't know. He was my happiest memory for such a long time. But it's been years, and by now, he mustn't still be alive."

"Would you want to see him, if he yet lives?"

Briella paused, thinking on the King's question for a moment, pulling her lower lip between her teeth. "I would. If only to get to say goodbye one last time." She felt his gaze lingering upon her lips.

"I may have a way." He stood suddenly and reached down for her hand. Briella did not hesitate to let him help her rise. Her curiosity was rapidly growing, and the chance to see one of her forever loves was not something that she'd ever refuse.

Holding hands, they exited the library via a hidden

doorway in the paneling. The King pulled Briella alongside him, guiding her steps. Together they traversed the lit staircase until they came to a stop before another ebony inky door. Briella felt tiny butterflies soaring throughout her stomach at the touch of the faerie and she decided that it was a feeling that thrilled her. Even if it proved dangerous to her heart in the future, in this moment his presence was magical.

Twisting the door handle and pushing the door open, the King led his seamstress into his private chambers. He escorted her to a settee that faced the fireplace and motioned for Briella to sit. She felt odd being in his private chambers but also curious at what possessions were within. Once she had taken her seat as directed, he walked through another door and was absent for just a few moments.

While he was away, Briella looked around the private sitting room. It was furnished in the Rococo style, with the chairs, settee and tables having scrolling curves along the arms and backs, which were meant to express drama and movement. *Within the dark shadows of this room, they look as if they are ready to move about at any moment.* The end tables held curved candelabras with dripped white wax upon them. The ceilings and walls were decorated with sculpted moldings and frescoes which were all dark. *It must have been beautiful once. There is still beauty to behold only now it's twisted.*

When the King appeared before her again, he held something behind his back. He breezed over to her and knelt, capturing Briella's hand within one of his own. His warmth encased her, making her feel safe and cared for once more. He smiled, met her gaze, and pushed a black looking-glass into the fingers of her other hand. The back and handle were decorated in full blooming roses, the coloring of the deep rich black made them stand out all the more. The looking-glass was truly a work of art. Words escaped her as she gazed into the glass, seeing her wide cerulean eyes staring back at her.

"This looking-glass has aided me in viewing the outside world, both in Faerie, and the mortal realm. One only has to direct it to your heart's desire. When the... When everything changed, this looking-glass appeared to me. I believe it was gifted to give me hope." King Ezekiel spoke so softly that his tone was almost reverent.

Drawing her delicate brows together, Briella looked up at him. "When you addressed me, you knew my name when no others in this land had that knowledge. How did you come to know who I am?"

"Ah, that is easy to explain. I knew it because I have known of you for a long while. There was a time when I sought other relations to the realm, ones who could rule in my stead. I felt alone in so many things." he paused for a moment and looked away. Briella bit into her lip, but remained silent, waiting for the King to continue. "That was the desire of my heart. For a new ruler to govern us all. It was a few years ago that I caught my first glimpse of you. I did not, at first, understand what you meant. I am still not entirely sure. But you, Briella, are the future of this Court. Of that, I am certain. The weaves of our life threads are being woven, and, somehow your destiny resides within Faerie." His mossy green eyes bore into hers. Briella swallowed, at a loss for words. His thumb began to stroke the back of her delicate hand. It was mesmerizing and delicious all at once.

"That... I... I cannot rule your Court. Your citizens would never accept me. I am not a full-blooded Fae and–"

"You are our hope. You are *my* hope, and are capable of such wonderful things, if only you believed in yourself."

"Did you not wonder how I would fit into your world?"

"I did at first. I knew that you were only half-faerie and I have no idea who your parents are. I was not provided with that information. But I did see enough of your character, Briella. I saw your grace in the face of cruelty. I saw you bear mistreatment and abuse and, through it all, you never changed the core of who you were. You have no idea how much I wanted to enter your world and tear apart those that harmed you. I wanted to avenge you, and it was the oddest thing, when I had never wanted to lift a finger to aid another before.

"I came to know you bit by bit, glimpse by glimpse, and it only made me want to know you better. When you entered *my* Court, I knew at that moment, that you were the key to my destiny. I knew at once, that things were never going to be the same. And while it both intrigued me and frightened me, I have never been more ready for fate to shake the very foundation upon which we stand. It's time for new things. It's time for everything to be different. And if I can gift you with this one wish, to see a loved one, then I shall." He left the looking-glass clasped within her careful grasp, freeing her other hand, and sat back upon his heels.

Briella swallowed the lump of emotion that formed in her throat. She missed the small contact of her hand in his. She did not know what to do. How was she to understand all that he had imparted upon her? Briella was not a key, not an answer to anything. She was broken and weary; time had not been kind to her. But he had seen so many of her weakest moments and still believed in her. It was humbling, and it was ruinous, and it was healing and beautiful.

Tomorrow she would ponder all that she had

discovered. Tonight, she would let her heart's desire seek out her beloved pet Bruno and see what followed next.

"What must I do to see him?" Briella asked, her voice wavering.

"Think of him."

Taking a deep breath, Briella thought about Bruno; she pictured him as she had last seen him, and kept the memory replaying within her mind. The black looking-glass began to alight; a bright golden glow lit up the room, blinding her. Briella turned away. A few moments passed before she peeked her eyes open and turned her head to gaze into the reflection. What she saw made her gasp. She dropped the looking-glass and let the tears fall.

Within a sunlit room, in a little brown bed, lay her best friend. He was shrunken and all of his brown hair had turned gray. He was asleep, but Briella knew by the gentle rising and falling of his chest that he was still alive. He was like a living skeleton and she wondered if it caused him pain to move. Was it even possible for Bruno to walk? Her poor companion looked so aged, that it was almost as if any breath could be his last. True, he was being cared for, he wasn't dirty, nor did he bear any signs of abuse.

But seeing him so altered took her heart and shattered it. She had not known that it could be broken further, even if she had suspected that the King could very well obliterate it. If only she had a way to hold Bruno one last time. To speak to him and soothe away any ache that might still linger within his heart. Answer any question his poor mind might still be holding onto. She wanted another stolen moment to bask in his presence. She wanted more than a mere moment in time, but if she could have only this, then she would happily accept it.

King Ezekiel rose to his knees and reached for the looking-glass. Seeing the aged animal within its depths, he said, "He still lives but is close to the other world. The veil is thinning for him. I am sorry, I wish that he was hearty and whole."

Shaking her head, Briella replied, "No. This is everything. This is a gift that I shall never forget. You have given me so much, and I'll treasure this forever. Thank you."

They both looked on for a few moments more as the glass continued its glow. Once it darkened and the reflection changed to that of the molded ceiling, which was the direction it was facing, the silence in the room became unbearable. It broke her. Briella could not cease the flow of tears that soaked her cheeks. She didn't want to. And she was grateful to know that the King was not judging her reaction as a weakness. He simply sat in the silence of the room awaiting her directions as to what came next. He radiated kindness, compassion, and strength. His presence was a comfort that she had never known simply being in the company of another could offer.

Silently, King Ezekiel rose and moved next to her. Briella leaned into his side, resting her head upon his shoulder. He wrapped his arms around her and let her lean into him. She felt a delicate whisper of a kiss alight upon her head. This was another gift he was giving to her. The feeling of being accepted just as she was. In this moment, she felt safe and understood; she felt as if her heart was gaining its own wings. She didn't know where this path was leading her, but if she greeted each new day with an ally by her side, then she could attempt to do the impossible. And that was another miracle to count among her many blessings.

They sat together for what seemed like ages. Briella did not want to move away from the tranquility of his embrace. It was a comfort that she had never experienced before. She had never had suitors, if that was even what she could think of the King as being to her. She knew that his tender actions went far beyond that which a friend possesses for another.

In a muffled voice, Briella commented, "I never would have imagined this."

"Being held by a handsome Faerie King in his private chambers?" he teased.

"Especially that part," she laughed, "but all of this really. I feel so tiny in comparison to everyone else. You have all lived so much more than I have. I haven't been on adventures or caused curses, or even fallen in love before."

"Now it seems as if it's the perfect time for all of those, well except for the causing curses part."

"Have you ever been in love?"

"No. And it's not something that I am even capable of," King Ezekiel replied. There was a note of heavy sadness within his voice.

"You can't love?" Briella sat up and away from his side so that she could look up at him.

"No. And before you ask, it's just a *me* thing. Faeries can and do fall in love, quite frequently." He looked down at her with sorrow rimming his expressive eyes.

"It's the curse then," Briella said aloud more to herself than him.

King Ezekiel said nothing, he simply watched her, watching him.

"And you can't talk about it."

He smiled at her and tipped his head to the side, quietly observing her.

"Which means if what you inferred is correct, that I am the key to solving this puzzle and putting your kingdom back to rights. How is one half-mortal girl to accomplish such a daunting task?" Her gaze looked from one mossy green eye to the other.

"Perhaps the *how* isn't important. Being yourself seems to work beautifully. I would advise you to continue to be you."

"If you cannot love another, how is True Love's Kiss even applicable to you?"

Drawing his brows together, he thought and then answered her, "I do not know. Fate would be cruel to saddle me with a lady that I am incapable of loving. Unless, maybe Fate is certain of how this is all to end?"

"Have you ever eaten True Love's Kiss yourself?" Briella eagerly awaited his reply; her heart was in tatters for the Faerie King who was incapable of love.

"No. It seemed an impossibility, so I never let myself indulge in it."

Sitting forward upon the settee, leaving the safety of his arms, Briella brought her arms around her middle. She did not like uncertainties and she was filled with them at the moment. A thought occurred to her, making her quizzical, and she voiced it. "Have you been able to use that looking-glass since I came here?"

His gaze flitted to the floor as he answered, "Uh, yes. Once or twice."

Briella gasped and demanded to know more. "When?"

"When you first were settling in. I wanted to make sure you were comfortable and that my orders were being followed."

"And… What did you see?" she pressed.

"That you were settling in and that my orders were being followed."

"Oh, that's not exactly what I meant." She covered her eyes feeling like a fool.

Taking her hand away from her face, he said, "I know. I only… It's just that, everyone is entitled to their secrets."

"Have you been spying on me while I've been bathing?" She felt a little hysteria entering her being.

"What? Good graces, no! How unfaely! What kind of a creature do you take me for?" He was turning pink from the tips of his pointed ears to his entire face and she wondered if that might be a new experience for him.

"So, you've never ever seen me in an indelicate state of dress?"

"I can't state that! I have seen you in tatters and rags and that, dear one, is quite unseemly. Have I viewed you as a lecher would? No... Well, once." He saw that her eyes were glaring at him and quickly rushed on to say, "But as soon as I discovered my mistake, I ended the vision."

Squinting her eyes, she inquired, "Then what secrets can you possibly be speaking of?"

"I meant your lack of seamstress skills."

"You *know*? And you've kept me on this entire time?" Briella brought a hand to her mouth in surprise.

"What else was I supposed to do with you? You weren't hurting anyone, and the mice have been instructing you. Your face while taking that inseam measurement was one that I shall never forget!" he chuckled at her.

Briella leapt up from the settee and covered her blushing cheeks with her hands. She did not know if she should be horrified or relieved that he knew and he wasn't hurling insults nor raging at her. But the feeling of his laughter was not pleasant, as it took her mind back to others' laughs that held malice and made her feel minuscule. She warred with herself, and stood there trying to quiet the rioting emotions surging through her.

Feeling arms encircle her, she leaned her head back

against the King's chest. She inhaled his mixed scent of spring and let herself draw comfort from him. He wasn't the villain, and she wasn't some damsel in need of rescuing. And maybe this curse would prevent him from ever loving her, but right now, in his embrace, she felt loved, and wanted, and that was all she needed to succeed. She would find a way to break this curse and, once it was banished, she hoped that he would be able to fall in love. And if she was not the one to bask in the warmth of his affection, she would still be herself and would thrive with or without him. If she built these beautiful moments in time with him, and occasionally withdrew them to treasure later on, she would regret nothing.

18

TEA AND CHATTER

The next days that followed were spent in a whirlwind of silks and lace. After the suit was completed for her mysterious male Fae patron, an inflow of orders threatened to swallow Briella whole. She spent her days learning her craft and her nights attempting to scour the castle for hints of how one breaks a curse. She had promised herself that she would stop being a fraud and really hone her craft. She did not want to rely upon others rescuing her. *And if by chance the King uses his magic mirror to spy on me, I want to show what I'm truly capable of.*

While wandering through the castle halls one afternoon, she turned the corner and came to a sudden stop, as the King and his retinue came from the opposite direction. As they were passing by her, Briella quickly lowered herself into a curtsey. As she rose, she met the Faerie King's gaze and he winked at her. It was thrilling to know that he still desired to carry on their flirtation, even when days had separated their last meeting. The smile that lit upon her face would remain with her well into the evening. King Ezekiel led his retinue down the way she had come from as they discussed some foreign policy.

The portly faerie, who had presented the disputing faeries to the King while he had held Court, was to his right, while a slim suave faerie was to his left. The slimmer faerie was tall and well dressed and had the air of one who knew others appreciated his good looks, though he did not appear to be conceited. He had auburn hair upon his head that matched the fur that rested at the tip of his tan tail. Dressed entirely in the color of gold, there was a glimmer in his kind dark eyes. The two faeries on either side of the King could not have been more different.

The other faeries who accompanied the party were all different in look and manner. They were covered in white fur and appeared more animalesque than humanesque. *Surely surrounding oneself with such differences must be the mark of a good leader.*

King Ezekiel had spent their hours apart trying to calm a matter that no one seemed to want to talk to her about. Her questions regarding what the mysterious matter was to Fleur and Cheshire, who seemed to know everything about the castle's inner workings, went unanswered. She had not seen the King at the dinner hour, nor had she caught him in the library. It was just as well. Briella was forming an attachment to the Faerie King, and some space would help her to think more clearly. She had a curse to break, after all. *And thoughts of kissable faerie lips would never solve a thing.*

One evening shortly thereafter, Briella began to make discoveries that allowed her to start piecing together more of the past and origins of the faerie race. She learned that the curse had taken place ten springs ago. For a decade, none had been able to leave the Spring Court's lands, and there were few who had ventured nearer than the woods.

It wasn't from any lips that these revelations were made; it was from the records room.

The Master of the Records, who recorded births, deaths, and mate bonds, was charged with accounting for who lived where. There was a record for every single being within this Court, and beside their names was a column detailing their trades or skill sets. Some were blank for obvious reasons, like Lady Bramley, who was a member of the peerage, and so just the act of breathing accounted for her skills. The gentry did not need to be listed as chattel, and so, their columns were bare.

The Master of Records was a grumpy, wrinkled faerie, who must have been very old to be showing such age upon his person. His hair was gray and his shoulders were stooped. He had silver whiskers on either side of his nose that twitched anxiously as he watched Briella look over the record books. He made no move to stop her from perusing the names and dates, and so, she kept reading until her eyes began to ache in the dim lighting. She supposed that the little information she had learned could be quite depressing, but she felt buoyed by the fact that she had discovered the little that she had. She couldn't be expected to solve a curse in just a few days' time. Especially, when there was no living soul within the castle that she could turn to for guidance.

What she had learned was that ten years prior, a celebration for Spring had taken place and representatives from the other five Courts were in attendance. They still resided within the castle and had not left. The King's parents had also died shortly thereafter. While Briella was piecing the information together, there was much that she did not yet know. She was trying to discover more regarding the curse but was hitting a wall at every turn. However, she was resolved to never give up.

Later, Briella would look for a book detailing the Six Courts of Faerie in the King's library. The collection of books seemed impressive; she felt certain that there were history tomes as well as philosophy. There was so much that she needed to learn, and so, the library was her next avenue to search. The shelves that she had perused had not yielded anything useful to her endeavors, yet.

The customs between the Courts varied greatly, and she did not want to cause any ill feelings should she encounter one of the representatives. There was much she should task herself with learning so that she did not cause any offense in an already volatile situation. If there must have been history books in the King's library, it stood to reason that Briella would also find something written about faerie customs. So far all she knew was that the six Courts were: The Spring Court, the Autumn Court, which bordered the Spring Court, the Winter Court, the Summer Court that was located along the other border of the Spring Court. Then there were the Courts of Lunar and Solar. Briefly, she wondered which Court Cheshire was from. She wanted to avoid that Court in the future at all costs given the feline's warnings about how mad the members of that Court were. The madness she had been party to here in the Spring Court was quite enough for her taste.

THE GARDEN WALKWAY WAS A BEAUTIFUL PLACE TO BE. IT must have been spectacular when flowers were blooming and butterflies were fluttering to and fro. The arched trellis that ran the entirety of the pathway was still lovely, even if it was covered in that oppressive ebony hue. Closing her eyes, Briella pictured how this space must have looked before the curse. She wondered if its beauty was taken for granted. That was often the case with beautiful things; one became used to them and hardly took notice. It was easy to become spoiled by the richness of beauty.

Turning the bend in the walkway, she came out upon a small, circular space that housed a long table and chairs. There were barren and bent trees twisted in varying directions as they stood silently guarding the party. Sitting at the head of the table, she saw Cheshire grinning madly as he waved his dotted teacup around, sloshing the tea inside from side to side. He wore a white ruff around his neck that a bronze medallion hung from. Seated on either side of the cat were other unclothed animals. The entire table seemed to be comprised of Unseelie faeries, and Briella suspected that her presence would not be welcomed. She forced herself to slowly back away onto the pathway, and as she did so a twig under her foot snapped, drawing unwanted attention toward herself.

Cheshire's grin grew broader. "Dear me! A visitor to our festivities. Do come and join us, my dear. It's rude to linger with one foot among us and one foot away," he purred.

Briella wondered if they would give chase if she simply turned and walked away. What a grand game for the uncivilized creatures! They could do very real harm to her and claim that she had injured herself. Or she could be brave and bold, and she could join them. Perhaps then, she could pry secrets from their mad minds and lips? She took the steps needed to reach the table and stopped before Cheshire, who was still grinning at her. It was enough to unnerve her, but there was nothing she could do.

A rust-colored fox jumped down from the chair on Cheshire's left and nodded to the chair. "Sit here. I was just going for a run. One can only drink so much tea before it muddles the mind," he said in a rich baritone voice that was oddly disconcerting. He took off in the opposite direction, crawling his way under the bramble.

Briella sat down in the chair and a new cup and saucer was placed before her. She briefly gave thought to the fox hair that would be adorning her backside, but at present, there was nothing to be done about that either. The forest green tablecloth was laden with dishes of decadent desserts. When Cheshire leaned toward her and poured tea into her cup, he politely inquired, "Milk or sugar?"

"Sugar, thank you." Briella watched as the cat used tongs to drop two sugar cubes into her cup. *How very civilized he seems.*

The whole table was silent as they looked at her. She smiled as she took a small sip. It was bitter tasting even with the sugar, but she made herself swallow it and said, "Delightful."

Nodding at her, Cheshire turned back to his guests and instructed a frog to continue on with his tap dancing upon his plate. A rabbit who sat beside Briella passed her a plate of small sandwiches, and she took one, placing it upon her own flower-patterned plate. She passed the sandwich plate to Cheshire, who took it while he was engrossed in conversation with the horse on his other side.

Feeling eyes upon her from across the table, she brought her attention to the face of a goose who wore a purple bonnet covered in blue flowers. The goose nodded and asked, "Do you miss your home?"

"Not at all. Do you?"

"I do," the goose sighed. "It's been so long since the storm dumped me here, and I haven't seen my goslings in such a long time. I imagine that they must think me dead."

"How tragic. I'm so sorry." Briella was not sure what

else she should say. *Missing one's family in such a horrible way must be so heart-wrenching.*

"Thank you. Are you enjoying your sojourn here?"

"It is a very entertaining Court, to be sure. I find that there is much to discover." Briella smiled at the goose.

"I say, my dear. I've heard that you are improving daily in your seamstress abilities. Well done! Too bad that I do not need any of your fine wares," Cheshire purred, giving her his full attention.

"That's perfectly fine with me. I've been quite busy. Besides, it seems that you found a way to enhance your creamy fur all without my aid," Briella commented, giving him her full attention. Her gaze alighted onto the medallion adorning his white ruff.

"Yes, it is charming, isn't it?" Cheshire pawed at the bronze medallion, making it swing back and forth. "I only wear it on special occasions. For, I cannot get another as it was created just for me by my very good friend, Hatter."

"Oh? You must miss your friend."

"I find that there is much to miss. But I feel as if change is in the air and headed our way, and that soon all will be set to rights. Tell me, how goes your sleuthing?" Cheshire waggled his bushy brow at her.

"Whatever can you mean?" Briella asked sardonically.

"Why, it's all over the castle, you're hunting for clues. To the…"

"Yes, Cheshire?"

"Uhm hum. Seems that I've caught my own tongue," Cheshire stated as he slid his pink tongue from his mouth, going crossed-eyed as he peered down at it. He then proceeded to lick his paw.

"I hardly think it's a secret. I've asked you what you know, how you came to be here."

"Twinkle, twinkle, little one. How you wonder where

you are. Up inside the castle set high, resides the heart that must be undone." A tiny voice sang out.

"That does not rhyme," mentioned Cheshire, who sounded unimpressed.

Briella followed the voice with her ears as her eyes landed on the teapot. She hesitated then removed the lid and peered inside. There, swimming in circles was a little yellow duck. Briella immediately thought of the tea that she had sipped and she felt her stomach churn. Had she been drinking the little creature's bathwater?

She heard Cheshire chuckle and the rest of the table's occupants joined in. She began to feel like she was the source of a joke, and did not wish to remain a willing participant in their entertainment. When she would have risen, Cheshire leapt from his chair onto the table immediately before her and placed a paw upon her shoulder.

"We meant you no disrespect, little one. If you succeed in your quest, you would be our heroine. We honor you. Anything that we can do to assist you, you only need to ask it. I sometimes forget our peculiarity to Seelie and that is my mistake. We don't mind the seasoning that little duckie gives to our drink. But perhaps it was bad form to present you with such unsavory brew. You have my word that no further trickery will befall you by my paw."

Taking a deep breath, she let the sincerity of the cat's words sink into her being. He was trying to make amends, and who was she to deny him? "I forgive you this time."

"My thanks," Cheshire said, nodding at her. He leapt back into his chair and picked up his cup, raising it to her in a silent toast before indulging in a large sip.

"Maybe what you seek can't be easily seen. Not everything stems from an outward sign. Perhaps you'll need to dig a little deeper into that part that feels more than any other," sang the little yellow duck from his bathwater.

Briella frowned. The part that felt more than any other would be the *heart*. She was, in theory, trying to get to the heart of the curse, and perhaps a heart was the source to everything. But who's heart? The King's? Does a castle have a heart? The castle seemed to be most affected, maybe that was the result of its ruler's heart being cursed. She had much to think about.

Briella spent another hour in the company of the Unseelie faeries with a fresh pot of tea brewed just for her in another teapot, which she desperately hoped was clean. They entertained her with dancing and riddles and all manner of talents. She no longer feared for her safety among these Faeries; they were not to be feared at all. When she finally realized this, Briella truly began enjoying herself. She had made new friends in the form of very unlikely faces and felt blessed to have stumbled upon their tea party. The chatter had been most enlightening, and the company amusing. She never would have expected that such depth of feeling would have resided within these beings. There were moments of madness, to be sure, but there was just as much joviality. If one became over-excited and threw a teacup or smashed a saucer, she was not alarmed. They were the most authentic creatures she had ever known, remaining true to themselves. If only the rest of the realms could learn from them, what would the world be like?

19

A GIFT FROM THE HEART?

Another two days had passed since Briella had last seen the King. He had not attempted to seek her out, and Briella had not ventured into any of his chambers except for the library. Her progress with locating a book to assist her was slow as she was still learning how the books had been categorized; there were just so many. A full-time keeper of the books would have been a welcomed addition to the glorious chamber in her opinion. But that faerie would have been impeding upon the privacy of the King, and she suspected neither faerie would have been thrilled with that idea.

Briella had not even had a glimpse of the Faerie King in the banquet hall during dining nor traversing the castle with his retinue in tow. With no further invitation to attend his Court, she stayed within her own sphere, content to let him choose when he would see her again. Their relationship was not ideal, that much was abundantly clear, and she didn't know the way forward. He had expressed such tenderness with her, but if she didn't break the curse, would there even be a future for them? Not likely. Desperately wanting to guard her heart, Briella was curious to see what the King would do next.

So, Briella had kept herself busy with creating clothing for the castle residents in decadent silks and sumptuous lace. Gustavious assured her that she was, indeed, becoming quite the seamstress and it was not something that he was ever certain that she would have been able to master. That was when Pernella had smacked him upon the back of his brown, furry head.

Fleur had spent the days fluttering back and forth between Briella's workroom and the King's side. Briella suspected that he was keeping track of her via the tiny faerie, and she was fine with that. The friendship between Briella and Fleur was back to what it had been, something that Briella was extremely relieved for. The oddity of Fleur's behavior had vanished, and she was once again herself.

In rare moments of quiet, Briella felt a presence near her, and a huge smile filled with pointy teeth, or a twitch of a cream-colored tail with lime green stripes, could be seen. She would smile and go back to whatever she had been doing, happily in the knowledge that there were many that were looking after her, even when their presence could not be seen.

After dinner one evening, which she and Fleur had taken in her room from a tray, she decided that a walk in the barren garden was needed to stretch her sore muscles. She had never been idle, and sitting over needlework for hours at a time was taking a toll on her physique. She grimaced when she thought that she might be putting on weight, and while she had needed to gain a few pounds to round out her womanly shape, she did not need to feel as if her new weight was impeding her person. Fleur agreed to accompany her, and so the pair set out.

"Besides," stated Fleur. "I can't very well keep an eye on you if you are gallivanting to and fro. It's much safer to have a friend whom you can depend upon at your side. As I am lovely, how could you object?"

"Why, Fleur, your enthusiasm for my welfare is touching," Briella replied, smirking.

"As it should be. We can't have a repeat of your abduction. I only have so much patience," Fleur said with a serious face. Her tiny wings fluttered rapidly to keep pace with Briella as they exited the castle and came to the garden entrance.

Briella shivered at the remembrance of her night in the woods. "Most certainly, let us not repeat that experience ever again."

They walked in silence until they reached the fountain which was half beast and man. Water spouted from its clawed hands. Briella sat upon its edge, while Fleur hovered over the purple, bubbling water. Briella gazed up at the teal stars and sighed. The pink-hued moon was shining upon all that its light touched.

"Isn't moonbathing divine?" Fleur asked. Her head was tilted up toward the sky as she peered at the moon.

"Is that what we're doing?"

Nodding her tiny head, Fleur said, "Exactly. If one can soak up the pinkish rays of the sun, why would not the same be done with the moon? Makes perfect sense to me."

"Hmmm," was all Briella commented.

There came a crunching upon the gravel that led the way toward them, interrupting their solitude. Fleur removed a tiny jewel-encrusted dagger from a holder hidden upon her thigh and flew before Briella, coming to a stop a few inches away from her head. She held a stance that told Briella that she was ready to fight. When King Ezekiel came into their view, Fleur gave a relieved sigh and reholstered her weapon. The King raised his pale eyebrows at her; his gaze flickering to where her sheath was.

"I cannot be at fault for feeling the need to get a bit stabby if trouble comes our way," Fleur primly informed him.

"As you should do. Protect yourself. Though, I'm quite glad that you didn't charge at me. It would have been a pity to make introductions with your blade." The King smirked.

Briella felt her racing heartbeat begin to slow its pace as she rose from her seat. She dropped her hands which had been clutched together over her heart. Briella curtsied to the Faerie King, while Fleur did so from the air. Briella straightened when a hand reached for hers to pull her to a standing position. Her gaze locked with the King's, halting her breath. So lost was she, that it took Fleur's voice to bring Briella back to herself.

"What a lovely night for a stroll, Your Majesty," Fleur stated.

Breaking his gaze from Briella's, King Ezekiel addressed Fleur, "It is," he purred. "Would you mind if I asked for your companion's company this evening? There is something I should like her to see."

"Your command is my cue to leave, I see. Never let it be said that I could not follow the directions of my King." With that, Fleur took off with her gossamer wings beating a steady retreat. Briella hoped that her friend was not upset with the dismissal.

Holding out his arm for Briella to take, the King smiled at her. The smile that broke across her face in return was radiant as warmth engulfed her heart. She wrapped her arm around his and let him lead her to his desired location. Looking up at his pale hair and the black glittering crown upon his head, he truly was every inch a commanding monarch. He exuded authority and a quiet will of iron. Where some may think him haughty or spoiled, she saw a male comfortable in his own skin with a willingness to rule justly. She had heard him lord over others, and had witnessed his fierce nature, but only when he needed to mete out punishment. And she supposed that there was a fine line he had to tow in order to attain his hold upon the Court. He could not be a friend and an authority figure; the two were a recipe for disaster.

"You are thinking so loudly, I can practically hear you," King Ezekiel teased her.

"Oh, I was, I suppose."

"What thoughts churn themselves within your mind?" He looked from the pathway they were treading, down to her eyes.

"Were you always this way? I mean, so dignified?" Briella asked. Ezekiel guffawed.

"Not at all. I had to grow into a king when I was not yet ready to lead. My father gave me examples to follow, but even he was flawed. I think I learned as the mistakes piled up. I learned that I had to distance myself from everyone else in order to command the respect to lead."

"Sounds lonely."

"Yes, well… It is my fault that I came to rule at such a young age. My actions were reprehensible. I am ashamed of myself and of my wasted youth. I had everything until it was gone, and then from the ashes I had to make a throne that I could be proud to sit upon. This Court is all I have, and I will defend it upon my dying breath. My subjects deserve to be treated fairly and to know a life filled with the little joys that make it worthwhile. And though I cannot give them joy, I can give them a just kingdom."

"I can't imagine you as this flawed youth." Briella gestured toward him.

"Trust me, I was this impossible being. I am glad you did not know me back then. Ah, here we are," he said, leading Briella into a small room.

The inky blackness was present, but with the glittering glow of the candles, the doom and gloom were far away. There was a settee in the corner of the room, situated near the dark marbled fireplace, where a merry blaze stood alight. There was a form resting atop a few darker pillows and blankets. Briella blinked her eyes to adjust them to the room. Though it was dark outside, this room and the corridor leading to it were well lit. Still, her eyes always needed a moment when entering a chamber to adjust themselves, unlike full-blooded Fae who seemed to possess perfect sight no matter the change of lighting.

"Go ahead and meet with your visitor," King Ezekiel spoke softly to her.

Looking at him and then looking at the settee again, she padded over to the piece of furniture. The closer she came, the more her heart began to wildly beat. It was practically leaping from her chest by the time she kneeled in front of the settee.

Before her rested Briella's dearest friend in all of the world. He was worn away from life, and frail so much so, that he could barely lift his gray head. His long thin tail showed an indication that he may still remember her as it waved back and forth in an erratic tempo. Bringing one hand to her mouth, she stifled the gasp. The other hand reached out to rest upon his furry forehead. She could hardly breathe, could hardly think; she was so stunned.

"Bruno," Briella quietly addressed her beloved pet. Raising her voice she inquired, "But how?" She felt the King's presence behind her.

"I could not let him leave this world without you having a chance to say your goodbyes and being able to cuddle him one last time. This I could do for you, the gift I could offer you both. But... I must tell you that the veil between worlds is thinning more with every passing moment. The journey was relatively easy on him, but his age is against us."

Nodding her understanding, Briella leaned down and kissed Bruno's forehead, and then she leaned her head against his. She retained her weight upon her knees, so as not to hinder him. She held onto her dearest friend and felt a tear fall from her eye onto his velvety ear. Bruno did not move, and she wasn't sure if he could see or hear her. But she felt in her heart that he knew it was she who was holding onto him. She let her heart speak to his and rejoiced in his presence just as much as she mourned their time apart. He was here and he was perfect, and he was all that she clung to. To have this chance to say farewell was a gift that she would never forget. He had seen her through the worst, and she would see him to the best that was yet to come; she would see him to a new world where he was spry and joyful. And with his death, she was certain her heart would never stop breaking, and she would forever mourn the loss of that one friend that always meant everything to her.

"Briella," the King began haltingly. "There may be a way to restore him, to keep him with you for many years yet. But I cannot guarantee its success, but... We could attempt it, if you wish."

Briella muffled from her position against his fur, "It wouldn't hurt him?"

"No, whether it works or not, it won't harm him, I vow this to you."

Raising her head and looking over her shoulder at

King Ezekiel, she met his stare and saw only sincerity and hope. It was enough for her to make a decision. *If it won't harm him and he may yet live many years by my side, how could I not take the chance?*

Her decisive nod was all that he needed before the King hurried from the room. She looked back at Bruno and begged him to hang on for just a few minutes longer. When Bruno closed his heavy eyelids, she felt terror flood her being. *Oh, no, no, no…* She begged whatever deity there was to keep him breathing, and while her prayers had never been answered before, she felt a calming presence settle down within her.

Briella couldn't say how long it was before the King had returned and knelt down beside her. He gently coaxed faerie wine into Bruno's mouth. Briella watched as the liquid dripped down his throat. The King's gaze was locked onto his task and Briella felt her heart reaching out to him. He was using such compassion and care to tend to her pet, and it left her feeling weepy and happy all at the same time. When no visible change occurred, King Ezekiel ceased with the wine and sat back upon his heels.

"I do apologize. I thought that there was a good chance that this would work. Perhaps I should have tried it before I came for you, but I wanted the decision to be yours." He hung his head.

Placing her palm against his face, Briella assured him.

"You did just as you should have. He is such an old fellow. Thank you with all of my heart for all that you have done. For me, for him. No one has ever attempted to gift me with anything so meaningful before. If Bruno could thank you, I am sure that he would express the same sentiment as well."

The King and Briella gazed at each other for a long moment searching each other's eyes. She dropped her hand from his face, but he caught it and turned her hand over to kiss her delicate palm. *How can one feel such despair and yet such a rightness all at the same time?*

Neither the King nor his seamstress were able to break the trance of the heavy moment between them until there was a blinding light that lit up the room and made the pair draw back from the settee. The King shielded her eyes with his arm and then did the same for himself. When the light began to dim, Briella pulled his arm away and gave a little cry. Bruno was lifted into the air and beams of golden light were emanating all around him. It was as if his soul was made flesh and was shining over them all. Glittering golden light swirled around his form, and in moments, the old dog was replaced with a younger version. His fur was no longer gray and his body had regained its youth. The gleam of happiness that shone from his rich, chocolate eyes made Briella sob.

Bruno was placed back onto the settee as the bright golden light extinguished. He rose to his feet, his tail wagging, and launched himself at Briella. The pair fell backward upon the dark carpet. Bruno licked her hands, her neck, and her cheek, all the while Briella cried. She could not fathom how this miracle was possible when all hope had fled her being. This was the Bruno that she had the most memories of. Not a puppy, but not an aged animal either.

King Ezekiel helped Briella sit up. Bruno leaped onto the King and gave him just as many kisses. The King laughed and patted the dog upon his head, trying and failing to quiet the animal down.

When the happy hound had given enough gratitude to his rescuers, he finally sat upon his haunches and waited like the obedient dog he had always been. Briella's sobs had abated, and she smiled at King Ezekiel when he handed her a handkerchief. She wiped her face and neck and breathed in the smell of the Spring Court. How was she to properly express her thankfulness to this beautiful faerie before her?

"I have no words that would adequately express what I am feeling. You have made my dream come true. I shall never forget this," Briella earnestly told him.

"You have no need to thank me. It was my fervent desire to reunite you both, and I am happy that all has turned out so wonderfully. Anyone can see the bond you share and it is admirable. Indeed, it is humbling. I once had my own canines, but I did not treat them as I should have. You humble me." The King bowed his crowned golden head toward her.

Briella was silent as she waited for him to once again raise his head and meet her gaze. She stared into his eyes for the longest moment when she was bumped from her side and fell forward into the King. Her hands landed upon his firm chest and her wide eyes looked up at his perfectly handsome face.

Looking down at how closely they were holding onto each other, the King spoke, "Bruno seems to be scheming. I can't say that I am confused one bit by his actions. He seems to know what I desire above all else."

Furrowing her brow, Briella inquired, "And what is that?"

The King seemed to hesitate a moment before he answered her. "I desire to invite you to dine with me tomorrow night. Perhaps you would agree to dance with me after and I can once again hold you within my arms."

"I should like that." Briella smiled at him with joy and sincerity brimming from her eyes.

Smiling back at her, he rose and offered his hand to pull her to her slippered feet. Briella took his large satiny hand and shook out her dress once she was standing. It was beyond wrinkled, and she could not bring herself to care. "What happens next?"

"You retire and become reacquainted with your dear Bruno. I shall not intrude upon this reunion. I think that he'd be happy to stay in your chambers. I will appoint a walker for him in the morning. You may still attend to your daytime duties, and only venture out of doors when it suits you."

"How can I thank you?" Briella looked into his mossy gaze.

"You already have, my lady. You need not feel indebted to me. Truly, this was as much a gift to you as it is to me."

Briella took his muscular arm, entwining their limbs together, and let him lead her from the room as Bruno trailed after them. They walked him out of doors to see to his needs for the night and then resumed their progress to her chambers. Once reaching her chambers, she unwound her arm from his.

"I will say thank you once again. I do not know how to stop myself. You have shown me such kindness and I cannot easily let that go." Briella gazed into his eyes and felt her heart turn over.

"Good night, dearest Briella." The King brought her hand up to his mouth for a kiss as her skin tingled. Her own lips parted on a gasp as she fought her body to remain in place; she wanted to reach up on tiptoe and place a kiss upon his lips. Intense feelings of longing coursed through her being. She felt breathless and weightless as if she could be carried away by the wind. Perhaps there was a great advantage to not wearing gloves. She could feel his velvety soft kisses upon her flesh. *He is thoroughly intoxicating.* Her eyes met his, and the mossy green hue of his eyes were more vibrant and darker than she had ever seen them before.

He smirked at her as he let her hand go. Taking a deep breath, he ran a hand down the front of his chest. Then he opened the door to her bedchamber and, seeing that all appeared well, he gestured with his free hand for her to enter.

Briella walked past him and she closed her eyes for a brief second as the scent of rain, grass, and charcoal met her. When she was on the other side of the door, she looked back at him over her shoulder.

"Slumber sweetly, dear one," he bid her.

Bruno followed and they watched the King close the door. Briella turned to Bruno and smiled. His presence was truly a gift of the heart. If the King's heart was part of the curse, how did this action fit into it all? She felt more confused by him than ever.

When Briella was readied for bed, she made a mound of blankets for Bruno at the foot of the massive four-poster bed, which he happily settled into. The day had been both long and exciting and she was ready for sleep to calm her mind and body. *How does he make me feel as if I matter more to him than any other? He does the most unexpected things, and I can barely believe what my heart tells me when I am in his presence.* She fell asleep to memories of kisses and a heart that was overflowing. She had never felt as if her heart was so near to bursting before, and she wondered at the fact that it could contain all of her joy. She had so much to be thankful for.

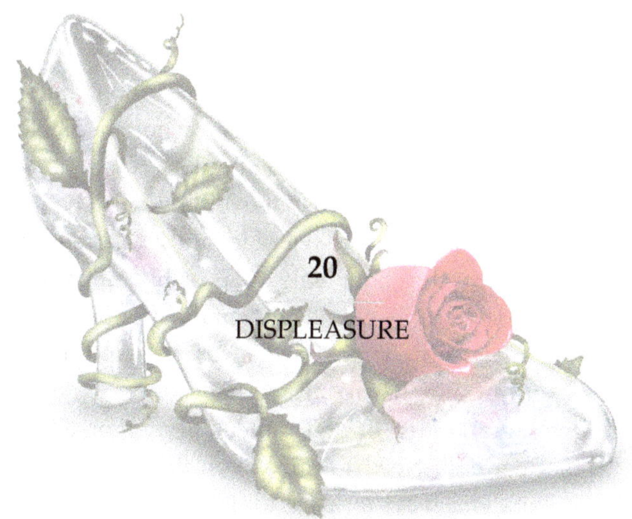

20

DISPLEASURE

"I'm displeased, really, very disappointed, and after all the careful considerations I have afforded you," Cheshire's annoyed voice floated in the air above Briella's head.

Briella rubbed the sleep from her eyes and tried to understand what the offended feline meant. Confusion quickly gave way to elation as she quickly recalled that Bruno was laying at the foot of her bed. Gratitude and love flooded her as she said, "Oh Cheshire! I want to introduce you to my very dear friend, Bruno."

"My dear, I am anything but pleased to make the mutt's acquaintance. I feel as if I might be sick this very instant all over your coverlet." Cheshire began to make heaving sounds and Briella quickly scrambled out from under the coverlet.

"Cheshire, don't you dare!" she screeched. Bruno stood from his spot and began to growl at the cat.

"'Tis not my... fault!" Cheshire groaned as he leaned over her pillow and coughed up a wet hairball.

Briella gagged at the mess and held a hand over her

mouth as she mumbled, "Bad kitty! I'm burning the whole thing!"

Straightening up and leaping to perch upon the side table, Cheshire questioned, "What? The whole bed? Now, that is a bit overdramatic, don't you think?"

"The pillow, Cheshire! Just the pillow." Briella took hold of Bruno, who raced to her side and was attempting to lunge toward the side table to possibly devour the offensive feline. Bruno seemed intent on upholding her honor. No matter how annoyed she was, she would never let Bruno or Cheshire harm one another.

"Oh yes, grand idea. That is rather a nasty morsel."

"It is a hairball. Need I remind you that it came from you? Perhaps you need to learn to not continually groom yourself," Briella huffed out in annoyance.

"Felines are notoriously clean creatures, it's in our nature to frequently bathe ourselves," Cheshire told her and then turned away from her.

Feeling dismissed, Briella walked over to her workroom door and opened it, then guided Bruno out from her bedchamber. Walking over to her bed and making a face of utter disgust, she grabbed the sides of the pillow and folded them together. She then walked over to the lit fireplace, and threw the pillow, case and all, into the blaze. It was time for a bath and to begin her day. She disliked the idea of keeping Bruno waiting and hoped that in her absence the walker would soon arrive.

"Don't be upset at me, dearest one," purred Cheshire. "In my Court, it's a sign of great respect to gift one with your offerings. Should it be permitted, long ago, I would've gifted you with a mouse or two. Only the heads are edible, you know. And I do so esteem you."

Not sure how to reply, Briella stood blinking for a moment or two before she entered her water closet.

WHEN SHE ENTERED THE PORTRAIT GALLERY LATER THAT afternoon, she knew exactly where to locate her father's portrait. This time, no meddling cat was trailing behind her. Instead, Bruno accompanied her. He had been well-behaved all day, even though his eyes were constantly alight on some Unseelie creature. He listened when directed to stay by her side. Briella felt more confident touring the gloomy halls of the castle with her beloved companion in tow. Her heart still felt near to bursting whenever she gazed upon him, and a giddy feeling that she had not felt in years lingered within her. She had avoided coming back to this gallery, she knew it would not change her destiny, but with a friend beside her, it didn't seem as daunting a task.

When she stood silently before her father's likeness, she did not know how to feel. Hollowness and disappointment for all that she had never known ate at her soul. She missed him greatly, but the secrets he guarded her from as a child had come as quite the shock. She was a half-Fae living in a cursed castle, and she was there to free them all. How was that possible? Looking up at her Papa, she saw so much of herself in him. She wanted to run her fingers along his cheek, but did not dare. What if she marred his portrait?

No amount of wishing him back would change her circumstances, and her heart could not take the what-ifs her mind was torturing her with. What if her father had not died? What if Bruno had never been taken away? What if her father had told her of his family? What if he had told her stories that would someday prepare her for his world? What if Mama had known the truth about her father? Would she have shared the secret with her? What if she never found a way to break this curse? What if she fell in love with the King, but he could never share her feelings? What-ifs were a waste of her time. She should be concentrating on the curse and how to break it. If she could do that, she need never be alone again, if the King was indeed her destiny. Ah, there was another if.

Knowing that it was time to return to her sewing, she said a silent farewell to Papa's portrait and led Bruno back to her workroom. She passed through the halls and felt the haunting eyes of the gargoyles following her progress. Briella didn't address them as she was still wary of their presence and didn't know what their intent was.

When she shut the workroom door behind her, she spied the mice in an argument upon the long worktable and walked to join them. Bruno happily settled down before the fire, he would soon be snoozing, and the thought sent another bolt of joy straight into her heart. *I shall never take his companionship for granted for he is the best friend in all the realms. The gift of his being beside me is an everlasting delight. And how I shall cherish my memories of the King as he brought this all to be.*

"I told you, I am done with this fluff and nonsense!" Jacques waved a furred fist in front of Gustavious's whiskered face.

"So, you're just going to quit? That's very unmously of you," Gustavious told him.

"I don't care what you think! This is the most I have ever worked, and I dislike it immensely!"

"Fine. Quit. But when you are fat and lazy and whining about how bored you've become, don't come back here." Gustavious turned his back to his friend and thumbed his nose.

"Why, Jacques, I had no idea you were so overworked. I should have realized it sooner. I am sorry to see you so out of sorts," Briella addressed her tiny friend. She felt terrible that she had been taking advantage of him. *Poor Jacques!*

Jacques looked up at her and said, "It's not your fault. It's this little dictator who thinks he gets to lord over us all. He forgets that it's splendid entertainment to run around the bramble unclothed and free. He's ignoring his animal nature and working like this goes against the grain. I am tired."

"But just think, in a few days it will be FaeWylde and we will have such delight then!" Pernella's small voice said. She had been standing off to the side watching the male mice disagree.

"What's FaeWylde?" Briella inquired.

"Well, it celebrates the most potent form of magic. It's where the Faerie World was created. We celebrate our creation and rejoice in the season of the Court in which we reside. Once upon a time, it was the grandest of all holidays. The butterflies and dandelion seeds floated through the air on the freshest of spring breezes. The rich colors of the blooming flowers and tiny wing beats of the hummingbirds filled the senses. It was a glorious riot of color and scents with breathtaking beauty. But now, it's not the same. The magic is dimmed. The color is gone. The magic is fading." Gustavious bowed his head and rubbed a paw under his nose.

Briella felt the sorrow that filled the room. They were all mourning what they had lost, and she was mourning what she had never experienced. FaeWylde sounded like it was spectacular. She wanted to view its beauty for herself. She wanted to vow to her friends that never again, would this holiday pass and not be as glorious as it had once been. But she dared not offer such hope when she had not broken the curse, and the idea of giving them hope when she might not be able to see this through would be cruel. Briella wanted to heal the land and give back to her friends everything that they had once known and loved.

LATER IN THE DAY, BRIELLA FELT THE DESIRE TO STRETCH HER legs, so with Bruno as her only companion, she ventured forth. They traversed the castle corridors until Briella spied a conservatory, which she had never visited before. Playing the pianoforte was a stout woman, who looked more Seelie than not. Upon closer inspection, Briella finally caught sight of the lady's eyes, which were large in their sockets and reminded her of an owl. That was her one true Fae characteristic. The faerie's eyes were a rich golden-brown combination and with her dark chestnut-colored hair, she was stunning. Her hair was arranged in an updo with cascading curls spilling down her back.

The music came to its conclusion and the faerie looked up at her and smiled. The action seemed friendly, but Briella felt a sense of false warmth that made her steps cease once she reached the edge of the carpet that was laid out under the instrument. Briella held her ground and waited for the silence to break.

"I know who you are. The entire castle is abuzz with news of you," the faerie addressed her, blinking her large owlish eyes.

"Oh? I hope it's nothing dreadful," Briella answered as she twisted her hands together. From her peripheral vision, she saw Bruno sit down on the floor beside her.

"Nothing dreadful about you. But do share with me your thoughts about our sovereign." The faerie tilted her head to the side and observed Briella from head to slipper.

"I hardly know what to say about the King."

"Truly? After all the time you've spent in his company?" she tittered. "I find that hard to believe. Tell me, has he shown you his temper, yet? His unkindness? His disdain for others?"

"I have been witness to his temper, but his actions were warranted," Briella thoughtfully replied and frowned.

"Were they or were they not? Was he defending you or himself?"

"You have such malice for him," Briella carefully remarked.

"It has been earned. You know nothing of his true nature. His cold heart should never know kindness from another when mercy is not in his vocabulary." The faerie was seething with rage.

"Will you not share with me what you mean? How you came to feel so strongly against him?" Briella was trying to tread with care. She had no desire to further upset the faerie.

"I will share a kindness with you that not many of my ilk would even bother with. You who are so far beneath us and so removed from our world. Why, you really are like a passing wind, here one day and gone the next. Your time is so short upon this plane."

Huffing out a breath, Briella made to speak when the faerie addressed her again.

"The King, he is not what he seems, nor is he what he pretends to be. He is a monster and should be eradicated." Then the faerie rose from her bench behind the pianoforte and marched directly past Briella without acknowledging her again.

Loosening a shuddering breath, Briella watched her exit the conservatory. Was this more madness? Was this rancor sincere or warranted? What had she meant to impart upon Briella… that King Ezekiel was a monster?

These doubts were swirling within her mind and she was not certain how she was to silence them.

When Bruno brushed his head against her leg she peered down at him. He had risen to stand by her side when the faerie began to be upset. He was awaiting Briella's cue to see whether this creature was a threat to their safety. Now that the danger had fled, Briella patted his head.

No, no she decided firmly. The King was not a monster and here before her was all the proof she would ever need. He had been nothing but sincere and kind to her. She had existed for far too long with real-life monsters wearing human skin, and she would dismiss this whole ordeal... It would never again have space within her mind or heart. *He is a just and good faerie, even if at times he doesn't seem so to his Court.*

21

AN EVENING OF FAEMANCE

Briella took a deep breath to settle her racing heart. She was moments away from dining with King Ezekiel. She knew that she looked beautiful in her rose gold ball gown. The color was vibrant, and the satin layers shimmered with each movement that she made. The dress needed no ornaments for decoration; it was superb all on its own. Her enchanted closet had created a work of art. As she felt this was to be a memorable evening, she wore her glass slippers. Forgetting how they appeared as if galaxies were spinning within the delicate glass of each slipper, she had gasped in awe when she had again donned them. They truly were marvelous. Choosing to wear her golden tresses down, they cascaded around her bare shoulders and back. Tonight, as in the past recent nights, she chose to forego her gloves, which left her arms bare all the way up to her puffed shoulder sleeves.

She took one last lingering look into the black full-length looking-glass and studied her face. There were striking changes to her appearance. Where before she had only suspected that her Fae heritage was showing itself, she knew that differences had formed. It was more in the coloring of her face. Her plump lips were permanently a darker hue, making them appear as if she had stained them with berry juice. Eyelashes that had grown fuller and darker, rimmed her eyes. And the gloves that she had arrived in no longer fit her fingers, which had lengthened. Everything else about her had remained the same.

Briella had held a secret fear within her heart that at any moment she'd notice whiskers appearing, a tail sprouting, or the shape of her tiny feet morphing into something more faerie-esque. At this point she didn't think anything more would change. She certainly hoped not.

There was a rap upon her bedchamber door as Briella quietly glided to it. She twisted the knob, pulling it ajar, and allowing her to view the King standing before her. He was resplendently clothed only in black. His royal bearing and breeding was formidable, instilled into every fiber of his being. His blond hair, natural skin tone, arresting eyes and eyebrows were the only color variation about him. Stepping forward and bowing at his waist, he addressed her.

"You are a vision of loveliness, Briella." His use of her name, maybe it was the manner in which he said it, caused butterfly wings to twirl within her stomach.

Briella rose from her curtsey and took the arm he offered, entwining their limbs together. "Thank you, Your Majesty." Her breathing was ragged as her excitement at just being within his presence set her pulse racing. That she was to spend an evening in his company was thrilling.

They walked to the twisted staircase, which they quickly ascended by one floor. They took their time as they meandered to the ballroom, neither one speaking to fill the silence. Briella did not feel a need to scramble for a topic of conversation, her mind was too occupied with thoughts of what was to come.

The ballroom was just as magnificent as it had been when Briella first spied it, only now, she and the King had the entire space to themselves. There, floating candles were giving an ambiance of romance, while the one small table set to the side of the room by the terrace doors was alight with a purple glow. Briella was curious as to where the purple light came from, and when King Ezekiel led her to her chair, she could not take her eyes away from the luminescent pearl that lay resting upon a layer of rich sand nesting within a glass dome. The vibrant pearl looked to be as large as her palm.

"It's a relic. When the Courts were established, each Court gifted another with a treasure from their lands. This was given to the Spring Court by the Summer Court, taken from the depths of their waters where the selkies reside. That was long ago but it's never lost its magical glow." King Ezekiel pulled her chair away from the table and indicated that she should sit.

Once she was seated and the layers of her dress were neatly arranged, she inquired, "Which Court received the Spring Court's gift?"

The King had efficiently seated himself and took no time in replying, "The Winter Court. They were given a flowering cherry tree that's eternally blooming."

"How lovely. How tall is it? Does it continually grow?"

"I believe it grew until it reached halfway to the vaulted ceiling, then grew no more. I've never actually seen it. The Winter King, the first one, built a special room just for the tree. It resides in the middle of their castle."

"How enchanting. Have you ever visited the other Courts?" Briella tilted her head curiously.

"Only the Summer, as that's our closest neighboring

Court. But… I was just a boy and that was ages ago." His voice held a note of melancholy.

"I see," Briella replied, and changed the topic to something happier as the look upon his face was causing her heart to squeeze painfully with sympathy. "Bruno is doing well within the castle. He has only chased one rabbit, who was very offended until Fleur handed him the bowl of carrots from our lunch. I had never heard a rabbit screech so loudly before. I hadn't remembered how wonderful it was to have someone you love continually by your side. If there is anything I can ever do–"

He stopped her right there by quickly stating, "You do not need to seek out an opportunity to repay me. Truly, I found him for you, yes, but I was gifted in return by your smiles and that, dearest one, was my prize."

Briella could not stop the smile that blossomed. Her heart was filled with these tender moments, these heartwarming words that were encasing themselves one by one within her soul.

Reaching his hand out to clutch hers in a gentle grasp, he stared deeply into her eyes. He held her hand so tenderly, but with a solid firmness that made the broken bits of herself want to fit perfectly together again. He was healing her heart with no physical magic; it was just done with the way in which he treated her. That he showed her how valuable and wanted she was. He seemed to delight in spending time with her, seeking her out, making time for her alone.

It was then that she heard the wheels of the silver serving cart. She didn't remove her gaze from the King's until the cart halted before their table.

Sebastian smiled with a twinkle swirling within his black eyes and bowed to them. "Your Majesty. My lady." He hurriedly leapt from the serving cart and scurried over to Briella, shaking out her napkin with a flourish before dropping it onto her lap. Then his tiny legs hastened to repeat the gesture for the King.

Once Sebastian was situated back upon his serving cart, he informed them that dinner would now be served. He moved his claw and the cart moved back the way it had come as a footman dressed in the black castle livery, passed and made his way to the table with a soup tureen.

The footman had long brown ears shaped like a rabbit's that twitched back and forth ever so slightly. He was tall and lean and otherwise seemed that his defining faerie characteristic was his furry ears. He spoke not a word as he gently ladled the pale-yellow soup into their bowls. When he had completed his duty, he bowed and walked backward a few feet until he turned and left to return to the kitchen.

King Ezekiel leaned forward and poured them each a goblet of faerie wine. Normally, that was a task for the footman, but the King showed that he honored her by performing the act himself.

"Where is Bruno tonight?" he asked.

"It seems as if the entire castle knew of my dinner invitation this evening. I have been a subject of curiosity today. Fleur informed me that she and Bruno had a dinner affair of their own to attend. But Fleur promised that he would be taken care of and walked before she returned him."

"I know that she will entertain Bruno. You need not fear," he said, and took a sip of the soup from his spoon.

Taking her own taste of the soup, which tasted like a mix of peaches and rich cheese, her senses became confused. Her brows furrowed while she tried to decide whether she enjoyed the soup or was repulsed by it. She mulled the flavors around her tongue before swallowing and taking a few more spoonfuls. The more she sipped, the more pleasing the flavor became, and Briella decided to be enchanted by it.

In the silence, Briella's mind wandered to the curse, as it was never far from her thoughts. "Would you mind if tomorrow I invaded your library?" She left out the fact that she had been invading it almost daily already.

"Briella, it's at your disposal, you need never ask. The room is yours." His eyes glistened with a tad bit of mischief as he continued, "Are you on a mission?"

"Indeed, I am."

Sebastian returned, as did the former footman, and they placed a platter of roasted meat into the center of the table. It smelled divine, and though Briella could not determine from which animal it came, she thought it looked very appetizing.

While it was customary for the head of a household to carve and serve the meat to his guests, here in the castle, that was never a task that the King undertook. It was the appointment of the dinner table server to carve and place the offering upon each guest's plate at any formal affair. While in the dining hall, it was the head of the table that carved.

Briella expressed her gratitude by smiling when her plate was filled, and the footman backed away from the table, having already served his king first.

"Enjoy," Sebastian said, clearing his throat.

King Ezekiel nodded his head and replied, "Well done."

Sebastian steered the serving cart away, but not before Briella thought that she spied red infusing his blueish cheeks. *The crab really does delight in serving.*

"I am surmising that Sebastian is from another Court. I

would hazard a guess to name the Summer Court as his birthplace."

"You are correct. Though, he should be conducting his orchestra in the Summer Court waters, he is here with us." Bringing the conversation back to the library, the King stated, "You can, of course, trust that I will assist you upon your bookish mission. What is it that you hope to discover?"

Dabbing her mouth with the napkin, Briella answered, "More information about the Courts. Their customs, their celebrations. I have just learned that you will soon be presiding over FaeWylde. It sounds intriguing."

"It is not what it should be, not what it once was. But we shall do our best to celebrate nonetheless."

They each took to their roasted meat with gusto and soon it was finished. They conversed about Briella's mother and some of the stories that she had told Briella were shared with King Ezekiel, who seemed to be amused by the imagination and cunning of the characters.

When they had their dessert salads placed before them, Briella only took a few tiny bites. She was much too full. Seeing her, the King pushed his chair back and crossed to her. He held out his hand for her to take and used his other to pull out her chair. He helped her rise, and then the two wandered until they stood upon the glass floor with the encased roses.

Briella still marveled that they stood upon such a floor. It was gorgeous and not the same darkness as the rest of the castle. Wondering what magic lay under her feet, she was startled when King Ezekiel stood before her and grasped her around her waist. Quickly regaining her wits, she held her right hand out for him to enclose within his own larger hand.

A waltz began from just behind them, and she cast a

glance to see Sebastian standing upon a raised wooden platform conducting a small orchestra that seemingly came from out of nowhere. *More faerie magic?*

Giving her attention back to the King, she looked up at him and smiled. He returned her smile and then led them into the steps of the dance. Briella tried to gaze away from the intense stare that their eyes were locked into. She could no more break away than she could fly. Within his eyes were dreams and promises, but there was something more lurking deeper and she was flummoxed as to what that was.

As they twirled and turned, their eyes always found each other. The butterflies seemed to magnify within Briella. She felt weightless and wonderful, never wanting to hear the notes of the music cease. The notes just melded from one song to another, again and again.

The candlelight seemed to burn a little dimmer, making shadows dance along the dark walls. Briella wasn't frightened, she was floating upon a cloud. When the King separated any distance between them, she leaned forward, turning her head and laying it upon his solid chest. She could hear the beating of his heart, and she was certain that her own heartbeats matched his. She felt him shift his head down toward her. When he placed a gentle kiss upon her forehead, the sincerity of it nearly made her weep. Never before, except within his presence, had she ever felt so treasured. Surely, a kiss such as this meant that she was precious to him.

Briella took her head from his chest and once more locked gazes with him. There was nothing more than their bodies pressed together, gently swaying, and the mossy green and cerulean eyes that could not look away from each other. She removed her hand from his arm and rested it along his cheek. And when he smiled, it lit up her whole being. Never had she desired a kiss with such longing before. There were parts of her heart waking up as if they had been in a deep slumber. She remembered upon first seeing him, thinking how enticing his lips had looked. She wanted her first kiss to be gifted to her by her Faerie King. She longed for his passion and his secrets in equal measure.

"My dearest, Briella. I cannot express what your presence here has done to me. I feel bewitched and beguiled and I can only add that I desire more. More of your smiles, more chances to hold you, more days and nights with you. More. Everything. Forevermore. And I am selfish. Tell me, are you happy here? Content?" King Ezekiel spoke so softly it was almost reverent.

"I'm more than content, Your Majesty."

"Would you stay here, with me, come what may?"

"If that would please you." Briella felt a blush creeping up her chest and settling into her warm cheeks.

"It would. It would make me the happiest of faeries. For you must understand that without you, I would never be whole again. Were you to leave, I don't know that I'd want to exist without you. You have completely undone me, and I have been perplexed, intrigued, and completely entertained by you. Say that you will always remain by my side, promise me this?"

Briella swallowed. She wanted to promise him, but had she not been warned to never make a promise to a faerie? No matter the circumstances? She longed to give him anything he asked of her. He had given her so much. Her thoughts swirled within her mind and without another moment to waste, she gave the King his answer.

"I will stay as long as I'm needed. That is a promise that I make to you. I have no desire to part from your side. I have never felt as if I belonged anywhere, but here within your Court, I feel as if this is where I am meant to be. I think I was always destined to be here with you. By your side with my hand in yours."

Swallowing heavily, the King stared down at her. His eyes roved from her eyes to her lips as he seemed to be memorizing every curve and dip of her face.

"I do not deserve you. I have done unspeakable things, uttered unsavory words. But I find that I cannot let you go."

Briella brought their clasped hands to her mouth and gently placed a kiss on the back of his hand. He was looking at her like she was the most magnificent creature he had ever beheld. She did not feel worthy of him, and it seemed that he returned her fear. What could be more fitting, more perfect, than two imperfect beings making their own happiness together? She wanted to discover how glorious they could be. She was choosing her own destiny, and she chose to entwine herself with him in however many ways that she could.

22

WHAT IS LOVE?

Briella was still floating upon a cloud of happiness when she opened her eyes the next morning. She thought of the King and all of the tender words that had been spoken between them. Neither had wanted to part from the other, even though the hour grew late, so they continued to dance. No further words had been needed between them. She was content to stay with him forever, promise or not. He had become her first thought upon waking and her last thought as sleep claimed her these past few weeks. Time was changing her, and she was willingly marching along. Though neither had voiced the deepest emotion possible, the attachment was mutually acknowledged. *Afterall, what are mere words when actions carry their own voice?* For so long words had cut just as deeply as the physical wounds that her stepfamily had inflicted upon her. Briella sighed as her thoughts quieted down.

When she stretched, Bruno woke and yawned while he lifted his head and wagged his long, thin tail. He had been curled up on the foot of her bed, in his usual spot, and was snoring softly when she had finally retired. What was most surprising was to see that Cheshire was also sharing her bed. While the two were at opposite ends of the bed with the striped cat once again claiming her pillow, they seemed to have come to some sort of understanding, and that further gladdened her heart. Being so very weary and not wanting to endure a scene or provoke either animal, Briella had lifted the pillow which Cheshire lay upon and moved it over slightly so that she, too, had room. She had ended up using her folded arm as her pillow and would need to request another pillow so that she did not constantly awake to aching muscles or sore joints.

"Could you possibly stop vibrating the mattress, drooly one?" Cheshire purred as he peeked one bottle-green eye open to address the dog.

Bruno simply looked at him and continued to wag his tail. There was no certain way to know how he felt about the cat's request. But he did stretch and jump down from the bed to stretch some more.

Satisfied, Cheshire closed his eye and drifted off to sleep once again.

Being as silent as she could, Briella climbed out from under the coverlet and stepped into her warm slippers. She rushed to the water closet to begin her day. There was much to accomplish and she was eager to get underway.

Before long, she dressed herself in a burgundy day gown that she had not requested from the enchanted cabinet. No, this was quite something to celebrate as this was the first complete dress that she had sewn with minimal help from Gustavious. The smile would not leave her face as she styled her blonde tresses into an elegant updo. While she saw to her duties during the day, it seemed so much easier when she kept her hair away from the scissors and needles that were almost constantly employed. Briella donned a pair of silver slippers, which perfectly matched the wide ribbon that rested just under her bosom.

Though there were many styles of dress that were worn within the Spring Court, she much preferred the design of the empire waist which was the height of fashion back in the mortal realm. On the rare occasions when Alerion had sent her into the village upon a task, Briella would always take notice of what was being worn. She had peeked through the modiste's shop to catch the colorful designs and to dream about a day that might never dawn; when she too may be arrayed just as beautifully. Now she was stunningly donned in such a dress. She ran a hand down the soft muslin material and sighed.

There was an expected rap upon her bedchamber door and Briella silently padded over to open it. The dog walker greeted her with a good morning and tied a leash around Bruno as he escorted him for his morning walk. She took a moment to wonder if Bruno had ever felt confused by the appearance of his official walker, as the male faerie had a tan tail and matching doglike ears that flopped with his movement. As far as she could tell, it never did cause Bruno one moment of alarm. He always greeted his walker with a wag of his tail and a dance of joy.

Briella nibbled a small pastry from the plate placed upon the worktable that greeted her upon her arrival to her work chamber. She took a moment to observe the room. It was tidy and well kept and she had the mice to thank for that. Well, except for Jacques, who had given up his position. Briella still missed him. *He has a good heart if only his temper would not get in the way of it.*

It was not long before Pernella and Gustavious entered

the room. They had been traveling via a series of tunnels that ran throughout the rooms of the castle. It had once made Briella feel uneasy as that was a wonderful way in which to spy upon your fellow residents, but it had ceased to bother her any longer. It was possible for the walls to be enchanted and to whisper their secrets, so what did the presence of a mouse or two really matter? There seemed to be so few secrets that were able to be kept under the stones that built the castle.

"My, it does look lovely upon you, Mistress," Pernella spoke as she scurried up the table leg and skidded to a stop upon the wooden table. Her tiny eyes took in the day dress Briella wore.

"Thank you! I am rather fond of it. I never could have undertaken such a task without your assistance. You and Gustavious have such real talent," Briella praised her friends.

Waving his mousy paw, Gustavious commented, "You had the talent all along, we just had to unlock it." The brown mouse skittered over to the button bin and rifled through it.

Dismissing him, Pernella inquired, "How was your evening with the King?"

Smiling dreamily, Briella told her all about the evening. The two females gushed over the shared endearments, whispered words said, and the romantic atmosphere.

"Still seems a mite ridiculous to me that you promised to stay. Needless really when we're all forced to be here," Gustavious huffed out as he climbed onto the table with a few buttons tucked under each tiny arm.

"Shhh, you! You will spoil our fun. It's romantic and you know that!" Pernella scolded.

"Women and their musings of the heart will forever remain a mystery to me," he replied as he shook his head.

"Maybe you could use those large mousy ears of yours and learn a thing or two about what matters to a female's heart. You won't want to be an imbecile when you finally get to claim your true love," Pernella told him.

"Aww, we've got time yet. Our circumstances have not changed."

Shaking her head, Pernella busied herself with her task of cutting out material for a suit that had been ordered by a male faerie who bore the head of a boar.

Briella smiled too as she worked upon the delicate lace hem that was to be edged along a gown's hemline.

It was late, and though Briella was weary from the prior night's dancing, she still found herself scanning the shelves in the King's library. King Ezekiel had yet to retire to his private chambers and she was content to continue her search. It was time to learn what she could to aid her in all matters of the Faerie realm. Turning to another shelf, she scanned the titles and picked up the one named, *The Courts of Faerie: Customs and Other Tidbits*. While it was not much of a title, she hoped that it was just the very book that she needed. Settling down in her favorite corner, she brought her feet up to rest against the cushioned settee and laid the opened book upon her bent knees.

Scanning the chapters, she decided to begin with the Spring Court as that was the most pressing of concerns for her.

The Spring Court was established by the first King of Faerie, Rubuious, who was a just ruler, but was easily taken advantage of by his peers. His Unseelie form was that of a rabbit, and when he first began to change to a Seelie form, his rabbit ears and tail were his marked faerie feature. As the years went by, he noticed marked changes in his Seelie form and discovered that one cannot go forever without changing forms, or one form is sacrificed. A true ruler of the Spring Court will always possess some shade of green coloring for their eyes, whether in Seelie or Unseelie form.

We can thank Rubuious for welcoming in the Fae traditions of the Faecrenzial Spring Equinox and FaeWylde. He resolved to never let his Seelie and Unseelie ways die, and so began these traditions to celebrate both sides of his heritage. The King of the Spring Court is gifted with the magic of new life and growth. It is his appointment to tend to the magic that thrives within his Court by always keeping himself tethered to the lands within his kingdom. A ruler must keep his heart pure to give back to the lands, and this is especially imperative to the Spring Court, as its ruler is the keeper of new life. We do not know what would occur if the ruler neglected his duties and was unable or unwilling to nurture his bond with the lands.

There was, of course, more to be read but Briella had to pause and give thought to the idea that no ruler of the Spring Court had ever lost his connection with the lands. Yet, this land was not as it should be. It was not thriving and brilliant with greenery. It was dying. So… King Ezekiel had lost his bond with the lands. And because of that, his land was a decaying wasteland that no new life flowed through. The matter of his predicament must lie within his heart. Whatever had taken place a decade ago had affected his heart, and thus the Spring Court. She now knew the source that needed to be corrected for this curse to be ended. Briella felt giddy and lightheaded with relief. Knowing how to correct this curse was still a mystery, but this information was the confirmation she needed, and that would pave her way forward. She had to heal the King's heart and save not only him, but his kingdom as well. It stood to reason that his heart was not capable of feeling love. How then, had she felt closer to him than she had ever felt to another? Was it not love that shone so brightly from his eyes? Her own heart argued the fact that no love was capable of attaching itself to his heart. She had felt evidence of his esteem for her, but no words stating *love* had ever been spoken. She was just as guilty of concealing the fact that she was falling in love. All could be well for everyone within this kingdom, if she managed to banish the curse. *Absolutely no pressure there. Only the fate of an entire kingdom that rests upon my shoulders, and our future happiness.*

Her musings begged her to answer the question of what love was. Was it a feeling? Was it a force that so slowly built itself? Was it a raging inferno? Did love happen so suddenly that one felt the full force of it and was astounded? And then, what did it mean to love? Did one treat others differently, or just the being that had brought the feeling to life? Did love make you act gentle? Did it make your words softer, kinder? Did it change the perspective of one's whole life?

She was deeply in thought when she saw movement before her vision. King Ezekiel was silently crouching down before her with a concerned look marring his handsome features.

"Are you unwell?" he asked.

"No, just very deep in thought," Briella told him.

"Can I be of assistance in puzzling out a solution?"

"I don't think so, at least, not this time." Briella pulled her feet from under her skirts and shook out her dress as she stood before him. Walking around him, she located the empty space on the bookshelf and reshelved the book. She was moving slowly in order to give herself time to form her thoughts, it would not do to ignore the King or simply bypass him and exit from the room.

Briella felt his presence behind her before she felt his hand upon her elbow. He urged her to turn and face him and she complied with his silent request.

"Have I done something?" he asked, locking gazes with her.

"I just have many disorganized thoughts, and I am attempting to sort them out," Briella replied, shaking her head. "Please do not fear that I have been upset by you or your actions."

The King carefully studied her face before he spoke. "I do not believe you. There are secrets swirling around within your exquisite irises. I will not press you for more than you are willing to give. But please know, that I am here should you have any need of me. I would do all I could for you at any time, my lady."

Swallowing the lump that rose into her throat, Briella tried to keep her tears at bay. It would not serve any purpose to become a watering pot. So, she nodded at him and stepped away. She padded soundlessly to the door and stopped before she turned the handle. "Have you ever desired something so much that you were disappointed when all you thought you understood was not actually how things were?" Pressing her forehead into the door, she awaited his answer.

"I have had moments of confusion and uncertainty. But Briella, if this is about you and I, I have no doubts. I have never doubted what this thing is between us."

Briella whirled around and faced him from across the library. "And what is this '*thing*' as you call it, that is between us? Is it friendship? Companionship? Something more or something less?" She felt the need to press him, to challenge him. If his heart was not able to love, then she needed to know that her discovery was correct.

He took a moment to reply. "It is what it is. Why must it be named?"

"Because it matters to me."

"I do not know what to call it. When we are apart, I find myself wondering what you are doing, and whether you are smiling or unhappy. I count down the moments until there is a chance that I may see you again, even across the crowded room. When I see you, I catalog every nuance of your person, learn every expression that your beautiful face presents. I strain my ears to hear your conversations, and my eyes will not willingly stray from you."

"And you do those things with what intent?" she asked.

"To know you better. To see where I may make a change to affect you or your circumstances. I never want you to be unhappy, and if I have the power to change any detail, it's my wish to do so."

"As my friend?" She would not look at him, instead, her gaze lingered on the carpet before her.

King Ezekiel gained the distance between them in a few quick strides. He reached his hand out to cup her cheek. "Briella," he began and stopped. "I want you. Must it matter what we label it?"

"It does. I find that I don't know how we are to go on. If it's just friendship, you would not object to my spending time with another. If it's just friendship, I may allow another to court me." She finally brought her eyes up to his face. She traced in her mind his plush lips and fine nose. His eyes burned brightly with an intensity that she could not yet name.

"I will not *allow* it!" he snarled. "*I* will not allow you to form an attachment with another. No one shall ever court you, nor even have the thought within his head to spend time with you. I would tear him asunder. I would merrily eviscerate him and never think of him again, and I would also make certain that he never filtered through your mind ever again. I will not allow you to ponder thoughts of another. For you do not merely belong to yourself any longer. Briella, you are *mine.*" The King brought his lips down to kiss her forehead, where he let his lips linger much too long. He then laid his forehead against hers, seemingly to calm his temper which seemed so at odds with the words he had so harshly spoken to her.

Briella squeezed her eyes tightly shut and choked back the sob that threatened to overtake her. "If you do not want me as more than your friend, please let me go. I have never felt for another what I feel for you, but if I am alone in the ability to single out my feelings, it is not enough. I have done the will of others my entire life. I do not wish to continue on unappreciated and unloved."

"You seek love? True love? I fear that true love, little one, is not something that I can offer you at present. I…" He trailed off with a look of pain across his features.

Reaching her hand out, she tenderly took his cheek into her palm. "I am sorry to cause you pain."

"No. No," he said softly. "You do not cause me pain. You are the source of where my…" He backed away from her and turned around with his shoulder slumping forward. "You should retire. It is late. I am a selfish being, Briella. I ask that which I am incapable of returning. If there is another that you wish to let court you, who you wish to spend your time with, I will allow it."

She wanted to rush to his side, to see his smile and teasing manner return. He stood so silent and motionless that she was completely lost at sea. But in the end, maybe he truly did not want her. Not as she wanted him, despite the prior words that he had cast upon her. Perhaps the feelings she invoked within him were the desire to conquer or rule over her.

The fire that seemed to almost consume her, did not burn for him as brightly. He simply desired to be friends and maybe nothing more, and here she was being a nuisance, trying to make him declare himself. What a fool she was. She had never been desirable to another, never cherished, so why would she expect a king to want her more than anyone before him ever had? It was laughable, this whole situation. How she wished that she too possessed wings that could carry her away! *I shall never be that which I want more than anything. I am unlovable and unwanted, and so very far beneath him,* she thought with absolute certainty. *I should not have pressed him so greatly for answers.*

Briella found herself facing the door and turning the knob. "One more thing, Your Majesty. Does the curse affect your heart? The land is dying, is it not? And the lands of your kingdom are tied to your heart? Is your heart dying or has it been missing for years?"

Only silence greeted her. Looking over her shoulder, she saw that he had not moved. "You cannot tell me. It's the binding conditions of the curse, I would guess. I will figure this out." With those parting words, she opened the door and resolutely walked through it.

It took great courage to walk away from something that she had longed for. Greater even still when she had laid her heart bare to another, and they were not ardently returning her affections. She would not give up. She would stop dawdling, and do her part in this destiny, because this wasn't just about herself, it was about a whole kingdom. Her heart might be broken once again, but this would not break her. Whether she was ever loved the way in which her own heart beat for another, or whether she was cast aside, it was time to act. If she could make him love her, she could break this curse and free herself in the process.

23

DREARY DAYS

The day was dreary, which was not overly surprising as most days within the Spring Court could be labeled as such. The mist hung heavily, shrouding the castle and the surrounding woods. The sadness that was now within her heart was a marked difference and made everything seem gloomier. The oppressive atmosphere of the castle was an apt companion to Briella's troubles. While she wanted to hide the day away in bed, she could not. She had never done so before, and would not start the practice now. She had so much to be thankful for. If only her heart would stop wallowing and look outward.

It began to rain and Briella looked out her window as the ping of the rain rang out against the windowpane. She rose from the bed and wrapped her royal blue robe around her shoulders. It did little to stave off the chill that the room held. Even donning her matching slippers could not keep the chill at bay.

The mossy green embers of the fire did little to cheer her up. The flames that danced before her were the same color as the King's unforgettable eyes. He would never love her as long as the curse persisted. He may never love her even if the curse was broken. But wasn't it better to love whole-heartedly and do the right thing, than to mourn a love that might never be? Not if, but when, she broke the curse, she would find the King. And if he never looked at her with love shining from within his eyes, she would be just fine. But that was the crux of the whole matter. He had looked upon her with love shining from his bright eyes, she was certain of it. It could not have been simply that she had longed to see such emotion; she had not simply dreamed it up. Those moments between them had been solid and real. But the fact remained that his heart was tied to the lands of the kingdom and they were decaying. The curse *must* be broken.

Bruno brushed against Briella's thigh and nuzzled his nose into her hand. With a lick, he greeted her and the smile she gave him was sad. The rap upon the chamber door announced the dog's walker, and Briella escorted Bruno into the care of the servant. When she closed the door behind the pair, she felt a little lighter. There were so many different kinds of love. She was certain that one day, she would find the love that she most longed for.

Once Briella was readied for her day, she straightened her posture and stepped across the threshold of her workroom. The mice had not yet arrived, and that was fine with her. She could do so many things that she never would have accomplished before she set foot into the Spring Court. Her time here in this room had not been a waste. She took out various fabrics and patterns, trying to decide what to create next. She stroked her chin as she thought.

Deciding upon a gown for FaeWylde, she chose a rich blue fabric that reminded her of periwinkles. Briella smiled to herself and began to pin the pattern to the fabric while she softly hummed.

The door creaked open and Fleur came flying into the room. Her dress looked like it was a mixture of mud and moss, and though it should have looked bizarre, it looked faetabulous upon her friend. "What are you doing?"

"What does it look like I am doing?" Briella replied, as she put the pin holder upon the worktable and looked down at the beginning of her gown.

Ignoring her question, Fleur commented, "It's a dreary day. The King isn't holding Court today, which is a good thing as his demeanor is horrid."

"Oh?"

"He has been yelling at us all since early this morning when he rose and started his day. I was having the best dream," Fleur sighed, as she came to rest against a spool of black thread.

"Really?"

"It was faetabulous!" Fleur started to drone on about a frog and a water lily, and Briella completely stopped listening to her as she measured out some lace to adorn the bodice of the ball gown.

"Unnamed!"

Startling, Briella gasped, "Hmm?"

"You have been ignoring me! That's very unfaely of you. And after I let you go on and on about anything you like."

Frowning, Briella thoughtfully looked at her tiny friend. "I am so sorry. I beg your forgiveness. When do I go on and on?"

"All the time… Well, there was that one time. I forget when or what it was about, but I am certain it was boring." Fleur patted her coiffure.

Briella smirked at her, but did not reply.

"Anyway, do you know what has the King in such foul humor? We all thought those days were bygone, but nope, they are here to stay, apparently. Maybe *you* know why."

"I have not the faintest idea. You could ask him."

"Are you mad? Has the castle finally addled your mind too?" Fleur flew up to bop Briella upon her nose.

Waving the faerie away from her face, Briella asked her, "Would it be such a horrible thing if I was mad? I think I would fit in quite nicely."

"*Pssh.* Next, you'll claim that humans were roaming the castle while a giant crane was leading a marching band stark naked."

"Now, that would be something dreadful."

"It would. Humans with their wrinkly skin and sagging bits. It makes me want to vomit." Fleur looked Briella up and down and frowned. "Why aren't you all saggy and old?"

Shrugging her shoulders, Briella said, "I guess I must have good ancestry to rely upon. Besides, I doubt that I have been here long enough to age drastically."

Flying up to look into one of Briella's eyes, Fleur scoffed, "You're something else! I cannot believe you have fooled me for so long! You are not just merely human."

"Why ever would you think that?"

"Reasons! Lots of them, now that I realize. You have changed physically and while that is common for a mere human, you have not just ceased with changes of age, you have changed in appearance. Your eyes are brighter, larger, and more exquisite. Your fingers are longer too! I am sure there are other changes that are escaping my notice at the moment. But it's there, in the very way you carry yourself. And it's not just from the shedding of past burdens either."

"Perhaps you are right." Briella threaded a needle trying to stall for time.

"'Tis a certainty! The curse affects you differently. Or, you are something more and that's the option that I choose to believe." Fleur folded her tiny arms across her chest and grinned triumphantly.

"You must not spread these thoughts you have."

"Unnamed! For shame. I would never spread rumors about my best friend."

"Rumors? Would you share truths?" Briella arched a golden eyebrow at Fleur.

"You take all joy and just shrivel it up. Here like a glittering jewel one moment, and then a hunk of dirt the next."

"Fleur, I do not mean to spoil your fun. That is not my intention. But you cannot tell anyone what you suspect; I am not ready to face ridicule."

"No one would dare ridicule you! I won't stand for it and neither will the King."

Feeling frustrated at the situation and for continually having to be on guard even while in the company of those she considered her friends, Briella went to rebuke her statement when a voice purred near her. "Fleur is correct, we will not stand for our friend, who is something much more, to be the source of conjecture." Cheshire's floating head was hanging upside down above the table.

"Do you know something that I do not?" Fleur glared up at the feline.

"Oh, I daresay, I know a great many things that you do not. But the one thing most of interest is the fact that a likeness of Briella hangs in the portrait gallery." Cheshire grinned.

"What? How have I missed this important tidbit?" Fleur looked at Briella woundedly.

"Don't be mulish, Fleur. Briella doesn't even know about this. Shall we all make our way to the gallery and search until we find the painting?" Cheshire shimmered as his full body appeared.

"Cheshire, are you certain?" Briella widened her eyes to attempt to implore him to change his statement.

"Oh yes, my dear. Let us go and view the portrait directly!" The cat floated to the door, then gave her a wink as he disappeared straight through it.

Fleur grabbed onto Briella's thumb and pulled her along after her flying form. Briella made her feet follow, but she was a riot of sensations. She knew that she was briskly walking, but paid no attention to anything before her as her thoughts tumbled within her racing mind.

Before she could make sense of the situation, the trio stood at the entrance to the gallery. Briella wanted to flee while another part of her wanted to stay. What if there really was a portrait that she resembled? What, if anything, would it mean for her? If others knew, would it change things? Would her situation become even more precarious?

Cheshire and Fleur both pushed Briella's lower back to get her to move into the room. They walked and scanned the portraits before them.

"If you know about this likeness, why are we searching for it?" Fleur demanded.

"It's more a feeling than a knowing." Cheshire grinned.

"Oh, for the realms sakes, Cheshire!" Fleur screeched.

"Let's keep searching. I know we shall find it."

Briella listened to the two bicker back and forth, but did not try to stop them. She had more important things to concentrate upon.

After an hour of various faces, both animal and

humanesque, Fleur gave a giddy clap. "Here! I have found her!"

Briella rushed to Fleur's side while Cheshire floated in the air spinning in circles until he, too, was before the beautiful faerie portrait. Briella could hardly bring air into her lungs. She was so stunned to see, what very much resembled herself staring back at her. The black plaque said it was Queen Faeira, but she could not decipher the date of her reign.

"You do look just like her! It's uncanny." Fleur breathed out quietly.

"Yes, it's as I said. You, my dear, were always meant to be here with us. You belonged to the Spring Court long before you were ever born," Cheshire purred.

"Let's see what she has to say!" Fleur raised her hands, palms up and a silver glow began to form. The orb of light lit from between Fleur's hands and floated away into the portrait.

"What are you doing?" Briella whispered harshly. She could not stand the thought of this portrait catching fire or being destroyed. It was an important piece of the castle's past and her ancestry.

"It's just an enchantment. It sometimes works and sometimes doesn't," Fleur explained.

The Queen in the painting blinked her blue eyes, and then seemed to focus on her guests. *"These are dreary days. You have come to save our home, blood of my blood."*

Briella had never seen such magic before. What Fairy Godmother had done was nothing quite like this. It was not even comparable. "How can you know that I am your descendent?"

A trilling laugh burst free from the Queen. *"You are standing before me. I know your face as well as I know my own, we share the same features. I am overjoyed to know that you exist and will save my beloved lands."*

"But how? How am I meant to save an entire kingdom? I suspect you had much more magic flowing within your body than I could ever imagine."

"There is more magic in true love, than in even the most powerful curse. You do not need faerie magic to ensure these lands live on. The darkness is bleeding into all of the Courts, I can feel its slow hand at work. You must save us, before time runs out."

"But… how? Why can't anyone tell me how?" Briella felt like bursting into frustrated tears. She felt like stamping her slippered foot.

"The most important deeds must be accomplished by the doer. It is up to you to discover what magic you can wield. The journey would not be worth the pursuit if all of the answers were freely gifted to you. You must search your own heart before you can ever hope to fix another's."

The silver orb exploded from the portrait in colorful light.

"No!" Briella wasn't ready for the magic to stop working.

"I am not as powerful as some of the older faeries. My magic doesn't always last that long as I am just a tiny sprite. I am sorry, Unnamed." Fleur touched her shoulder.

"Thank you," Briella told her and she meant it with her whole heart. She had found family. It was silly to feel like this momentous thing had occurred, when she had family who had resided within the castle walls. After all, her father's portrait hung here as well.

Laughing like a twinkling bell, Fleur exclaimed, "Do you realize what this means?"

Briella looked at Cheshire, who just shrugged his

shoulder, then began to lick his striped leg, which he thrust out before him.

Fleur rolled her eyes and stated, "Unnamed is more royal than the King is! She has more royal blood flowing in her than even he does! It is she who belongs on the throne!"

Briella wrinkled her brows together, and just looked at Fleur.

"'Tis a pity she possesses no magic. Think of all the wondrous things she could accomplish." Their feline companion agreed.

They turned away from the portrait and began the trek back to the workroom. Each seemed to be lost amongst their own inner thoughts. Briella was loath to part from her ancestor's likeness but also longed for the solitude of her chambers. Briella felt like a million ants were marching up and down her body. She could not make the feeling abate.

Once she reached her workroom she padded straight for the wooden table. She looked at the beginning of her ball gown and sighed, having no desire to finish it.

Fleur entered the room behind her and sat upon a spool of thread near the dress. The tiny faerie seemed to be lost in thought. Briella didn't know where the feline had gone, but she was glad that he wasn't there to taunt or tease her. She was free to let her thoughts roam where they may.

The idea that she was descended from the faeries of long ago was chilling. All she knew, all she thought she knew, was constantly changing.

24

SPOKEN WORDS

Briella took dinner in her bedchamber. She felt like her mind was overtaxed and being good company was not something that she was capable of. Her heart was sore and her body was weary. Even Bruno was not enough to pull her away from the maudlin mood she was experiencing. A talking portrait had informed her that time was running out to break the curse, and this was not welcomed information. Was love enough to surmount a curse? Was something wrong with the love she bore for the King? Could her heart speak to his, thus breaking the curse?

Pushing her dinner tray away from her, she considered Bruno. He was a prime example that the King had a heart. For saving Bruno for her was a beautiful gesture that could only have been a thought of the heart.

She began to pace the length of her chamber when a rap came upon her door. Wanting to ignore the intrusion, she waited a moment to see if they would go away.

"Are you in there, dear one?" came King Ezekiel's voice.

Surprise overtook her and she did not know if she wanted to open the door or bolt it closed forever. She did not expect to see him after last evening, though she knew that they had to mend the hurt that lingered between them. She could do this even though her heart was beating erratically and her hands were shaking. Briella took a deep, steadying breath and felt herself calm enough to face him.

Briella's steps took her to the door, which she opened to the sight of the King. He always stole the breath from her body, and it took her a moment to remember that air was a necessity. While his handsome visage fed her eyes, she needed to breathe so that she could continue to take his measure. His face was sorrowful and his green eyes looked tortured. This was not the faerie that she was used to seeing. Before her, stood a beaten-down being. *How my heart aches for him!*

He stood before the threshold to her bedchamber and waited. He did not step foot in nor utter a word. Briella took his warm hand into hers and brought his hand up to her mouth, where she kissed his palm as her eyes searched his.

He gave the faintest of smiles and leaned against the door frame, bowing his head. "I had to see you," he whispered. Briella swallowed the lump of emotion that had formed in her throat and let his hand go back to his side.

"I'm glad that you're here. Our parting last night was appalling. Be it between friends or not, it was poorly done."

"I agree."

The firelight cast a glow onto his golden head and black crown. He seemed at a loss for words and, try as she might, her mind was not supplying her with the words either. So, they simply stood and stared at each other.

Bruno came forward and greeted the King with a lick on his hand. King Ezekiel looked down at him and then crouched to level his height with the hound. He patted him atop his head and rubbed his stomach when Bruno flopped down upon his back.

"He really likes you," Briella observed.

"He certainly seems to," mused the King.

"Would you care to come in? Stay for a while. We could…" She looked around her room, trying to find an activity fit to capture not only a king's attention, but a faerie's as well.

"I do not wish to intrude upon your inner sanctum."

"You never could, Your Majesty. Please, do make yourself at home. The entire castle is yours, after all." Briella gave him a teasing smile and moved backward away from the doorway. She padded over toward the fire and waited to see what his decision would be.

King Ezekiel straightened up and came into the bedchamber. He turned to close the door quietly behind him. When he moved toward the center of the room, he looked at all of the furniture before he, too, came to stand before the marbled fireplace. "I wanted to apologize."

"You don't need to."

"I do. I need to apologize because I have confused you. You are the one being that I never want to injure. All of my instincts compel me to ensure your well-being. I have failed in the very basic manner of guarding your heart." He spoke softly with a sincerity that left no room to doubt how deeply conflicted he was.

"I am sure you did not mean to," Briella turned toward him.

He stared into the mossy flames and said, "Never. You must understand that what I feel for you, is not what it should be. It is less than you deserve, and that is not something that can easily be corrected."

"Because the curse prevents you from falling in love, from feeling with your heart?" she softly confessed though she voiced it as a question.

Turning to her, his tortured gaze captured hers. "I… cannot… that is to say… that your statement is accurate, and I am unable to rectify the constraints placed on me. There is nothing that I can say to alleviate this distance between us."

"Perhaps you can be content in knowing the feelings of another, where yours are so complicated. I must admit that I have fallen in love with you. I can't say when it began, only that I was in the midst before I even knew what to do with the discovery. I do not wish the feeling away. If you cannot love, let my feelings be enough for the both of us." She brought her delicate hand up to clasp his jaw, but his hand wrapped around her tinier wrist.

"No, my sweet Briella. You deserve so much more than I can ever give to you. It's not right to take from you when I can offer you nothing in return."

"Your regard? Your kindness? That is hardly nothing. The way you've protected me, you've shown me a completely different side of yourself, that no one else has been a witness to. You are strong, you are a leader, you are gentle and kind. With me, I feel your heartbeat, and that is enough for me. Let me love enough for both of us."

Shaking his head, he said, "No. I will not let you have less, when you could have so much more."

"What of True Love's Kiss? That vision showed me you. *You* are my destiny. I will break this curse, and you will be freed. Whether or not you ever return my feelings for you, I shall never regret my honest feelings, nor my telling you of them."

"True Love's Kiss is a dessert, Briella. It could be enchanted though it very well could mean *nothing* just as easily."

"Or, it could mean *everything*. Why won't you fight for us? For what could be?"

When he reached out to touch her face she backed away from him. He was shaking and his breathing was erratic.

"What is ailing you?" Briella asked as dread and fear filled her entire being.

"I am running out of time. I can feel the days slipping through my fingers. I cannot be with you because my time, as I am, is almost at an end," he spoke harshly, making her flinch.

"It is not too late. May I try to break the curse? I have an idea that might work, but you must trust me." Briella leaned closer toward him.

He looked down at her and nodded, his golden hair flopping forward into his eyes. Rising onto her tiptoes, she lightly brought her mouth to his. He tasted of honey, faerie wine, all the joys of Spring, and all-male. He made a guttural sound as he reached for her and brought her body flush with his. The King opened his mouth against hers, and his tongue slipped along her lips to gently taste them. Briella had never been kissed like this before, and her heart began to beat so fiercely that she thought it might leap from within her chest. In return, she opened her mouth, and he took the invitation to slide his velvety tongue against hers. Briella grabbed onto his sturdy shoulders, digging her nails into sinew and muscle. She could not get close enough to him. Their tongues were dueling in a dance that was both intoxicating and forbidden. Her blonde locks, which flowed down to her waist, were fisted in his grasp; this, coupled with his arduous attention to her mouth, made her moan. It was such a shock to hear herself, that she wrenched herself away from his embrace.

Briella brought her hands to her face and looked at him. He was breathing raggedly as was she. But he looked the same as he had before she had initiated the kiss. The kiss did not cure the curse. Maybe they really were doomed, and True Love's Kiss *was* utter nonsense. Her heart began to crack into tiny pieces that all fought to destroy her from within.

"You understand now how the possibility of us is not meant to be? We were always in each other's destiny until the… Until things changed. I am your future no longer."

Briella felt the crack in her heart burst open. Tears slid down her cheeks as she broke. She did not need to be stoic or strong. No, her heart needed to mourn so that she could reach all the lonely tomorrows that would greet her after this night.

"Was it all deception? Did any of our time together mean anything to you?"

The King spoke through his body's shudders, "Every *moment* meant something. Every *word* spoken between us meant something. I have never deceived you. The Seelie are incapable of deceit. I let myself hope that forever existed for me alongside you. I deceived myself as well, it would seem."

Briella sank to the floor in an ungraceful heap. She was beyond words. She was unaware that he had left the chamber until a horrible howling sounded from the woods outside of the castle. Briella jumped, stifling back her sobs, and looked for the King, but he was gone. She was alone with the frightening sound of a wounded beast that could not reach her. Briella was left forsaken to gather the pieces of her shattered heart.

25

CURSE BREAKER

The next two days and nights kept Briella in a daze. She neither saw nor heard from the King. She existed in this sphere where she went through the motions of her tasks, putting neither her heart nor her mind into anything that she accomplished.

The preparations for FaeWylde were few. Without the proper greenery to decorate with, the holiday was just not as festive. The spirits of those residing in the castle were very low. The candle's glow seemed to be dimmed; the mossy green flames in the fireplace seemed to be more subdued; the inky blackness had never been more oppressive.

When Briella took her walks with Bruno, even he seemed unlike himself. She suspected he missed the visits the King had taken the time for. How she wished for some wise counsel to console her. But none was forthcoming.

When Briella ambled through the castle grounds, the gargoyles looked more disgruntled, if that was possible. Their wings seemed to hang a little lower, and their dark eyes did not follow every movement she made. It was as if they ceased to take an interest in what would come next.

It was all so wrong. So many things that should have been were now fading away into a new existence, and Briella could not keep at bay the dark thoughts and predictions as to what would happen next. She still desired to break the curse, but she was no one of importance. Destiny had gotten this all so horribly wrong. She could no more break a curse, than the moon could float down to her and carry her away. How ridiculous all of her posturing had been. She had been so sure of herself, certain that she would be so important that she could cure the lands. *What absolute poppycock. I'm nothing more than a fraud.*

Cheshire had visited her, but she had so bored him, or offended him, that he never stayed within her presence for too long. That was just as well; she was horrible company and dull-witted as… Whatever was dull-witted. It seemed that she was, indeed, rather insipid and vacuous. She felt so very low and her unkind thoughts sunk her further. She was a worm, an insignificant thing, only useful to do as she was directed.

This was not a fairytale and she was no rescuer. Her place was precarious, at best. She ate, bathed, dressed, and she slept when her mind allowed her.

If ever there was proof that she possessed a real beating heart, it was in her every waking moment. It was destroying her from the inside out. She loved a faerie and, in all the ridiculous tales ever to be told, she would forever be an example of a fool. For her one true love would never love her back. It stung down to the marrow of her bones. This was not supposed to be how her story was to end. Tried she had, but she was not the author of her own story. Fated mates were not ever going to be real for her. No one would ever fill this void left within her withering soul.

When it was time to dress for the evening celebrations of FaeWylde, she chose to wear the dress that she had first worn when she entered this Faerie Court. It seemed appropriate. The ball gown still fit her curves and dips and looked like a dream. With a wistful smile, Briella realized that the glowing silver stars upon her ball gown matched the silver stars that twinkled along the vaulted ceiling of the library. Wasn't it peculiar that the twisted vines along the middle panel of her gown resembled those that one could easily view when out of doors? Briella surmised that there was a reason why her Fairy Godmother had created the ball gown thusly.

Briella placed the sheer lace gloves into the enchanted wardrobe and thought about them stretching to fit her longer fingers. When she retrieved them and put them on, they fit perfectly. With only her glass slippers to don, she was ready to see what the evening would bring. She did not expect King Ezekiel to single her out, it would be too painful for each of them. Still, she wanted to look as beautiful as possible. Once she had her glass slippers on, she took another look at her golden tresses. Deciding that no jewels would adorn her hair, she stood before the full-length rosewood mirror and inspected herself. She was different in so many ways from the first time she wore this, with changes both minuscule and substantial. She was more beautiful, she knew that was undeniable. Her Fae heritage was on full display.

When Bruno came to her, she bent over and tied a golden bow around his neck. He was to accompany her, as she had decided that he was never to leave her side except for his morning walks. He was a beautiful hound with short brown hair that was glistening in the candle's light.

His chocolatey, brown eyes were kind and always curious. Bruno was ready for any adventure that came their way. Briella was fortunate that he provided her with a great deal of affection and protection. His devotion and love for her were unquestionable.

Straightening up again, Briella walked through her bedchamber door into the hallway and ascended the staircase with Bruno in tow. Their destination was the ballroom, but for some reason that she could not name, Briella felt compelled to visit the throne room. She had only been in it once, but when she reached its threshold, her eyes went straight to the stained-glass windows.

The story they told held her captivated.

On the first glass that she viewed, there stood a figure with a golden crown atop golden curls. It was the sneer the figure wore that made this window look ghastly. The male faerie was pointing at his subjects and standing over their prostrate forms. The second glass showed a beautiful faerie with cobalt-colored robes, teal eyes, gossamer wings, and flowing sea-colored hair. From her palms, poured purple flames that she directed at the crowned figure, whose outstretched hand reached for a pile of ash. Moving onto the third glass window, Briella gasped as it showed the castle with its turrets being twisted, and gargoyles descending from the sky. *This is the story of the curse,* Briella realized. The fourth glass depicted a rose with petals falling, floating down to land upon the twisted trees and brambles. Within the center of the rose's petals was a heart that was crushed and misshapen. The fifth glass showed glowing red eyes that peered out from between the twisted trees. The last glass window was a burst of golden light. That was all it contained, as if it was not yet completed. If the curse could be broken, what might it render? If time ran out, as the King had mentioned, what would happen with the last window?

Briella thought back to her last encounter with the Faerie King. He had been shaking, as if it was taking all of his strength to maintain control. Was he the beast portrayed within the glass? Had he seen her arrival in the courtyard with his glowing scarlet eyes, and then became the King again to meet with her? Had he already been in his beast form the night she had been abducted? If she did not break the curse, would he remain forced into the beast form forever? A perfect looking-glass to his actions of the past. Chills attacked her body, and Briella began to shiver. The answers were right before her, and yet, she was still missing a vital piece of information. *What am I missing? I must figure this out!*

Briella felt numb. Her mind was reeling and her body was stunned, rooted to the spot in which she stood. She could stare at the stained glass windows the entire evening, and knew the last clue was not to be found within them. Taking a moment to center herself, Briella closed her eyes. Making her feet move, she soon stood before the two large granite doors that had wilted roses carved into them. She had not seen their beauty when entering the chamber those few minutes ago. The compulsion she felt had vanished the moment that she stood before the windows.

"Come along, Bruno," Briella cooed as she stepped from the throne room.

The pair quickly reached the ballroom, which was lit with floating candles as the scent of rain filled the air, welcoming them in. Rainbow-colored bubbles were drifting along the floor while couples and children gathered around the massive fireplace. They stood roasting meats and toasting confections with the aid of the mossy green flames that seemed to dance to the tune that the minstrels played. Looking at the walls, Briella noted that the shadows looked more monstrous and foreboding. If time was against them, the castle was showing its dismay.

Off to the side, against the black wall, stood tables displaying various foods. There were meats, cheeses, and breads, some having been previously cooked and some not. The dessert table was always the favorite, and the decadent desserts served would put any bakery within the mortal realm to shame. Of course, the faerie wine was flowing freely as the faeries were already deeply into their cups. There was a fountain between the tables that circulated the wine and was almost as large as the fountain, which gurgled water in the courtyard. There were no tables nor chairs as one was to eat, dance, and welcome in the holiday on foot. It had always been this way and likely would always be so, as long as there was a Spring Court to celebrate.

There were tiny glowing lights that floated just above the tallest faerie's antlers and they went on for as far as Briella could see. She took in the faeries that were gathered all around her. They were conversing, some dancing, but they did not look merry. They too looked sorrowful as if their hearts felt broken like hers. Some faeries were completely Seelie and in the lower lighting she could not spy their one defying Fae quality. She spied several Unseelie, and though she did not fear for her safety when in their company, she still did not seek them out. It was a curious thing to view so many beings together with so many differences between them. *I hope that all of the Courts are as inclusive as this one.*

Fleur met her at the dessert table and greeted Briella,

"My, you are lovely! What a shame that everyone is so gloomy tonight. Of course, I completely understand."

"Is there something to understand?"

"The curse's end is near. Can you not feel the change within the air?" Fleur tilted her head to the side. She wore a white dress that resembled daisy petals, and her red hair was flowing freely.

"I felt something, but I did not understand what it meant. What happens when the curse ends?" Briella pulled her lower lip between her teeth, hoping for some sort of confirmation of her earlier discoveries.

"No one knows. That's the thing with curses, you never know how they will play out. There are always unknown variables."

"Do you mean it will simply end or must it be broken?"

Giving her whole attention to Briella, Fleur stated, "I suppose that all depends upon you."

Briella turned away from the tiny, but mighty, stare of her friend. She felt the beginning of a headache alongside the ever-present frustration of not understanding how she was to become the curse breaker. Panic began to set in.

Fleur flew down toward Bruno and offered him some Faerie Floss before Briella could stop her. Fleur rolled her eyes and said, "Let him enjoy the evening."

Briella watched as Bruno became boisterous and started leaping and jumping around. Fleur directed him to an empty space, and the two danced around each other while one was bound to the ground, and the other fluttered in the air. The sight made Briella smile, and it was the first happy moment that she had participated in for quite some time. She would let them have this time together and be content to watch. She had no room at present in her heart for frolicking.

She felt the air change first, and then felt his presence behind her. She did not want to acknowledge him, but how could she not? He was like the beacon on a foggy eve; she was helpless to halt the current that passed between them. Briella gravitated toward him for protection and warmth, not wanting to ever disappoint him. She slowly turned and looked into the King's eyes.

King Ezekiel closed the distance between them and held out his hand for her to take. When Briella moved into his arms, he directed them to the center of the embedded rose and glass floor. Encircling her waist with his free hand, he led her into the dance steps of a waltz. She floated on a cloud waiting for it to burst, to change everything for the worse. They locked their gazes, and his emotion of sorrow and loss were reflected within her own eyes. She was broken, and so was he. They were two individuals who had been created for each other, but their time apart had not been kind. They had led such vastly different lives, making very different choices. And it was as if every moment was leading up to this one slip of time.

King Ezekiel brought his lips to her forehead and gave her a tender kiss. His lips were warm and soft. She closed her eyes and deeply breathed in the scent of him as they danced.

He made a sound of discomfort and Briella almost tripped over his boot when he ceased turning them about. Bending forward, he exhaled harshly before immediately straightening up and earnestly looking at her face. Briella felt like she was being studied, and it was like she was being memorized for a final parting.

"What is wrong?" Briella entreated, willing him to answer. She moved to stroke his jaw and he let her.

"I feel the change is coming on. I used to be able to choose when it overtook me. I could distance myself, hide away. Briella, you must flee. Run to your bedchamber and lock the door. You must go now." He pushed her away from him and tried to step away, but he folded in on himself again.

Briella looked around at the gathered crowd. Could someone be of assistance? She could not leave him, not like this. She knew what the change would do to him, and she refused to be afraid. *I will not cower! Nor shall I flee from his side. I will bear witness to this cruel twist of fate.*

Briella closed the short space between them and touched his back. He was trembling and his breaths were coming in shallow pants. She heard the fabric of his jacket and trousers rendering apart. His boots fell away from his feet as they morphed into massive, clawed feet with dark fur covering them. Briella gasped.

The King was changing into a beast before her eyes. His clothing fell away as fur sprouted from every inch of him. He was snarling, and drool was falling from his muzzle. He whirled around to look at her and growled out, "I told you to *leave*! I am the *monster* you should fear. I destroy everything and I will destroy *you* too." He took two steps toward her and roared.

Briella shrank away from his hot breath. The ferocity in his gaze frightened her, but she would stand her ground and not show her fear. "I shall do as *I* please. You have no right to behave this way. You are still *you*. I shall never run from you, no matter the face you wear or the skin that covers it."

Scowling at her, the beast taunted her, "And who do you think *you* are? You who came from nothing. You who thought you could break this curse. You are *nothing* to me. But perhaps you would be an excellent morsel for me to devour."

Briella scowled back at him. "You are a monster, every

inch of you. But you are *my* monster. I shall never turn away from you."

He shook his head and the drool fell onto the glass floor between them. Briella looked down at the sight and noticed that tonight the roses within the glass were black and shriveling. A sure sign of the crossroads that were directly before her.

Meeting his intense gaze, she did not flinch.

"You are delusional if you believe that any kind of a future, could ever exist for us now. No happily-ever-after will ever present itself now. You may think you could stand me in this form, but I assure you, that you could not. For, who could ever love a beast such as I?" His gaze was riddled with pain and longing.

Briella clasped his massive jaw in her palm and made him look at her. "I could. I *do* love you. You, who are so much more than even you know. You might not understand the depth of my affections for you. No difference in appearance could strip you of who you are inside. Your inner *you* still resides. If only you could view yourself from my eyes. I have always seen the real you. And you will always be deserving of my affection, esteem, and adoration."

"You think too highly of me. I could never have risen to the heights that you raised me to. I am unlovable, undeserving, unwanted and I always have been. Even when this face was more beautiful to behold." He was issuing forth growls that rumbled his massive, furred chest.

Briella's hand fell away from his face as he turned his back on her. She could see the dejection that covered him completely. Had she not felt that same way almost every day of her past? She, too, thought herself to be unwanted, undeserving, and completely unlovable. It dawned on her that she was none of those things. Her stepfamily were all of those things but not her. It had never been her faults that they threw at her and taunted her with, but their own. And it was not until her bitter and broken heart learned to unfurl itself, that she found her place. She found her home among these beings. She was every bit as worthy as any of them. And the one that she loved most had felt the exact feelings that she had allowed to take root inside her soul. He was not any of the things he spoke of. He was so much more, and she meant to share this discovery with him.

For, if she could learn to love herself, surely, he could too, no matter the form he was in. *I not only like myself, but I love the person that I have become. I value the decisions I have made. Whether they were right or wrong, they have taught me lessons and made me who I am. True love begins with accepting myself just as I am.*

Briella felt her whole body tingle. A wholeness that she had never before felt, settled into her bones. She had accepted herself and, in doing so, she had broken the block upon the magic that flew through her veins. A wisp of air swept through the castle grounds as it breezed her golden hair in every direction and tugged at the hem of her ball gown. She had never felt freer. She was worthy of a happily-ever-after and she meant to have it.

The beast, no, her King, took in the shimmering air that was blowing all around him. He slowly turned to look at her and his jaw fell open. "Oh, my fates," he breathed out. "You're magnificent!"

Briella felt joy and love, so much love flooded throughout her that she could not contain it all. She happily giggled. "As are you, Your Majesty." She closed the distance between them and saw the awe that lingered within his mossy green gaze. It was for her. "I have discovered something very valuable. You see, I have found that in order to love you better, I had to learn to love myself first. For, how can one give their heart away when it's not whole? In loving you, I learned that I do have value and worth and am worthy of your love in return. Now I can gift you with my entire heart, because it's wholly yours as it was always meant to be." Briella was smiling brightly through her tears.

She reached up to brush her hand through the wild mane of dark hair that rested atop his head. She was careful to not touch either horn that rested along each side of his head. The crown he always wore was missing, forgotten somewhere upon the ground where it had fallen. Rising to her tiptoes, she clasped his large face between her hands and pulled him toward her. Then she smiled again with all the love she possessed and placed a kiss upon his beastly lips. She did not mind the fur nor the slick surface of his lips. Briella poured every bit of herself into this kiss, believing that she was the curse breaker and that this was just the beginning of their love story. A feeling like heat raced through her and it made her gasp. She fell back onto the pads of her feet and watched as golden magic seeped from her body to encircle him. It swirled with stars and sunlight about him until the King began to roar.

The faeries surrounding them scattered as the volume of his roar rose. The golden magic lifted him into the air and tore through his fur, revealing the King she knew was hidden beneath. Briella watched as his fingers and toes curled and shrunk back to their appropriate sizes. She caught sight of a tail with a puff of white hair at its end, which she had only seen once before, in her True Love's Kiss vision. Briella smiled. That was his one defining Fae characteristic. How had she not remembered that detail?

She would encourage him to never glamour it away again. She positively loved it.

When the golden light started to cease its flow from her body, it settled into the male faerie that stood before her. The very *naked* faerie who stood before her. Briella watched the joy that radiated from his handsome face. The smile she saw was genuine, and she could practically feel the happiness that shone from within him. She dared not lower her eyes, she had never viewed a naked male before and now was hardly the time to ogle him. Briella knew that to the Fae, nakedness was nothing to take much notice of. It was simply a state that they had become accustomed to.

King Ezekiel leaped toward her and encircled her within his arms. He spun her around in a circle as he laughed with such glorious joy. Then, he stilled and said, "Thank you." He closed his eyes and leaned his forehead against hers. Briella reached up to kiss him again. The King eagerly returned her kiss. His velvet tongue danced with her own and she never wanted to part from his lips. He was caressing her back with his long fingers as he held her firmly against him. He kissed each corner of her mouth and then her nose. Briella sighed with the sweetness of his appreciation.

Clapping and shrill whistles broke their enchantment with each other so the King slowly lowered her to her glass-slippered feet. Turning around in front of her true love, Briella blocked his front from view. Faeries were not modest by nature, as many shifted into their other forms unclothed, but Briella felt a possessive need to protect him from prying eyes. He was hers and hers alone.

From the center of the crowd, she spied the lady faerie whom she had encountered in the conservatory. Her owlish eyes were blinking at them as she walked to where they stood. Her dark chestnut hair began to unravel as she floated into the air. Before their eyes, her gown changed into a cobalt-colored robe, which covered her hair, but nothing could hide the gossamer blues of the wings that sprang from her back.

"Fairy Godmother!" Briella exclaimed, clutching her hands to her middle.

"You know this Enchantress?" The King demanded.

Looking over her shoulder at him, she nodded and smiled. "She is the reason that I am here. She appeared to me with her magic on the night I arrived for the ball." Turning her attention back to her Fairy Godmother, Briella reached down for the hem of her gown to reveal one glass-slippered foot. "I have taken care of them."

Fairy Godmother smiled back at her. "As I knew you would."

"Wait..." King Ezekiel spoke hesitatingly. "How can you be her Fairy Godmother and the Enchantress?"

Waving her silver wand through the air, Fairy Godmother pointed it at the King and said, "Bip and bop and boo, let us get some clothing upon you!" Silver magic swirled from the tip of her wand to shoot toward the King, enveloping him, and within moments, he was dressed in a forest green tailcoat, brown trousers and boots that matched with all the appropriate clothing in between. "So much better! Now we can converse without any dangly bits being a distraction."

Briella covered her mouth in an attempt to stifle her giggle. She willed herself not to blush. *Oh my stars!*

Patting his chest, King Ezekiel addressed the faerie and with regal dignity said, "Thank you."

"My pleasure. To answer your question, I am many things to many beings. I am here and there and everywhere. I know the comings and goings of all who reside within the faerie Courts. If one needs assistance, such as a lesson learned, I shall step in and make it my priority to assist. And I must say, I have assisted you both, splendidly."

"Were we always meant to find each other?" Briella asked with uncertainty.

"Absolutely! But you both had a lesson to learn regarding matters of the heart. Briella had to learn to love herself, and my dear, you were faetastic. And our beastly King needed to learn to serve his people and not his own self-interest first. Along the way, he forgot to keep love within his heart. And so, you understand, you both needed me." Fairy Godmother smiled beamingly at them.

A troubling thought occurred to Briella. "What shall I do now that so many know my name?"

"Search within your heart, and you shall discover that your true name remains hidden. Briella was never your true name." Fairy Godmother came closer to take Briella's chin into her palm. Then she gave Briella a kiss upon the cheek before whispering, "Thank you, darling, for awakening the magic of the Spring Court."

Briella smiled through happy tears and nodded her head.

"What happens next?" the King asked as he reached for Briella's hand, which she willingly gave to him with a radiant smile gracing her face.

"What happens in all of the best Fairytales? You live happily-ever-after."

EPILOGUE

THE ENDING

King Ezekiel walked with his tail trailing along behind him, hand in hand with his beloved, who slowed their course several times to take in the blossoming beauty of the Spring Court. Color was in every direction one gazed, whether it was found in the flora or fauna; the transformation that had taken place amazed them both. Once the light of day greeted the new morning, discoveries of wonder began to be reported. It was not an instantaneous change, but the Court was awakening and blooming once more with the encouragement of its monarchs and with the castle once again coming to rest upon the leveled ground. Every day greeted them with new wonders. Learning how to wield the magic he had inherited from his father, was humbling and awe-inspiring. In quiet moments, he was certain he felt the distinct magical essence of his father and it was like being wrapped within his warm embrace again. He would honor the lessons his father had tried to teach him. He would never fail to love those whom fate had placed into his path.

As for the Spring Court, its King was attuned to every border, every soul that existed within his kingdom; even the earth was connected to him. He delighted in the new life that was springing up everywhere within his Court. His heart was light, and his purpose was finally realized.

The Faerie King laughed when Bruno chased a butterfly, then ran in the opposite direction when a bee charged after his curious nose. He watched the butterfly for a moment, never having seen one colored quite like it before, with white wings that appeared to have a red rose pattern. Turning his mind to other matters, he continued onward.

Every day granted him new love for his Queen. She was breathtaking to behold, and the added glow that accompanied her acceptance of her powers made her ethereal. His favorite activity was to hold her, to simply bask within her presence. It was like a dream where he feared that at any moment he would awaken and be left bereft without her. He still had some work to do to repair his mind, and yes, his heart as well. His Queen was helping to heal him every day and he was doing his best to put her first in all things. Never again would he be selfish.

He could not say that he missed the gargoyles nor the darkness that coated his life, which had immediately departed upon the breaking of the curse. He was a better faerie, a better king with his true mate and bride-to-be beside him. Since faeries did not partake in the human custom of weddings, but because Briella had been raised as a human, King Ezekiel planned a lavish affair for his one true love. Briella had readily agreed to a mating ceremony, which was the custom of joining lives throughout the land of Faerie. The Enchantress had presided over the ceremony, which took place under the glow of the pink full moon on the night that Queen Briella broke their curse. King Ezekiel and Queen Briella celebrated the new dawn together, and neither was ever far from the other. It was a love match to rival any before, and a marvel to match for any that would come after.

Queen Briella spent her days as the Queen of the Spring Court learning just what it was that her magic could do. Growing and seeding new life was her new forte. She was skilled with the knowledge of what each plant, flower, or tree needed in order for it to thrive. And indeed, the Spring Court was thriving beautifully. The King's own heart was a garden that blossomed more with each passing day.

Picking up her pace, his Queen matched her stride to his as she came back to his side. Finally reaching their destination of the rose trellis, which was beautifully blooming, they caught sight of the Carpenter. He had dark hair and teal-colored eyes that were kind and considerate. His brown clothing was well-worn. He was a skilled faerie who could work marvels with any material. The King was exceedingly pleased to have had his help with all the tasks that needed to be attended to. The Carpenter had been busy repairing the castle and its grounds.

To the right of the Carpenter, was a faerie that he had not met with in more than a decade, dressed just as outlandishly as usual.

"The Duke of Barclay, what a wonderful surprise to see you here!" The Queen rushed over to stand before him.

The Duke bowed before her and kissed the back of her bare hand as he straightened. "'Tis my honor to be here. You remember me telling you about my very good friend, the Carpenter?"

"Indeed, I do." Queen Briella smiled with warmth.

"Once he finishes his repairs, we shall set off to the Summer Court to enjoy their freshwater oysters. I did inform you that that is the only way to dine." The Duke's twinkling beady chocolate-colored eyes blinked at her.

Briella nodded her reply.

"You old walrus! You were always fond of the sea!" boomed the King's voice as he greeted the Duke, and clapped him upon the back before the faerie could bow.

"Right you are! It's the sea for me. Now that I have my fellow adventurer back, we can go about our old haunts again," the Duke's shrill voice rang out.

"Tell me how you came to know my Queen," directed the King.

"Oh, we are old friends. I came to offer for her hand while encouraging her to reach for the stars and dream. Of course, I was directed to her by a mutual acquaintance. I shall congratulate you on winning her hand, Your Majesty. We had planned a large family, so it's now your task to see to that." The Duke winked as he gave him a toothy smile.

The King bowed his head and hid the smile with his hand as he rubbed his mouth with his tapered fingers. The idea of Briella wed to the faerie was an amusing thought, the two would never suit, and he suspected that the scheme was a direct result of the Enchantress' curse. The lady really was in the midst of everything. And as far as children, he had that well in hand as well.

The King and Queen soon left the friends to themselves and made their way back into the castle with Bruno happily keeping pace beside them. They repaired to the library, which was jointly their favorite room. Queen Briella sat upon the settee and was immediately pulled into the arms of her beloved once he had sat beside her. Bruno settled at their feet, content to take a nap.

He had a flash of a memory that made him cringe. When he had first addressed her, it had been grumpily, and with the impression that he wished for nothing more than to see her leave his Court. In truth, he had sensed her presence and it both frightened and enthused him. With the dangers of the madness running amuck and his inner beast being almost uncontrollable, he really did fear for her safety. He was uncertain that she could remain unscathed until the curse was either broken, or ran its course. So he was rude and uncaring. It had cut him deeply to see her become wary of him, but in that unexpected moment he had let his fear have reign. But now, all was well and she was his forevermore.

"Finally alone," he wiggled his blond eyebrows at her, then leaned toward her for a kiss.

"Ah ah ah. No kissing if you please. We have things to discuss," came the Enchantress's voice before she appeared from the air to stand before them.

King Ezekiel straightened in his seat and gave his full attention to the faerie. Never again would he dismiss her; he had learned that lesson well. Hopefully, he would never turn away another soul who was ever in need. He resolved to work upon that matter at a later date. "What needs to be addressed now?"

"I am leaving, for one, and that's all you need to know. The darkness from this Court has leached into the other Courts. The Lunar Court suffers the worst. I shall go directly there," the Enchantress informed them.

"Can we offer any assistance to you or the Lunar Court?" Queen Briella asked as she sat forward.

"Not as of yet. But this is not the last that we shall meet. Take care of your hearts, you never know when there will be one who exists to steal them away." The Enchantress waved her wand and began to disappear, but before she could entirely vanish, a grin and a striped tail greeted them from around the back of her neck.

Queen Briella gasped and held up her hand to stop the pair from vanishing. "A moment, if you please!"

The Enchantress turned around and waited.

Gaining her feet, the Queen quickly erased the distance between them. "Cheshire? Are there to be no parting words between us?"

From his perch upon the Enchantress's shoulder, Cheshire's entire body appeared. He straightened to his full height and jumped. The Faerie Queen managed to catch him as her reflexes had greatly improved thanks to her Fae abilities.

Putting a striped paw to her cheek, Cheshire told her, "I loathe goodbyes. While I long to return to Wonderland, I know that my heart shall miss yours, My Queen. I believe that the fates will see us reunited once again. It has been my honor to guide you, little one. You have surpassed all my expectations."

Smiling brilliantly, the Queen leaned forward to kiss the feline upon his furry head. "Goodbye, my friend. I shall miss you."

With that, the cat leapt into the air and disappeared all but for his large smile.

The Enchantress smiled and, with a nod of her head, together she and Cheshire vanished.

Queen Briella turned and made her way back to sit beside her fated mate. She snuggled her head into his chest.

This shall be a painful parting for her, he thought. He would do his best to ensure that she never felt loneliness nor dwelled in the realm of sadness if he could help it. In his heart, she was far too lovely to ever be unhappy; her heart was pure and just.

Cheshire was just another name added to the list of those who had left the Spring Court to return to their home Court. The influx of those returning to the Spring Court had kept the couple busy, and truthfully, he had not thought about all those who had departed. The King had felt relief that those that were so unhappy, could return to their Court. He had even let the faerie who had abducted Briella free with the condition that he never enter the Spring Court again. He hoped that the madness that had plagued his Court would now be squashed forevermore.

There was one matter that still had to be addressed, and that was his mate's stepfamily. He had plans to remove them from the chateau and return it to the true daughter of DuBois. And if in the process the three men suffered, it would only brighten his heart. They deserved no kindness. It was a pauper's life that loomed in their future. He would show them the mercy that they had bestowed upon his Queen.

The chateau was rightfully, and even lawfully his Queen's. Their children might someday make use of it. Not all of the Queen's memories were fraught with horror or tied to sadness. She had created some beautiful memories of her mother and father, and he wanted her to have the estate because someday she would want to revisit it. He would never take her happiness for granted and would strive every day to be a better faerie, King, fated mate, and soon-to-be husband.

Life was a grand adventure, whether be you human, faerie, or something in between. King Ezekiel planned to live a long life with his true love by his side. What the looking-glass had long ago shown him, had come to pass. He was utterly in love and his heart's desire was right by his side.

~

Thank you for reading A Court of Broken Dreams and Curses! If you're interested in continuing with the next story in the Courts and Curses series, preorder the second book A Court of Broken Promises and Nightmares today! Also, join my reader group Michelle's Dashing Heroes and Compelling Heroines to chat all things regency romance with me!

AUTHOR'S NOTE

Dear Reader,

Thank you for reading this book. It means so much to me that you did. I hope that you've enjoyed your time in the Spring Court and have fallen in love with a character or two.

Please keep an eye out for A Court of Broken Promises & Nightmares releasing in 2023! Hatter is currently keeping me company as we sip tea and plot.

Supporting indie authors is important and appreciated. Self-publishing is a huge endeavor and the best way to support an author is to leave a review. Honest reviews can help others decide whether a book is right for them or not. Also, if you love a book, shout it out to the world. Share it with your friends and family and even with your book club. Books make wonderful gifts too. Sharing your love of reading inspires others and may even assist another with finding their new favorite author.

Happy Reading,

Michelle Helen Fritz

ACKNOWLEDGMENTS

A massive thank you to YOU! You took a chance on this book and I am forever grateful to you. I hope that you enjoyed this story.

To my Handsome Hubby who toils away so that I can daydream and raise our littles, thank you! You will always be my dream come true.

Thank you to my four beautiful children. You inspire me. I would be lost without you cheering me on. I love our storytimes and your giggles gladden my heart.

Thank you to my mother whose wonder never dims. You have cheered me on and been such a huge part of this book coming together. I promise that a book is coming soon that will be dedicated to you.

Thank you to Cortney who was a cheerleader for this book before anyone else was. You are amazingly kind and such a faetabulous friend and boss.

Thank you so very much, Heather! You are an extraordinary being and a wonderful friend and inspiration. You never cease to be kind and willing to help where you can. Thank you for the encouragement and for sharing all the things with me.

Ericka… I will forever be grateful to you for believing in me and encouraging me and for all the things. I treasure you.

A huge thank you is due to Paranormal Depths Editing for taking my book baby and making it shine! Your thoughts and questions were invaluable.

Thank you to Brittany Smith, who has a golden heart and a ready wit. You are so faely and I am so glad that you commented on my post!

Thank you to Wanderlust Ink & Tomb L.L.C. for being so amazing with the cover design and all of my ideas. You made my dream come true!

Samaiya Art! You beautiful lady! Your art is superb! Thank you for creating my pretties and for making them out of this world.

Thank you to my sister Cathey who made this one phenomenal book. Your attention to detail and thoughtfulness has been such a huge gift to me!

To Shannon who is the sister of my heart! Thank you for being excited for me and for thinking that my published books were fantastic. I love that I get to share this with you, even though we are miles apart.

Thank you Fandom Fealty! Your pop of Briella is faetabulous and I love her! You always take my breath away with your creativity and skill. Also, thank you for being so supportive and excited for all of the other books too!

Tuesday! Thank you for asking me if I would ever write. You made me think that maybe I should and here we are! I absolutely adore you! Thank you for listening to my dollie pop requests and creating works of art. I love that we can share all bookish things.

I can't end this without a huge well of gratitude to Paullett Golden. So… Thank you so very much, dear lady. I don't know of many authors who are as generous with their time and guidance as you. You have inspired me and lifted me up. You are exactly what I aspire to be.

Thank you to Amanda and Book of Matches Media for all of your careful planning with this new release. I am so excited that we got to work together! Amanda, you are kindness itself and I have been blessed to know you. Thank you for being the example.

Thank you to all the social media peeps! Authors could not do what we love, if not for you!

Merrit! Thank you dear lady for all the excitement and support! You have been amazing and I thank my lucky stars for you!

And finally thank you to my Creator who gifted me with imagination and a love for literature.

ABOUT THE AUTHOR

Michelle Helen Fritz began her literary career as a personal assistant to Indie authors. She enjoys being immersed in the process of turning an idea into a complete and published book. Michelle loves to write about dashing heroes and the compelling women that tempt them with a bit of intrigue and an abundance of romance, creating swoon-worthy characters and stories for her readers to enjoy. Occasionally, her characters talk to her and change the entire plot. Maryland is where her humble abode resides, housing her four home-schooled children along with her jaunty hero-husband who makes all her dreams come true. Michelle fully believes in happily-ever-afters and wishing upon stars.

Ways to Connect:

Facebook Reader Group

Instagram

Follow on Amazon

Follow on BookBub

ALSO BY MICHELLE HELEN FRITZ

A Bramley Hall Regency - Clean & Sweet Regency Romance

Love At Last

Love That Lasts

Love Ever Lasting

Courts & Curses - Clean Regency Fairy Tale Retelling

A Court of Broken Dreams & Curses

A Court of Broken Promises & Nightmares - Releasing 2023

www.ingramcontent.com/pod-product-compliance
Lightning Source LLC
Chambersburg PA
CBHW070549310726
48982CB00011B/1522/J

* 9 7 9 8 9 8 5 2 8 8 1 6 2 *